A Sticky
Situation

Also by Kiki Swinson

Wifey

I'm Still Wifey

Life After Wifey

Playing Dirty

Notorious

Sleeping with the Enemy (with Wahida Clark)

Published by Kensington Publishing Corporation

A Sticky Situation

Kiki Swinson

Kensington Publishing Corp.

http://www.kensingtonbooks.com

DAFINA BOOKS are published by

Kensington Publishing Corp.
119 West 40th Street
New York, NY 10018

All Kensington Titles, Imprints, and Distributed Lines are available at special quantity discounts for bulk purchases for sales promotions, premiums, fund-raising, and educational or institutional use. Special book excerpts or customized printings can also be created to fit specific needs. For details, write or phone the office of the Kensington special sales manager: Kensington Publishing Corp., 119 West 40th Street, New York, NY 10018, attn: Special Sales Department, Phone: 1-800-221-2647.

Dafina and the Dafina logo Reg. U.S. Pat. & TM Off.

ISBN-13: 978-0-7582-3892-4
ISBN-10: 0-7582-3892-4

First Dafina mass market printing: May 2010

10 9 8 7 6 5 4 3 2 1

Printed in the United States of America

My kids mean the world to me so I'm dedicating this one to them. I love you Shaquira, Lil J & Kamryn! To my cousin Lex, from Wilmington Delaware, you truly have inspired me as a writer to come harder on every book I do. Thanks for the love & all the hype you throw out there to the world when you let everyone know that we are related.

Maxine

The First Mistake

"Tell me you love me," Seth insisted as he pushed his huge dick through the walls of my vagina like he owned every inch of my pussy. Sweat leaked from the pores of his body onto my 130-pound frame. His brown eyes locked onto mine as he waited for my response.

"Baby, I love you," I finally told him, my words riding on the same waves of the motion in which he was penetrating me. The way he was fucking me was undeniably good. The feeling I was experiencing was all too powerful, and I was finding myself falling deeper and deeper in love with this guy, even though I knew it was forbidden.

For eight years, I had been a federal probation officer, and the men and women on my caseload knew that I was nothing to play with. From the first day they entered into my office, they knew that I had been assigned to monitor their transition back into society. I didn't tolerate any form of fraternizing, nor was I into giving second chances. I played strictly by the book. So never in a million years could anyone have told me that I would be sleeping with one of my parolees, because if they had, I would've laughed in their faces and told them to go straight to hell. Because you know what? They would've been right. But who could predict the future?

The sad part about all of this was that I couldn't see the forest for the trees when I was around him. He truly had me open. And to make matters worse, the man was fine. He looked just like Mehki Phifer, had his smile and his swagger. I resembled the actress Nia Long, so when we were in public together, people always complimented us on how good we looked together. On another note, my two childhood friends Heather and Danielle weren't impressed at all about how good we looked together. They were displeased with the idea that I got involved with him from the start. They believed I was dealing with some self-esteem issues, so they were constantly reminding me that he was not on my level and that I deserved so much better. Not to mention, I could lose everything I worked so hard for if my superior ever found out. But what could I say, other than I'm in love? I guessed that was why I just cosigned for Seth to get a brand new Dodge Magnum.

The only problem I had with Seth was that he couldn't keep a job, so I had to make two of his car payments. All he knew was the street life, which wasn't a problem in the beginning because I was from the projects. I practically lived there all my life. My mother and father used to work together at the factory warehouse, and they sold five-dollar bags of marijuana out of our apartment when they got off. My father was a well-respected man around my way. He always had some type of hustle. He was a sharp guy, and what little power he had, he knew how to use. The women loved him, but he respected my mother, and that's why I looked up to him. He had such a swagger that wouldn't quit.

What was so crazy is when I met Seth for the first time, I saw that same swagger in him. I guess that's what attracted me to him. So, as soon as he could get it together all the way around the board, he and I could definitely make this thing official. I told him this all the time, but he wasn't trying to hear me, which was why I proposed to him that he and I go into business together. He acted like he was down with the idea, but so far, he hadn't made any attempt to sit down with me so we could go over possible business ventures. It bothered me, but hey, what could I say? Seth was your typical man who didn't like to feel like he was being forced to do something, which was why I never tried to pressure him. He was not receptive at all when he felt like his back was against the wall, so I said what I had to say and left it alone.

The issue about him moving into my condo always got him on edge, so he tried to avoid the subject as much as possible. At the time, Seth was living at home with his mother, Mrs. Richardson, which I didn't approve of. Granted, her home was beautiful and she was living there all alone before his release, so having him around gave her something to do.

But lately, she had become very codependent and couldn't do a thing without him. Plus, she called his phone non-stop, wanting to know what time he was coming home so she could ask him to pick up a few things while he was en route. It had gotten to a point where it was beginning to affect our relationship, so I thought it was time to cut the umbilical cord. Seth and I had a fucking life together now, and I wanted to take it to the next level.

Today marked our one-year anniversary, so he and I decided to spend the night inside and have dinner by candlelight. Afterward, we retired to my bedroom with a bottle of Veuve Clicquot Ponsardin I picked up on my way home from work. From then on, we made magic.

"This is my pussy, right?" Seth asked, his strokes getting more and more intense.

I was able to belt out the word *yes* before he took another direct jab at my G-spot.

"Well, act like it and throw this shit back at me!" he demanded.

He loved talking to me this way. It got his dick really hard. When I was responsive, it even gave him a source of power. So without further delay, I locked my legs around his waist, tightened up the walls of my vagina so I could put his dick in a chokehold, and then bucked back at him like I was a wild rodeo rider. The way I was grinding on him was like a person sharpening her pencils. Emotions of all sorts were popping all around, like fireworks. The juices from my pussy even made popping sounds of their own. It was beautiful. And after fifteen straight minutes of tongue kissing, hard fucking, and sucking, we both climaxed and called it a night.

The next morning I got up around six-thirty and went to take a shower. I would've asked Seth to join me, but he looked like he was sleeping peacefully, so I elected not to bother him. Besides, I didn't have any intention of being in there any longer than I had to, since I knew I had to be at work by eight. I jumped in, took care of my business, and hopped out in less than ten minutes. To my surprise, Seth was awake when I returned from the bedroom. He was lying on his back with his hands propped up behind his head.

"How was your shower?" he asked.

I smiled, dropped my towel to the floor, and revealed my entire wet body. "If you were awake, you would've found out."

He smiled back. "Yeah, a'ight! Be like that."

Holding a bottle of lotion in my hand, I walked over to his side of the bed and turned my back to him. "Just be quiet and lotion my back," I instructed him.

He took the lotion bottle out of my hand, squirted a dab of it into his palm, and massaged it into my skin. When he was done, he smacked me on my ass.

"Ouch! That hurt!"

"Ahhh, stop being a baby and bend that ass over so I can get me a quickie," he commented, grabbing a hold of my arm.

"I know your quickies! And they aren't quick at all," I told him, releasing his grip from around my arm.

"Come on, baby, please!" Seth began to beg, but I ignored him because by then I was applying lotion to the rest of my body. I wasn't about to stop just to give him a shot of ass before I left for work. No way. I had too much to do, and I didn't have a lot of time to do it, so he was going to have to take a raincheck.

"Are you going for that interview today?" I asked, changing the subject.

Seth hesitated a bit. "Yeah, I'ma go since my homeboy got his peoples to put in a good word for me. But I ain't feeling it, for real."

Disgusted by his lack of ambition, I asked him, "Why not?"

"Because it's summertime, and I ain't trying to work outside in the fucking heat. And then that little bit of money they paying niggas to slave out there at some construction site ain't making it any better."

"How much are they paying?" I wanted to know what a "little bit of money" was.

"Eight-fifty an hour."

"Well, you got to start somewhere."

"Yeah, I know. But, I don't want my start to begin there."

I sighed heavily. "So, what are you going to do?"

"I don't know."

"Well Seth, you're twenty-nine years old, and you're not getting any younger. So, you need to hurry up and think of something fast, because if you don't, sooner or later you're gonna get a rude awakening and it's not going to be pretty."

"A'ight now, don't start beating me in my head," he commented sarcastically.

"I'm not trying to beat you in your head. I'm trying to get you out of that street hustler mentality and make you understand that in a legitimate world, you've got to crawl before you walk."

"But I keep telling you that you don't have to do that."

"So, what do you want me to do? Just stand around and watch you let opportunities pass you by?"

"Maxine, I told you, I got this," Seth replied nonchalantly.

"Well, I wish you would act like it, because I am tired of covering your ass with all the unnecessary paperwork when my boss gets the urge to go look through my case files."

"I told you what to do."

"Seth, don't be naïve. You know I can't release you from probation until you've served at least half of the time you were sentenced. And not only that, you've got to meet a few more requirements as well."

"Like what?"

"You just don't get it, huh?" I asked, staring at him in amazement.

Seeing the expression on my face, he knew he was pissing me off, so he came at me with a different approach. "Hey listen, don't get all bent out of shape. I'm going to the interview later, and if they hire me, I'm gonna take the position."

"You getting the job isn't the big issue. Keeping it after they hire you is your biggest problem. I mean, you have been through five jobs already, and that right there is a sure sign that you lack commitment and you have no work ethic."

Annoyed by what I was saying, he said, "A'ight! You made your point."

"Too bad it's going to go in one ear and right out the other," I commented.

I went into my walk-in closet to get dressed. I thought he was going to come in the closet behind me so he could get the last word, but I was wrong. Seth kept his ass right in that bed. Good for him, because I was completely turned off at that point and needed a breather. Immediately after I got dressed, I grabbed my briefcase and car keys and headed out the front door. While I inhaled the interior smell of my brand new, fresh-off-the-showroom-floor, candy-apple red C-Class Mercedes Benz, my cellular phone rang. It couldn't have been anyone else but Seth, so I neglected to look at my CallerID and answered it.

"Hello?"

"I just called to tell you I love you."

Taken away by his charm, I smiled and said, "I love you too."

Maxine

Unnecessary Drama

Every single time I walked through the doors of the United States Probation Office—located on the second floor of the federal building in the heart of Norfolk, Virginia—I always made sure I was drop-dead gorgeous. This morning I decided to show off my new, navy blue Dana Buchman wrap-around dress I ordered online from Saks Fifth Avenue a week and a half ago. The way this dress conformed to my body sent a clear message that not only was I a professional businesswoman, but also a sexy one. My nosey-ass colleague, Carolyn Granger, would have something to say the moment she laid eyes on me. Her office was right next to mine, so she saw every move I made. That was why I had to be very careful when Seth came in for an office visit. I couldn't have her blowing my cover because if that twenty-six-year-old cracker was given the chance, she'd definitely take it.

The beef between she and I started two months ago when she found out that she and I both applied for Karen's position. See, Karen just accepted a position as a Director of Legal Affairs at the U.S. Probation Office in Newport News, so she would be leaving this office in less than ninety days. Now whoever got her job would be the boss over everyone in this entire office, so Carolyn wasn't looking forward to me telling her snotnose-ass what to do. But, she'd better get with the program because I was bound to take Karen's position, especially with the education and all the experience I had. Carolyn and I both had the same type of degree, but she hadn't been there as long as I had, so I had a huge advantage over her. And later on that day Karen would be giving me the good news. I just hoped she would tell me right in front of Carolyn so I could rub it in her face. Seeing a frown on her face would bring me so much joy and I'd cherish that moment forever.

Aside from that, I pretty much was low key and I minded my business because my job was pretty simple. Every day I came to work, saw my clients, took a couple of urine samples every now and again, made a few judgment calls, and then my day was over. Now, there were some days when I had to make a few home visits. And if I had to collect a urine sample from a male parolee, then I had to have one of my male colleagues accompany me on that visit. All we did was go in the home, check out the scenery, ask a few questions, and then we collected the sample. It was not complicated at all. In fact, I enjoyed working in the field more so than I did at the office, so I tried to get out as much as I could. Today would not be one of those days, though, because I had clients scheduled to come see me all day long.

My first appointment for the day was Nicole Simpson. She was a very young and beautiful woman who had been released for some time now. According to my file, she got mixed up with her cousin Kira's husband, a guy by the name of Ricky Walters, and started trafficking large quantities of crack cocaine to different drug houses in the city for large sums of cash. After making more than a handful of runs for this guy, she eventually got an assigned route. She was stripped of that when one of Norfolk's narcotics detectives got a call and was tipped off by an informant. Not too long after her arrest, federal agents took over her case, and when that happened, she brought down everyone affiliated with her.

Her cousin Kira was given a chance to cooperate before the gavel went down on her. She turned, and when the ball dropped, a lot of people got some serious time, including her husband Ricky. Unfortunately for him, though, some very powerful and well-connected people put a hit out on his life, and he was murdered by a couple of hit men disguised as U.S. Marshals. Kira was put in protective custody while Nicole remained in the limelight, which in turn brought out the men who were the major drug suppliers for their entire organization and responsible for the attempted murder on Kira. So, when they resurfaced, more people were murdered, including their elderly grandmother. I knew that had to be devastating. And probably even more devastating because it was their lifestyle that brought on that tragedy. But now that that chapter of her life was closed, Nicole requested to relocate to Houston, Texas, so she could rebuild her life. After heavy consideration, my senior officer and I gave her the green light. The purpose of today's visit was to give her a travel permit and bid her a farewell. I just hoped she didn't get herself caught up in that same type of drama down there, because her new probation officer was nothing to play with. From what I'd heard, he was an Uncle Tom who was constantly looking for promotions. Nicole had better keep her nose clean, or else.

Earlier, when I walked into the office, I noticed that Nicole was sitting out there in the lobby. After I got situated and pulled her paperwork from my file cabinet, I brought her into my office.

"Have a seat," I instructed her, admiring both her diamond necklace and the multi-colored, oversized Salvatore Ferragamo handbag she carried. "So, how are you doing?" I asked the moment I sat in my chair.

"I'm doing OK."

"I am so sorry about the loss of your grandmother."

"We all are," she replied.

"How is your cousin taking it?"

"She wasn't doing too well in the beginning. But as the days pass, she's starting to come around."

"So, how does she feel about you relocating?"

"She's excited about it. That's why she's coming along."

"Oh, really?"

"Yep."

"Do you think that'll be a good idea?"

"Yeah, I think we'll be all right."

"Have you thought about what kind of work you're going to get into?"

"Well, since Kira is going to use the money she got from her husband's life insurance to open up another salon, I'm going to help her run it."

"What did she do with the other place you guys had on Newtown Road?"

"Well, you know her friend Rhonda got murdered too, so she felt there was no need to keep it open, which is why she shut it down and sold every piece of equipment she had in there."

"What about your parents?"

"Whatchu mean?"

"What are they going to do now that your grandmother is gone?"

"Well, they just put her house on the market, so they said as soon as they sell it, they're going to take the money and move down south to Florida."

"What about their house?"

"They're going to keep it and rent it out."

"How are they taking the death of your grandmother?"

"They don't talk about it. But I do know that they blame Kira and me for it."

"Do you think that this will put a strain on y'all's relationship?"

"I'm expecting my father to love me at a distance. But, I don't think my mother is going to change at all."

I sighed before I said, "Did you ever go to see that psychiatrist I referred you to?"

"No."

"Why not?"

"Because I thought it would be a waste of time."

"But after all you've been through these past eight months, you don't think you need to see someone?"

"I'll be all right," Nicole insisted.

"Well, if you say so," I replied.

After I went over a few more routine questions, I wished her luck, and before she got up to leave, I looked her straight in the eyes and said, "Technically, I am not your P.O. anymore, so you can come clean with me and tell me exactly what happened the day you shot Syncere in your grandmother's house."

Caught completely off guard, Nicole said, "What are you talking about?"

"I'm talking about the two firearms the police officers confiscated from the crime scene."

"What about 'em?"

"Well, it's been kind of hard for me to believe that he would bring two guns with him, just to kill one person."

She became a little agitated. "So, what are you saying?"

"I'm saying cut the crap, Nicole. You and I both know that you had that other firearm in your possession way before your boyfriend got there."

"No, I didn't," she replied with sincerity. "Syncere had both of those guns on him when he entered into my grandmother's house. I was just lucky that I was able to get to the smaller gun before he was able to pull the trigger on the other one."

I laughed. "Sticking to your story, huh?"

"That's what happened."

"Yeah, all right. Get on out of here," I told her.

Right when she was about to walk out of my door, she turned around and winked her eye at me. "Take care," she said.

"I will. But I'm not the one you need to be worried about," I replied nonchalantly.

"Oh, don't worry about me. Trust me, I am going to be fine," she assured me. I begged to differ. With that track record she had, trouble was bound to follow her. I guaranteed that as soon as she touched down in Houston, Nicole and Kira were going to hook up and become *wifey* to a new set of street thugs. And when that happened, all hell was going to break loose. For them, it was like a game of Russian roulette—the kind of lifestyle they wanted to live.

My next client, Todd Warner, was late. He was thirty minutes late, to be exact. Come to think of it, this was not his first time being late, so I was going to rip his ass apart and make an example out of him. The only thing that would save him was if he was laid up in somebody's hospital bed. Other than that, I was going to violate him. I mean, it was not like he was trying to conform to the rules of his probation anyway. Like Seth, he couldn't keep a damn job. At least Seth had never lied on job applications about never being convicted of a felony, like Todd had. What got me was that Todd knew I was going to find out about it. But, his simple ass didn't care. He'd been back on the streets for about eight months now and had absolutely no clue at all how to readjust to society.

He knew how to embezzle millions of dollars, though. Todd's pre-sentence report indicated that he was a pro at embezzlement. As an investment broker, he was able to steal over $15 million from clients at a brokerage firm. When FBI agents finally arrested him, they seized his million-dollar home in the Pungo area of Virginia Beach, a $250,000 Bentley coupe, an $80,000 Porsche Cayenne, and a half-million-dollar boat—only to auction them off. The rest he was going to have to pay in restitution. I didn't know how Todd was going to get the money, but if he didn't figure out a legitimate way of doing it, he was going to have to suffer the consequences for that as well.

After waiting in my office for over an hour for Mr. Warner to show up for his appointment, my receptionist buzzed me through my intercom system. "Ms. Shaw, I have Todd Warner on line three, waiting to speak with you."

"OK. Thank you." I immediately picked up on line three. "This is Ms. Shaw."

"Ms. Shaw, this is Todd. I just want to apologize for being late and to let you know that I am on my way to your office, as we speak."

"Don't bother," I interjected.

"Why? I'm only five minutes away."

"Mr. Warner, your appointment was over an hour ago, and I told you that if you were late again, I was going to make you regret it. So as far as I'm concerned, you're a no-show."

"Ms. Shaw, I have a legitimate explanation."

"Save it, Mr. Warner, because if you weren't in a life-or-death situation, then I don't want to hear it."

"Ms. Shaw, I got in a little fender bender off South

Military Highway, so I had to wait on the police to take the report."

"What time did the accident occur?"

"I'm not sure but the time on the police report says eight fifty-nine."

"Your appointment was at nine o'clock."

"I know. And I would've been there if this woman had not run into the back of me. Besides, it took the officer about twenty minutes to get to the location."

"So the other driver was at fault?"

"Yes."

"Well, why didn't you call me sooner?"

"Because my phone wouldn't get a signal."

"Were you seriously injured?"

"No. I'm fine."

"OK. Well, bring me that report, so I can stick it in your file."

"Will do," Todd assured me and we both hung up.

Seven minutes later, he arrived in my office with the police report he needed to back up his story. After I went over a few things with him, I sent him on his way since I had another client out in the lobby waiting on me.

That next appointment went smoothly, and before I knew it, it was time for me to go to lunch. I gathered my keys and purse and headed toward the elevator. En route I bumped into Marcus Finley, who was a federal marshal. He was escorting a man in handcuffs in the direction of the elevator. That man was none other than a parolee I used to monitor by the name of Dwayne Harris. That short, stubby-ass nigga used to give me so many problems, I had to trade his ass off to another one of my colleagues. By the looks of things, Mrs. Huggins was probably sick of his ass too, which was why Marcus had his ass hemmed up. It was no secret that he was on his way to jail. Judging from Marcus's expression, I could tell that he wasn't in the mood to take Dwayne, especially since it was going to be a long process. To put a smile on Marcus's face I said, "Cheer up! Trust me; it can't be all that bad."

"Only one thing will put a smile on my face."

"And what's that?"

"If you tell me you'll go out with me."

"Marcus, you already know I don't date men I work with."

"Come on now, give me a chance," he pressed.

"Sorry. You know the rule," I told him and proceeded toward the stairway. I figured this would be my only escape from his constant badgering. Granted, Marcus was handsome with a nice body and made over $65,000 a year, but I was totally not interested. As I walked by them, Dwayne leaped toward me and headbutted the hell out of me. The impact from the blow sent me tumbling backward, and I lost my balance and fell down on my ass.

"Yeah, bitch! How does that feel?" Dwayne roared as if he hated my guts. I couldn't respond. I was dazed.

Marcus quickly put Dwayne into a chokehold and wrestled him to the floor. "Stay down and don't you move!" Marcus ordered him.

"Look at you now," Dwayne managed to utter to me while his face was buried into the floor. "I don't hear you running your motherfucking mouth now!"

Applying pressure to the back of Dwayne's head with his knee, Marcus roared, "Shut up right now!"

Dwayne started laughing. "Oh yeah, dawg. She gon' really give you some pussy now."

"Say one more word and I'm gonna send you straight to the hospital!" Marcus warned him.

While all the commotion was going on, other colleagues of mine began to fill up the hallway. As soon as I regained full sight I allowed Karen Wheeler, my duty officer, to help me stand.

"Are you OK?" she asked me.

"I think so," I replied, blinking.

"What happened?" she asked.

"That asshole headbutted me." I felt my head for the growth of a lump while I watched Marcus drag Dwayne onto the elevator.

Karen looked in the direction of Marcus and said, "Where are you taking him?"

"I was getting ready to take him to jail, but now, I'm going to put him in one of the holding cells downstairs while I file my report."

"OK. Well, Maxine and I will be coming behind you in a few minutes."

"All right." Marcus pressed the button to close the elevator doors.

"Can you walk?" Karen asked me.

"Yes, I can walk," I assured her.

"Well, follow me into my office."

Once in her office, I took a seat and she grabbed an ice pack from her first aid kit and handed it to me. "Here, put this on your head," Karen said, taking a seat on the edge of her desk. "So, tell me what happened."

Trying to gather my thoughts, I took a deep breath

and said, "I really don't know. I mean, he just charged right at me and headbutted me for nothing."

"Wasn't he one of your problem cases a while back?"

"Yeah, he was."

"What was his name?

"Dwayne Harris."

"Oh yeah, I remember him. He was the one you violated for making those harassing phone calls to you, and who threatened to assault you in your office over a year ago."

"Yep, that was him."

"So, you guys didn't have any words?"

"No, we didn't. All I did was say a few words to Marcus."

"Well, did you look at him in any way?"

"No, as a matter of fact, I didn't."

Karen scratched her forehead. It was apparent that she was in deep thought. I sat there with the ice pack pressed against my head and waited for her to say whatever it was that she was thinking about.

Finally she said, "Are you able to go down and file charges on him?"

"Oh yeah, I'll be filing them as soon as I get out of here."

"OK then, do that. And when you're done, take off the rest of the day."

"What about my other clients? Karen, I have a boatload of people to see today."

"Call them and reschedule."

"OK," I said, and as I was about to get up Karen told me to hold up a minute.

"What, you need me to do something for you before I leave?" I wondered aloud.

Karen gave me a weird look and then she retrieved a typed document from a manila folder placed on her desk before her and handed it to me. "I know this isn't a good time to tell you this, but my conscience would've killed me if I would've allowed you to walk out of here without knowing who would be filling my shoes after I left this office."

Anxiety crept into my stomach, but I remained calm. "I got your position?" I asked as I grabbed the piece of paper from her hand.

But, Karen remained silent as she watched me read the document.

I scanned the letter in less than thirty seconds. It took me no time to find out that I didn't get the promotion. I was furious, and my expression showed it. "This can't be the final word," I protested.

"I'm afraid it is," Karen said.

"So, you're telling me that Carolyn got the position?"

"I'm afraid so."

"But I thought I had it in the bag. I have been here a lot longer than she has. So, how did she get the promotion over me?"

"I'm not sure."

"Well, who made the decision to give the job to her and not to me?"

"My boss and Carla Perry from personnel."

Angry, I stood up from the chair. "Can you call them both and set up a meeting so I can ask them what the hell was on their mind when they decided to give Carolyn your job?"

"Maxine, I'm afraid it doesn't work like that. You're just gonna have to accept it and move on. And who knows, another promotion could come up and they'll give it to you. So, don't be upset. It just wasn't your time."

"I understand all of that, Karen. But, I worked my ass off in this office. I have gone by the book from day one, and I haven't gotten one written complaint from any of my clients, including the ones I violated. And not only am I doing a damn good job, I just got my ass kicked by an ex-client to prove it. So, where is the justice?"

Karen stood up from her desk and walked around it to pat me on my back. "Maxine, I understand your frustration, but believe me, your time will come. But, until then go home and get some rest."

"Yeah, right!" I said and turned to leave.

Immediately after I exited Karen's office I made my way downstairs to the U.S. Marshal's office. Marcus was sitting down behind his desk when I walked through the glass door. He had Dwayne handcuffed to the chair in which he sat—which was approximately four feet away from Marcus—but his back was facing me. There were three other marshals huddled around, drinking coffee, talking amongst themselves. Marcus's boss, Tom, was one of them. To avoid any more confrontation with that asshole Dwayne, I walked to the other side of their office and gathered up the appropriate paperwork I needed to file charges against Dwayne. Looking at that motherfucker sitting there with a smirk on his face made my blood boil. I wanted so badly to go right over there and punch him right in his damn face, but I knew Marcus's boss Tom wasn't going to allow it. That cracker was strictly by the book, so I guessed I was going to have to get that fat, stubby bastard in court.

It didn't take me long to fill out the paperwork, and when I was done, I handed it to Tom, waved at Marcus, and turned to leave their office. As soon as I grabbed the doorknob, Dwayne turned around and said, "Bitch! Do you think I care that you filed charges against me? That shit ain't gon' do nothing but make me madder."

"Shut your mouth, Mr. Harris!" Marcus warned him.

Dwayne refused to listen. "Yeah, you thought I forgot about when you violated me, huh? I don't forget shit! And I'm gon' get your ass again, because you took me away from my daughter when you did that shit to me." His threats continued as his face turned blood red.

Instead of entertaining his bullshit, I kept walking. Thank God Karen gave me the green light to get the hell out of there. As soon as I got back to my office, I made contact with everyone who was scheduled to see me today, grabbed my things, and left.

When I got inside my car, I pulled out my phone and called Seth to see where he was. He answered on the second ring.

"What's good?" he asked.

"Where are you?"

"I'm on my way to your place. Why?"

"Just curious. So, how was your interview?"

"It was cool."

"Did you get the job?"

"Yeah. I got it."

"Well, at least somebody got some good news today," I commented.

"Whatchu talking about? What happened?"

"After all the shit I've done for this office I was just told by my boss that I wasn't gonna take her place when she left."

"Who did they give it to?" Seth asked.

"They gave it to this bitch named Carolyn, and I know she's gonna rub it in my face when she finds out."

"Why would she do that?"

"Because for one, she knows she's gonna be my boss. And not only that, she's just a petty-ass bitch!"

"Don't let that bullshit get to you. But didn't I tell you them crackers didn't give a fuck about you for real?"

Dreading the fact that I had to answer his question, I sighed and said, "Yes."

"Where are you at right now?"

"Sitting in my car, why?"

"Where you getting ready to go?"

"I'm on my way home."

"Good. Because we need to talk."

"About what?"

"About this job shit!"

"What about it?"

"Maxine, I can't get down with that company pimping me to work for them for eight-fifty an hour."

"Seth, I understand all that. But, it's a start, baby."

"For who? Some ol' lame-ass nigga who ain't ever had nothing," he struck back.

"Look, Seth, I am not trying to start an argument with you. I just simply wanted to make a point."

"Yeah, I know whatchu was trying to do. But I ain't in the mood for that right now."

"Well, what are you in the mood for?"

"Some real money. And if I don't get it sooner than later, I'm gonna lose my motherfucking mind."

"I told you what we need to do."

"You told me a lot of things."

"I'm talking about opening up a business."

He sighed. "What kind of business, Maxine?"

"I don't know. Maybe a Laundromat or something."

"Do you know how much that's going to cost?"

"Yes."

"How much?"

"Probably close to fifteen grand, if we can get some of the washers and dryers used."

"And how much do you have?"

"I got six grand in my savings."

"That's it?"

"Yes. But I can get a loan from my bank for another ten grand, if I need to."

"That's cool and all, but what kind of nigga am I to let my woman put up all the dough for a business, when I can come up with my own?"

"Well, if you can come up with your part of the money, then how come you haven't gotten it yet?"

"Because you won't let me go out and do what I need to do."

"I know you are not talking about going back into the streets!"

"I'm sorry, Ma, but that's all a nigga like me know."

"Look, I can't talk about this right now." My blood was boiling. "Stay at the house, I'll be there in twenty minutes."

Maxine

Love Conquers All

Seth was in the kitchen, sipping on a can of energy drink when I walked through the front door of my place. Before I could open my mouth, he rushed over to me and said, "What the hell happened to you?"

"This stupid-ass fool I used to have on my caseload ran up and headbutted me," I replied while Seth examined my forehead.

"What, y'all had some words or something?"

"No, we didn't."

"So, what happened?"

"Well, when I was walking down the hallway, he was standing by the elevator in handcuffs with one of the U.S. Marshals. So, as I walked by them, I spoke to the marshal and then—out of nowhere—this guy leaps right at me and headbutts me."

"What did the marshal do?"

"He grabbed the guy by the neck and slammed him down to the ground."

"So, what's going to happen now?"

"I filed assault charges against the asshole, so he'll be thrown back in prison for about five more years."

"Come sit down," Seth urged me as he led me toward the kitchen table. "Did you put some ice on it already?"

"Yeah, my boss gave me an ice pack earlier."

"Well, I think you might need some more because that thing is big," he insisted, going to the refrigerator. He placed a couple of ice chips in a Ziploc bag, handed it to me, and sat down at the table next to me. "You know I'm mad about this shit, right?"

"Trust me. You're not the only one, because I am furious right now."

"What's that nigga's name? Because I am going to kill him!" Seth roared.

"Look, don't get yourself all upset because there's nothing you can do about it. He's in federal custody, and he's going to be there for at least five years."

"You think I care about him being in their custody? Shit, I can get that nigga done at the drop of a hat if I want to."

"Please stop talking like that," I begged him. "I'm gonna handle it."

"On some real shit, I ain't trying to hear that! I want something done to that nigga."

"Shit, I want something done to him myself. But, since I'm a federal probation officer and an officer of the court, I can't do anything. We're gonna have to let it go and let the system handle it. Anyway, we need to continue where we left off from our telephone conversation earlier."

"It ain't shit to really talk about, unless you gon' let a nigga go back to the streets."

Frustrated by his irrational thinking, I said, "I don't know why you even went there. I am your probation officer."

"Yeah, but you're my woman first."

"True. But how will I look letting you go back and hustle drugs?"

"What? Your conscience is going to have you feeling all fucked up inside because you supposed to be upholding the law?"

I was getting irritated. "Don't go there, Seth."

"It's too late for that. That law shit went out the door when we started fucking with each other, so you can go ahead on with that bullshit."

"It's not the same."

"How is it different?" He pressed the issue. "What's the difference between fucking me and letting me go out into the streets to grind for a couple of weeks so I can scrap up some dough? You can get in trouble for both of them. And at this point in the game, you shouldn't even want to be there after how they played you with that promotion by giving it to that other chick."

"Oh trust me, I'm not gonna be there much longer."

"Well, there you go. Now, we ain't gon' have nothing to worry about."

"Seth, I'm sorry, but I can't do it. That shit is illegal, and I'm not going to be involved in it."

"But you're not. I wouldn't even bring the shit around you."

"That's not the point, Seth. Just knowing about it makes me responsible and I could lose my job. Better yet, I could get locked up right with you."

"Fuck that job! I don't want to hear nothing else about it. Those crackers don't give a fuck about you. And yet, you're around there hunting down motherfuckers for them to lock up and getting your ass beat up in the process. You're just a pawn in their eyes, and they ain't gon' ever give you a position over another cracker. I don't care how smart you are. It just ain't gon' happen."

"You're probably right. But, I'm still not going to change my mind."

Seth stood up from the chair and got down on his knees. "Please, baby, I know you're against what I'm trying to do. But if you give me just a week out there on them bricks, I promise I'll bring you all the dough I make so we can start up that business, and I won't ever ask you to let me do it again."

I shook my head. "I'm sorry, but—"

Before I could finish my sentence, Seth placed his finger against my lips. "Baby, all I need is one lick. That's it! And just so you'll feel better, the shit I'm trying to move ain't nothing but a few pounds of weed."

I hesitated for a bit. "And who are you supposed to be getting this weed from?"

"You don't need to worry about all that. The less you know the better off you'll be."

"Well, where are you going to get the money to purchase that stuff?"

"I don't need any money. I got a few peoples I can see."

I sighed heavily. "Seth, I don't know about that. You could really be getting into some major shit if you go back into those streets."

"I got this, baby. Don't worry about it," he assured me as he started massaging my face.

"I still don't know. I mean, what if those guys you're talking about are being investigated, and you get caught right up in it?"

"Will you stop being so damn paranoid? Believe me, nobody is investigating them."

"How can you be so sure?"

"Look, let me tell you something," he said in an aggravated way. "I could've gone back to the streets a long time ago. Niggas been trying to put me on since the day I came home. But I told them nah, 'cause I was trying to do shit a little different. And what's so crazy about that is the road I've been trying to take ain't been treating me right. So when those niggas approached me with the same proposition again, I'm like, 'Damn, here's my chance to get back on my feet.' Plus, I figured I could help you out."

"But I don't need your help," I interjected.

"I know you don't. And you constantly throw it in my face all the time."

"No, I don't."

"Listen, I ain't trying to get into that with you. All I want to do is get back on the grind one more time. Rake in a nice chunk of dough and be done with it."

I refused to comment. I sat there and remained silent.

"Whether you realize it or not, I could've got back

in the game without even telling you. But that's not how I want shit to be between me and you. I want to be honest with you about everything, especially if we're going to be together. Now, what do you say?"

"You promise it's going to be a one-time thing, right?"

Seth smiled. "Yes, baby! All I need is one shot."

Before I answered Seth, I thought about what he said and how I was treated at work today, and it became very clear that they didn't respect my work around there. And since I was gonna be resigning soon, I smiled at him and said, "You know what? Fuck it! I don't care! Go for what you know. But, please, be careful."

"I will, baby! And I promise, after I make this move, I am going to take your pretty ass on a cruise," Seth assured me as he jumped to his feet.

"Yeah, yeah, yeah," I said as I watched him make a call from his cellular phone. I continued to sit there while he was engaged in his conversation. I could hear the excitement in his voice. After only a few words were exchanged, he hung up.

"I just got the ball rolling," he told me, and then turned around to leave.

"Where are you going?"

"Those niggas just told me to come and holler at 'em."

"What are you going to do about that job?"

"What do you mean?"

"Are you going to take it?"

"Yeah, ain't shit changed about that."

"OK," I said.

After Seth dashed out of the kitchen, I sat there

in disbelief. I mean, I couldn't believe that I had just given him permission to go back to the streets and hustle. What in the hell was wrong with me? Was I insane? Or was I just plain fucking stupid? I did know that I loved the hell out of him. All I could do was hope I wouldn't have to suffer the consequences for using my heart to make decisions where they concerned him.

Seth

Back To My Roots

As soon as Maxine gave me the go-ahead to get my grind back on, I hauled ass out the crib before she changed her mind. She was known for changing it at the drop of a hat, and I couldn't afford to let her pull the plug on this one, because I had a lot at stake. Not only that, but I gave them niggas my word that I was coming into the fold, so I couldn't turn back now. Once I revved up the engine on my money-green Dodge Magnum, I sped out of her neighborhood within a matter of seconds.

In the middle of my drive, I thought about what it was going to be like to be back on the grind. I knew that times had changed, so I wouldn't be able to do the same shit I used to do back in the day. I also wondered what it was going to be like working for Mike and his right-hand man, Jay. I had only known these cats for a couple years. I met them both while we were all doing time at the federal camp in Petersburg, Virginia, and when we found out that we were from the same area, we started working out on the compound together. They got released about two years before I did, but Mike gave me his number and told me to look him up when I came home. I did. Now we were about to have a little reunion.

Before I would be able to catch up with them, I had to find out where they wanted to meet. I called Jay. "Ay yo, Jay," I said the moment he answered. "Where you and Black want me to meet y'all?"

"Come out to Portsmouth."

"Where at?"

"Meet us in Prentis Park."

"Which side?"

"We gon' be parked outside this white house on the corner of Lincoln and Richmond Avenue."

"A'ight," I said and hung up.

After twenty minutes of constant traffic, I finally made it to my destination. From the second I drove up and saw Mike posted up by his Hummer and Jay standing next to his 2008 Chrysler truck sitting on twenty-two-inch rims, I knew shit was about to be on. Without hesitation, I got out of my car and joined them. I walked up and greeted Mike's big, black, husky ass first. "What's good, dawg?" I said, giving him the proper handshake.

"Just trying to make moves, son," he told me, revealing a diamond bezel Chopard wristwatch.

The shit damn near blinded me, but I played it off like the shit didn't faze me. I mean, how would I look, sweating that nigga's shit? That's some ol' bitch move. After I let his hand go, I walked over to Jay and greeted him too.

"Ready to go to work?" Jay asked me.

Before I answered him, I looked at his tall, skinny, Puerto Rican-looking ass, dipped out in a three hundred-dollar pair of Red Monkey jeans with a brand spanking new white tee and a fresh pair of white Air Force Ones. The only piece of jewelry he had on was a gold rope with an iced-out cross dangling from the end of it. Jay wasn't the flashy type of cat like Mike, but he wasn't too far behind him.

"Yeah, I'm ready," I finally said.

"A'ight. Well, follow us."

I hit the alarm button on my key chain and followed Mike and Jay into the white house. From the outside, the shit looked run-down with the chipped paint and all. But on the inside, they had it kind of hooked up.

"Whose spot is this?" I asked.

"This is my girl Trina's crib," Mike said. "She don't be here that much anymore since I got her a bigger spot out on Churchland."

"Must be nice."

"For her, it is. But you know I just bought my wife, Lacy, a crib out on Virginia Beach."

"Yeah, I remember you telling me a while back. How is she?"

"She's a'ight. Can't wait till she drop that load. Shit, it feels like she's been pregnant forever."

"How many months is she?"

"Eight."

"So, what y'all having?"

"As big as she is, she looks like she's carrying two big-headed boys," Jay interjected and laughed.

"Yeah, he ain't lying. But she ain't carrying nothing but one. When she had the ultrasound, they told her she was having a girl."

I smiled. "That's what's up!"

"So, whatchu trying to get into?" Mike changed the subject while Jay disappeared into the room down the hallway.

"I was hoping you could hook me up with a couple pounds of weed."

"Nigga, I ain't got no weed! Shit, it's been a drought for about four months now."

"So, whatchu got?"

"I got whatever you can move."

"Well, a'ight. Hit me off with a couple ounces of hard white."

Mike laughed. "Ain't nobody getting high off crack anymore. The fiends around here either use dope or powder."

"Well, give me a couple ounces of powder."

"Who do you know get high off powder?"

"Come on, man. You know I've been out of the loop for a while."

"I know. That's why I'm gon' hit you off with a couple grams of dope. My shit is a missile, and all the fiends call it Black Label."

"Man, you know I don't know shit about heroin."

"Don't worry about all of that. Jay is in the back putting some shit together for you right now. As soon as he's done, I want you to take it and go set up shop at my spot in Dales Homes. A chick named Melody is going to be waiting for you."

"Who is she?"

"She's just a Section 8 chick I fuck every now and again. I kick her a few dollars here and there, for letting me use her crib as one of my spots."

"She got kids?"

"Yeah, she's got a little boy, but he ain't never there."

"Good, 'cause I don't like to do business around kids." I noticed Jay walking back down the hallway. "Damn, nigga, I thought you got lost!" I commented and smiled.

He smiled back and said, "Nah, son, I was just trying to get you straight."

"How many grams did you give him?" Mike asked.

"I broke off three from the egg," Jay replied. He handed me a small, quart-sized Ziploc bag filled with a brown powder substance.

"What am I going to do with this? I don't know how to bag this shit up!" I blurted out.

"Don't worry about it. That's Melody's job. She's going to put the shit in caps. When she's done, she's going to introduce you to my street team so they can start bringing the money to you. Believe me, when those niggas get the word out that you've set up shop with my dope, the fiends gon' go crazy."

"So, what's my take on this?"

"Just put it like this: I'm giving you this shit wholesale. So that means you gon' make five dollars off every pill of dope you sell. So if you sell five hundred of them, I'm gonna hit you off with twenty-five hundred. It's that simple."

Smiling at the thought of instant success, I sighed

and said, "Yo, son, give me the address to home-girl's crib, because I'm ready to get this paper."

Both Jay and Mike smiled back at me.

"I want you to call Jay if you happen to run out before he comes out there to check up on you," Mike instructed me as he walked to the front door.

"A'ight," I said as I followed him. Outside we exchanged a few more words and then parted ways.

After I pulled off, I got Maxine on the phone. "Hey baby, whatchu doing?"

"I just got out of the shower. What are you doing?"

"I'm on my way to go and take care of some business."

Sounding a little worried, she said, "Please be careful."

"Baby, I got this, so don't worry about me. I'm going to be fine."

"What time are you coming back this way?"

"I'm not sure. But I'll let you know."

"OK. But if I don't hear from you soon, I'm gonna call you, all right?"

"That's fine."

"OK. Give me a kiss." She made kissing sounds into the phone. "I love you," she told me.

"I love you too," I replied.

It didn't take me long to make the trip out to Dales Homes. It was only a hop, skip, and a jump from Prentis Park. When I drove past the sign that said, WELCOME TO DALES HOMES REDEVELOPING HOUSING AUTHORITY, I knew I was in ghetto heaven so I was going to have to go into street mode. Time to become the nigga I used to be before I caught my fed beef a while back. It was a known fact that you couldn't be soft out there. You had to let those motherfuckers know you meant business because if you didn't, the fiends, the bitches, and the snitches would swallow your ass right on up. And I couldn't have that. I had shit I had to do and a goal to make, so I was going to stay focused.

As I drove by the long row of one-floor apartment buildings made out of cream-colored stucco, with air conditioners posted up in one window of every house and surrounded by nothing but dirt and cement, I couldn't imagine why those people wanted to live like that. The kids were playing outside in the dirt— I assumed they were making mud pies—while the cats made their trades a couple of feet away. The kids' mothers were nowhere in sight. The whole scene was crazy. And I knew right then that I wasn't going to be able to take much of it. The sooner I could get my dough up, the sooner I could kiss this place goodbye.

The moment I turned my car ignition off, I noticed the front door of this chick Melody's crib was open, which wasn't a good look since I had to be in there with all this work. Anybody could bum-rush that crib at the drop of a dime . . . and what the hell would I be able to do about it? Nothing but stand there and look stupid as a motherfucker. When I got right up to the screen door I yelled out her name. "Ay yo, Melody!"

"Yeah, who is it?" she said.

"Come open up the door," I replied instead of yelling my name out loud.

In less than three seconds, I heard shorty walking toward the front door. When she appeared on the other side of the screen door, she smiled, showing me every last one of her pearly white teeth and the dimples in her cheeks. I mean, the chick was drop-dead gorgeous with her light brown eyes and soft caramel skin tone.

"So, you ain't gon' tell me your name?" she asked sarcastically.

"I didn't say it because I didn't want them niggas over there to hear me," I told her, referring to a couple of young cats I saw a few feet away. They were huddled around by a tree, making wisecracks at each other.

"That ain't nobody but my brother and his friends."

"Oh, so that's why you got your door wide open?"

"Yeah, that's one of the reasons."

"Well, I'm Seth, and if you don't mind, I would prefer if you kept it closed, especially while I'm here."

"Mike told me to look out for you, so I will," Melody commented, giving me a cute little smirk.

"I'm glad to hear that," I replied as I walked into her place.

I stepped away from the door, giving her enough room to close and lock it. Then Melody said, "Come on, let's go into the kitchen."

I followed her, and believe me, I got the chance to get a complete mental picture of her entire frame, which got me to wondering how she got all that ass into them little-ass shorts. My dick was getting hard just watching her cheeks hang from the bottom of them joints, so you know I was fighting myself to keep from grabbing her around her waist and pulling her back to me, so my dick could rest up against her. I wanted to feel how soft her ass was so bad, but I knew I couldn't.

When I took my eyes off her ass and look backed at her again, I got weak just thinking about what I could do to her. And what was really crazy was that homegirl looked just like Melyssa Ford. She was a shorter version, but she had the same big titties, small waist, and fat ass. I was really trying to figure out why Mike only fucked with this chick to use her crib as a spot. She was a keeper, if you asked me. If I were in his shoes, I would take shorty's pretty ass out of this hellhole and set her up somewhere where her kid could go outside and play without worrying about getting shot. But hey, I guessed Mike had his reasons.

"Where the shit at?" Melody asked once we were in the kitchen.

"It's right here." I handed it to her.

"A'ight. Well, take a seat right there." She pointed to a set of chairs placed at the kitchen table. "I'm gon' get started over here." She grabbed a face-mask, a coffee grinder, a clear bottle of empty capsules, and a plastic bag of white powder.

"Is that white powder cut for the heroin?" I asked.

"Yeah, it's baby laxative," she told me and immediately went to work.

Watching Melody mix that dope and baby laxative like she was in a lab turned me the hell on. Shorty was definitely about her motherfucking work. She was fast, too, because it took her less than an hour to mix and cap up fifteen hundred pills of dope. The only thing I didn't like about the whole process was the smell. I mean, the fumes were strong as hell, and if you inhaled enough of it, you were bound to start fucking with it. I couldn't have that 'cause I didn't get back into the game to become a dopefiend.

"You a'ight over there?" Melody asked, right after she dumped all fifteen hundred pills into a Ziploc bag and closed it up.

"Yeah, I'm fine. But the next time you start mixing that shit up, I'm gonna need to wear one of them masks, too."

She laughed. "That shit is strong, ain't it?"

"Hell yeah." I stood.

She removed her mask and sat it on the counter-top. "Here you go." She handed me the plastic bag. "Go in the living room and sit down while I clean up this mess."

"A'ight." I went into the living room and sat on the sofa.

Meanwhile, I got a call from Maxine. She was blowing my phone up, too. I started not to answer it, being as though I didn't want homegirl eaves-dropping on my call; but then I figured "what the hell" and answered it after the fourth ring.

"Why did it take you so long to answer your phone?"

"Because I was doing something."

"Are you OK?"

"Yeah, I'm fine. Stop trying to make something out of nothing!" I said, becoming agitated.

"Where are you?"

I sighed heavily. "Come on now, don't do that. I told you I was fine. Now, I'm gon' have to call you back."

"What time?" she asked.

"I don't know," I snapped.

"Listen, baby, I am not trying to get you upset. I just want to know where you are."

"And I'm not telling you. Now, didn't we have an agreement?"

"Yes."

"OK, well, let's stick to it. Before you know it, it's going to be all over. A'ight?"

Maxine hesitated and then she said, "All right."

"Well, look, I'ma holler at you later."

"OK. But please be safe."

"I will."

"I love you."

"I love you too," I replied, but I said it as low as I could. It didn't do any good, though, because Melody definitely heard me.

"So, you're in love, huh?" she asked the moment she walked into the room.

"Nah, I ain't in love."

"So why did you tell her you loved her?"

"Because that's what she wanted to hear."

"So you lied to her." Melody stood directly in front of me with her hands on her hips and her legs wide apart, revealing every angle of her fat pussy.

"I guess I did," I responded nonchalantly, but I was very obvious about what I was looking at.

"You mean to tell me you're playing with her emotions?"

I looked down at her pussy once again and then I looked back at her face. "Does it matter?"

"Yeah, it does matter," Melody protested in a cute way, pointing her finger at me. "But what I really want to know is, what are you staring at?" she asked, even though she already knew the answer.

I smiled. "I don't know. You tell me."

"I ain't gotta tell you because you already know. So stop playing games."

I got up, walked over to her, and stood right in front of her. My body had to be less than an inch away from hers. I was close enough to hear her heartbeat, and when I heard that first thump I said, "You are the one playing games. I mean, look at you, walking around here with them little-ass shorts on, getting a nigga's dick all hard. I bet you put them joints on right before I pulled up."

"My shorts ain't little! And no, I didn't put them on right before you came." Melody rolled her neck as if she had just made a point.

"Yeah, you'll tell me anything," I said, getting closer to her.

At that very point, our bodies connected. My dick swelled up the instant it brushed up against her pussy. The shockwave of emotions started running rampant inside my dick. When I realized that Melody wanted me just as much as I wanted her, I put both of my arms around her waist and lowered my hands down to her ass. I cupped each cheek in my palms and pulled her closer into me. Ten seconds later, I had my tongue right down her throat, and boy, was I having the time of my life. But you know what they say: all good things come to an end because right when I was about to rip her shirt off, a loud knock rattled the front door.

Aggravated by the sudden intrusion, Melody yelled, "Who is it?"

"It's me, Jay."

"Oh shit! What is he doing here?" she wondered aloud, pushing herself away from me.

Wanting to know the answer to that very same question, I quickly straightened up my shirt and tried to reposition my dick. "Are you gon' answer the door?" I asked her.

"Nah, you answer it while I run in the back and change."

"A'ight." I strolled over to the door and opened it. Jay immediately walked in.

"Damn, nigga, what took you so long?" he asked, giving me a suspicious look.

"Shit, I started not to answer it at all," I told him. I walked back over to the couch and took a seat.

"Why not?" Jay pressed as his eyes wandered around the living room.

"Because it ain't my crib."

"Where is Melody?" he asked.

"I'm right here," she blurted out. She'd changed into baggy cargo shorts.

"You a'ight?" Jay asked.

"Yeah, I'm fine. Why?"

"Black just wanted me to stop over here and make sure everything was everything."

"Yeah, everything is cool."

"What about you, Seth? You a'ight?"

"Oh yeah. I just got my shit bagged up, so I'm definitely a'ight."

"How many pills did you get out of them three grams?" Jay asked Melody.

"Fifteen hundred."

"A'ight. Well, that shouldn't take you long at all to

get rid of, so when y'all get down to three hundred, call me and I'll bring a couple more grams through."

"I'ma need you to go to the health food store and pick me up a couple more bottles of those vitamin C capsules, so I can clean them out and get them ready for the next batch."

"How many you got now?"

"Probably close to a hundred."

"A'ight. Well, I'ma send one of them niggas outside to get it before I leave."

"OK." Melody went back into the kitchen.

"Does your brother and those other niggas know the work is ready?" Jay yelled.

"No, but I was getting ready to tell them," she yelled back. "You can tell 'em, since you're standing by the door."

"You know you're slacking, right?"

"How is that when I just finished?" Melody's voice echoed throughout the house.

Instead of responding, Jay shook his head in disbelief. I could tell that he was getting frustrated with her. But after he poked his head outside the front door to let his peoples know the dope was ready and came back in, he seemed like he was coming around. I didn't notice this at first, but I thought Jay might be a little intimidated by me. When we were at Mike's other chick's spot, the nigga acted like he was cool. Now, he was gritting on me like me and him had beef. The more I sat and thought about it, the more I realized that this nigga had an attitude with me because he sensed me and Melody was in here doing something we ain't have no business doing. Since he didn't have any hard-core evidence, he was pissed off.

Shit, the way he was acting made me believe that the nigga wanted her for himself, and knowing him the way I did, he probably already hit it. He wasn't going to tell me, though, just like I wasn't going to tell him. I guessed we were going to all have a few secrets in our back pockets.

A few minutes later, Melody's brother and his friends began bringing money to me, and the ball started rolling. When Jay saw how fast those pills of dope were going, he decided that he couldn't sit around and babysit me and Melody anymore because he had to leave and go re-up for us. When he got up to leave, I pretended not to notice his expression. I just handed him all the dough I had made and let him carry his ass.

"I'll be right back," he informed us.

After Jay sped off in his truck, I thought Melody was going to come back at me so we could finish what we started, but she kept her distance. She did wink at me every now and then, though. I guessed it was her way of showing me that she didn't forget about what happened earlier. To let her know that I didn't forget it either, I made a few comments about how good I would've made her feel if Jay had not showed up. I smacked her ass a few times, too. Other than that, I left her alone since Jay was still in the area and he could sneak back up on us at any given moment.

At the end of the day, I pumped out twelve grand worth of heroin. That's twelve hundred pills of dope, to be exact. By the time I left the spot, it was a little after nine o'clock. I had been out there for a total of eight hours and walked away with six grand. I was happy as hell, so I figured it was worth it.

"Damn, we had a good day," Jay commented.

"Yep, we sure did," I agreed, stuffing my profits deep down inside my pockets.

"You think you could do this again tomorrow?"

"You damn right!" I assured him.

"Well, holler at us then," he said and then we both parted ways.

Maxine was pacing the floor like her mind was going bad when I walked through the front door. As soon as she was able to hold me in her arms, she felt better. And after I got her into bed and fucked the shit out of her, she completely forgot what she was worried about. When she drifted off to sleep, I took my money out of my pocket and counted it over and over again, just to make sure that bitch-ass nigga Jay didn't sucker me out of a couple hundred dollars. When I convinced myself that the count was right, I stuffed every dollar back into my pocket and turned over to go to sleep.

"What a helluva day!" I said under my breath, thinking about the many ways I could've fucked Melody if that cock blocker Jay hadn't showed up. Then I thought, *There's always another day,* and closed my eyes.

Maxine

Gotta Keep The Dog On The Leash

It was Thursday and the sun was shining bright. The weather was really nice for it to be in the smack dead middle of fall. Plus, I was happy as hell about my man waking up next to me this morning, and since I refused to let the moment die, I decided to take today off. My boss, Karen, didn't have a problem with it, especially after I lied to her about having a migraine.

"Take it easy," she said. "And if you're not feeling any better tomorrow, just call and let me know."

I assured her that I would and ended our conversation. I crawled out of bed and went to the kitchen so I could surprise Seth with a nice, hot breakfast. He loved blueberry pancakes with a juicy T-bone steak and a side of scrambled eggs with cheese. That was his favorite breakfast, so I hooked it up. Once everything was done, I poured him a glass of cranberry juice, grabbed utensils and a bottle of syrup, and placed them all on a wooden lap tray.

"Baby, wake up. I got you some hot breakfast," I announced as I entered the bedroom.

Seth turned over and rubbed his eyes a bit to regain focus. "Damn, that shit smells good as hell!" he commented and then yawned.

Excited about how much he loved my cooking, I said, "I got your favorite."

"I see." He smiled, taking the tray in his hand and setting it across his lap. "How long you been up?"

"Not long."

"What time is it?"

"Eight-thirty."

"You ain't going to work today?"

"No. I decided to stay home today, so we can spend some time together."

"Well, whatever you want to do, we're gonna have to do it early because I have to go back out to the spot around one o'clock."

Disappointed by the mere thought of him leaving me there again, I snapped. "So you mean to tell me I am going to have to sit around here on pins and needles all day long, worrying if you're OK?"

"Maxine, don't do this shit, because you're getting ready to piss me off!"

"Do you think I care about you getting pissed off when I got to sit around here, knowing my man is out on the fucking block selling drugs, so he can come up with his part of the start-up money for our business?"

Seth removed the tray from his lap, set it on the other side of the bed, and got up. "I ain't got time for this bullshit!" He grabbed his pants from off the floor and stormed out of the bedroom.

I followed him. "So, what, you running home to your mama?"

"Don't worry about it," he replied sarcastically as he slipped on his pants and sneakers in the living room.

"Fine, I won't worry about it," I snapped back. "But know that I'm pulling the plug from your little street hustle after today."

"Yeah, whatever."

"Oh, so you think I'm playing, huh?" I screamed, running behind him as he opened my front door to leave. "Do you know I can have your ass hauled back to jail if I wanted to?"

"Do it! I don't give a damn!" he roared and walked off.

Heartbroken, but disgusted at the same time, I just stood there in disbelief as I watched Seth get in his car and leave. I wanted so badly to run behind him, but when I noticed that my nosey-ass neighbor, Lisa, was standing outside her door, sweeping her welcome mat, I decided against it. I'd die before I gave her the pleasure of seeing me air my business out in the neighborhood. I sucked it up, closed my door, dashed over to my living room sofa, and snatched my cordless phone from the base of the charger. I pressed the speed dial button for Seth's number. As I waited patiently for him to answer, I began to rehearse in my mind what I was going to say to him the moment he said hello. Unfortunately, my rehearsing was in vain because he refused to answer. I called four times, back-to-back, and still he didn't answer. I also sent him a text message, telling him it would be in his best interest to call me back, being that I held the keys to his freedom. Again, he chose to ignore me. I was even more pissed off and the only way I was going to be able to blow off some steam was if I could see that bastard face-to-face—and there was no better place to do it than at his mother's house. She was definitely going to have a fit when she found out that I was there to curse her silly-ass son out, but if she knew like I knew, she had better keep her fucking opinions to herself or else she was going to find herself getting cursed out too. I was dead serious.

Thank God, I already had on a pair of sweatpants and a T-shirt. After I slipped on my sneakers and grabbed my keys and purse, I was out the door and in my car in five minutes flat. The way that I sped off in my car drew the attention of Mr. Thomas, another one of my neighbors. I knew he could tell that I was in a foul mood because normally when he waved his hand in greeting, I'd stop my car and chat with him about his grandkids and about the latest news concerning the war in Iraq. This time, I blew my horn and kept it moving. In the middle of my drive, I called Seth's cellular phone again, and just as I expected, he didn't answer. I hung up and called his mother's home number, and I got no answer there. My intuition told me that someone was there, and that was enough incentive for me to keep driving in that direction.

My intuition was right. As soon as I turned onto their street and drove within three hundred yards of the house, I could see his car and his mother's car parked outside. I parked at the curb in front of the house. As I began to walk up the sidewalk, I noticed someone peeking through the living room mini-blinds. I knew it couldn't be anybody but his mother because she did it every time she heard a car door close. That was just how nosey her ass was. You would have thought that after she saw me walking up to her door, she would have the courtesy to open it and welcome me in, but she didn't. I figured she ran and told Seth I was outside and he told her not to answer the door. It was something he would do, being the coward he was. I wasn't going to let them play me out like that, so I knocked on the door with a lot of force because I intended on getting my point across today, if that was the last thing I did.

Finally, after the fifth knock, Mrs. Richardson's tired ass opened up her door. "Hi, Maxine, how are you?" she said and greeted me with the fakest smile her phony ass could muster up.

"I'm not too good. Where's your son?" I asked, cutting to the chase.

She stood directly in front of the doorway. "He's in the shower right now."

"OK, I'll wait for him." I took a couple of steps toward her so she could let me in, but this lady didn't budge. "Are you going to let me in?"

"Well, he said he didn't want to see you."

I was infuriated. "Mrs. Richardson, I don't care what he said. I want to see Seth right now."

"Maxine, I really don't want to meddle in y'all's business, but Seth told me not to let you in this house."

"Whose house is this, his or yours?" I snapped.

"You better stop letting him run over you like you're his child."

"Now Maxine, I don't think you should carry that tone with me."

"Mrs. Richardson, I'm sorry for yelling, but I'm a little frustrated. Now, all I want to do is come into your house and talk to your son for a few minutes so we can work a few things out."

"I understand what you're saying, but I still can't let you in."

"Mrs. Richardson," I roared, "do you know that by being Seth's probation officer, I can come into your residence, while he resides here, as often as I choose to?"

Dumbfounded, she said, "No, I didn't know that."

"Well, I can. Now, will you please step aside so I can come in?"

Out of nowhere, Seth came from behind his mother and told her to excuse him. "I got it, Mama. You can go back in the kitchen now."

"You sure?" she asked.

"Yes, we can handle it from here," I interjected, giving her an evil look. When she disappeared around the corner, I ripped into Seth's ass. "Why the fuck you always got to hide behind your damn mother? You never sit down and have a discussion with me without running out on it, and I am tired of it."

"Don't you think I'm tired of you trying to run my motherfucking life? It's bad enough I got to have you all down my back about sticking to the rules of my probation, but to have you trying to tell me what to do like you're the man and I'm the woman is a bit much, and I ain't gon' put up with it anymore. If you wanna violate me for that, then go ahead."

"First of all, I've never treated you like you were the woman and I was the man, so you can cut that out. All I've been doing is trying to look out for your best interest so you can be successful in your life. I mean, what kind of woman would I be if I just let you continue to work at dead-end jobs, where there are no benefits and no room for growth?"

"But it ain't about you; it's about me," Seth explained. "I want to get back on my feet on my own so when I look back at my achievements, I can really feel good about myself."

"I understand all of that, but look at how you're doing it," I replied, trying to give him a mental picture. Of course, he couldn't see it. After ten more minutes of a long debate, he got more frustrated than ever and said, "Look, I am tired of standing here and going on and on about this. I done already got my feet wet yesterday and came out with over two grand in my pocket, so I'm definitely going back. If you want to violate me for that, then stop selling me wolf tickets and go ahead and do it."

Seeing how seriously fed up he was, I realized that my tactics weren't working. I knew that if I didn't back off and let him finish doing what I had agreed to let him do, he would eventually defy my authority and shit would get really ugly. After mulling over the pros and cons of this situation, I came to a conclusion. "All right, you win," I finally said.

"But it's not about who wins or loses. I just want to do what I need to do and that's it. End of story."

"OK, and you will," I commented in a soft tone, hoping it would defuse all the tension between us.

Before Seth could respond, his cellular phone started ringing. He pulled it out of his front pants pocket and looked at the CallerID screen. "I'll call you later, because I gotta take this," he told me and tried to close the front door in my face.

"Wait a minute. Who is that?" I snapped.

"It's my peoples. Now, I gotta go," he snapped back and closed the door.

Mortified at how he had just treated me, I stood there in complete shock. My first thought was to kick the front door down, but I elected not to do it. His mother would love to call the police on me and charge me with breaking and entering. That wouldn't be pretty at all. It would also be just my luck that my boss would find out about it. That would definitely be a scandal and a half, so to avoid all of that, I counted to ten and walked away.

When I got into my car, I took one last look at their house and then pulled off. Before I could get far enough down the block my mind started going into overdrive. I wanted to know who these people were that Seth was working for. I want so badly to at least get a name and find out what they looked like. I would never be able to get any information from Seth, so I guessed the best thing for me to do was to do some investigative work on my own. There was no better time to start than right now. I immediately turned onto the next block and pulled my car over, because I knew it was only going to be a matter of time before he left the house to meet the caller, and I wanted to be there when that happened.

Meanwhile, as I sat there and waited, I got a phone call from my girlfriend, Heather. She had been in my life forever, and it seemed she knew me like the back of her hand. People said she looked like Gabrielle Union, but just a little taller. Because of her height, I had always tried to encourage her to pursue a career in modeling, but she chose to be a psychiatrist instead. She's worked as a licensed psychiatrist for six years and felt like she knew everything about people and their behavioral changes. No one could tell her anything. Not even a man, which was why she was still single and had no children to go with that fully loaded BMW truck she drove and newly renovated, three-bedroom home she lived in.

"Hello," I said, trying desperately not to let on that I was upset.

"Haven't heard from you in a couple of days. What are you doing?"

"Out running errands," I said, lying through my teeth.

"Where at? Because I'm out, too."

"I'm in Chesapeake with Seth," I lied again.

Heather's tone changed. "That figures," she said. "So, why aren't you at work?"

"Because I had a migraine when I woke up this morning."

"You probably got it from that nigga and you don't even know it."

"For your information, I was assaulted yesterday at work by this asshole. That is the sole reason why I woke up with a migraine this morning."

"Oh my God! What happened?"

I told her what transpired without going into excessive detail.

"Wait a minute. You mean to tell me you got headbutted by one of your old parole clients? And you didn't do anything about it?"

"What could I do? The motherfucker hit me so hard, I crashed to the floor."

"Well, I know you're gonna press charges on him, right?"

"I've already done it," I assured her. But that wasn't enough, because she started going on and on about how dangerous my job was getting and that I needed to think about changing careers.

"Heather, you know I can't change careers. I got a lot of years invested, so that wouldn't be a good thing to do right now."

"I thought you wanted to go into business for yourself?"

"I do, but that's gonna take some time."

"What, you need some money?"

"No, I'm fine. I've got a nice sum of cash in the bank. Besides, Seth said he was going to put up his part too."

"You've got to be kidding me. Now, how in the world is he going to come up with enough money for you to go into business for yourself?"

"Well, he just got a job, for one."

"OK, and how long is he going to be employed this time?"

"Heather, I know you mean well, but please, lay off Seth. He's really trying hard to readjust to society."

"Maxine, you just need to face the music that you're involved with a thug and all he knows is the streets. He isn't going to ever be a productive citizen; it's not in him. The sooner you realize that you are not going to ever be able to change him, the sooner you can get on with your life."

"Why are you always so negative?"

"I am not negative; I'm a realist. The sooner you become one, the better off you'll be."

"Do we always have to fuss about him every time we talk?"

"No, we don't."

"Well good, let's talk about Danielle," I said, changing the subject.

Heather hesitated a moment, but then she asked, "What about her?"

"Have you spoken with her since she and her kids flew back to Florida to be with her husband?"

"I spoke with her briefly this morning while I was on my way to work, but she was having a hard time hearing me because her husband was standing next to her, fussing at the kids. I just told her I would call her back."

"How did she sound in the little bit of time you spoke with her?"

"She sounded OK."

"You think he's going to cheat on her again?"

"Knowing him, he probably will. But who knows for sure?"

"Well, the last time I spoke with her—which was the day after her plane landed—I asked her how they were doing, and she said that they were fine. But I didn't buy that for one second."

"Both of y'all are the same."

"And how is that?"

"Y'all don't mind taking up for y'all's man."
Heather laughed.

I laughed too, because she was right. Danielle and
I both protected our men. I guessed it had a lot to do
with how long we'd been with them or the amount
of love we'd invested. I couldn't speak for her, but I
knew that my man loved me, so I would do whatever
it took to protect him. Of course, Heather wouldn't
understand it, which was why I kept things of that
nature to myself. It would be a moot point to her
anyway, so why even bother? Our conversation went
on for another fifteen minutes. We talked about
everything and just when the conversation was about
to get juicy, I saw Seth getting into his car. I cut
Heather off in mid-sentence. "Hey girl, let me call
you right back," I said.

"OK, call me later."

"All right." I immediately disconnected our call.

I gotcha now! I said to myself as I dropped my
phone into the passenger seat and sped off to follow
him. The entire drive, I kept my distance and allowed at least two to three cars between us at all
times. There was one time when I thought that Seth
was onto me, but I soon figured out that he made
the abrupt lane switch because the driver in front of
him was driving five miles under the speed limit.
That made me feel a lot better. Nothing would have
made me feel worse than for him to know that I was
following him.

When we got into the residential section of
Portsmouth, I realized that I had to fall back a little
more and allow traffic lights to catch me for the
rest of the trip, since there weren't a lot of cars driv-

ing through this area. It ended up not mattering because he soon made his first stop. I followed him down Lincoln Street, in the Prentis Park section of Portsmouth, and watched him make a right turn on Richmond Avenue. I put my foot down on the gas pedal and sped up, but by the time I reached that block and saw that he had parked his car at the corner, my heart dropped. I didn't know whether to stop or keep driving. *Keep driving,* my mind told me, and that's what I did. As I passed the block, his car door opened. I don't know what happened afterward because by the time he was completely out of the car, I was gone. I didn't go far, though. I made a right turn on the very next block so that I could circle around and catch Seth on the opposite end of Richmond Avenue. By the time I was able to turn onto that street, however, he was nowhere in sight. His car was parked in the same spot, but he was gone. I figured that he had to either be in the light blue, two-story house sitting on the opposite side of the street or the white, one-story house on the same side as his parked car. To find out which one he was in, I knew I had to pull over and wait.

While I waited, I noticed that there was a Hummer parked directly in front of Seth's car. Since there was no other car parked within two hundred yards of his vehicle, I assumed that the Hummer had to belong to the people he came to see. I kept my engine running and waited. After about ten minutes, Seth and some big, black, tall, linebacker-looking guy came strolling out of the white house. They said a few more words to one another, shook hands, and went their separate ways. The guy driving the Hummer made a U-turn and left. Seth got in his car and followed him. I was glad that he went in the opposite direction, because I didn't know how I was going to duck down in my car without being seen if Seth decided to exit the street from where I was parked. Lucky for me, things were working in my favor. My luck continued, and as soon as Seth made the U-turn to get back onto Lincoln Street, I was back in stride. I followed him for another two miles, and when he entered the Dales Homes housing projects, I knew that this had to be his final stop.

Dales Homes was one of the oldest projects in the city of Portsmouth, and it was known for its heavy drug traffic. I used to visit this place often when I had a parolee who resided out here with his mother. I warned him all the time that it wasn't a good place for him to be if he really wanted to keep his nose clean and stay off the street. Sorry to say, he didn't listen to me. After about a year, I got a call from a Portsmouth Narcotics detective, informing me that he had just busted my client and a few other guys for selling crack cocaine to an undercover police officer. Needless to say, things didn't work out for him, because after the state judge handed him a six-and-a-half-year prison sentence, I violated him and gave him the other four years he had over his head. He had been gone now for almost two years, so I hoped he learned his lesson this time. If he hadn't, he was going to spend a lot more time behind bars than he would on the streets. The only thing I could do for people like him was wish them well, because my main focus right now was Seth. He was a major priority for me. Finding out exactly where he was going and who he was affiliating himself with would take precedence over everything I had to do today. How I would go about doing it was another issue, but I knew I couldn't be too eager.

The apartment buildings were built side by side in the form of a horseshoe. There was one street that traveled in a semicircle, called Dale Drive. As you drove around it you couldn't see what was ahead until you actually drove up on it, because you were constantly turning your steering wheel to the left. I figured if I wanted to avoid running into Seth, I needed to park my car and walk the rest of the way. Something told me not to walk down the block with my Dooney and Burke bag, so I tucked it underneath the driver's seat of my car. After I got out, I activated the alarm so I wouldn't have any problems. As I strolled down Dale Drive, I had to pass an array of people standing on the corner. I walked by a young woman who looked like she wasn't more than twenty-one years old, sporting a blonde and blue, hard-wrapped wig. She was cursing out her two sons because they kept running in and out of the house. I also walked by this guy beating the hell out of his girlfriend. What was so crazy was that the block was filled with people, and no one broke it up. From the sound of things, he was whipping her ass because he caught some guy in her house. All I could do was shake my head and keep it moving.

There were a lot more people I came in contact with who were in really bad shape. One person who really stood out among them all was this light-skinned woman, who looked like she used to be attractive at one point in her life. She looked like she had one foot in the grave, and it wasn't going to be very long before the other one joined it. As I walked in her direction, I put my head down to avoid eye contact with her. I felt like if I looked at her, it would appear that I was staring at the condition of her body, and I didn't want to do that. You could never tell how these people would react if you looked at them funny, so, I wasn't going to take any chances. I found out that she wasn't going to let me by without stepping to me first.

"Excuse me ma'am," she said between coughs as she stood up from a green metal utility box. "Do you think you can spare some change?"

"I'm sorry, but I don't have any," I told her and began to pick up my pace.

That didn't matter to her, because she wanted to get my full attention. She got it when she reached out and grabbed my arm. The shit startled the hell out of me, and I honestly wanted to jump out of my fucking skin. I mean, to have this lady get up enough balls to grab me with her abscess-infected hands made me damn near pass out. Without even thinking twice, I stopped in my tracks and snatched my arm away from her.

"Please don't do that," I warned her.

"I'm sorry," she said, releasing my arm. "But all I want to do is tell you not to do it."

"Do what?" I asked, wondering what the hell she could be talking about.

The lady got closer and said, "I used to walk around here looking just like you, wearing nice clothes, thinking I was high and mighty because I was beautiful and had a long, healthy head of hair.

I had a nice body and all the men wanted to be with me. But at the blink of an eye, my world got turned upside down when I started hanging out in places like this."

"But I don't get high," I interjected.

"Yeah, that's what we've all said. Now look at us." She pointed at different drug addicts in our immediate vicinity. "We all got a story to tell. But mine is by far the worst, if you ask me, because I was an assistant principal at a performing arts school, making damn good money. But because of my heroin addiction and hanging in that motherfucking candy shop over there in Norfolk, I lost my husband, my daughter, and my home in Virginia Beach. The repo man took my 2007 Jaguar after I let the dope boys tear it up. I used to rent it out to them for days at a time, for a couple measly pills of dope," she continued as tears began to build up in her eyes.

"I'm sorry to hear about your loss, ma'am, and I would love to stand here and listen to you, but I'm sort of in a rush."

"Don't call me 'ma'am'. My name is Faith."

"I'm sorry, Faith, but I've got to go," I told her and abruptly walked off.

"I hope you take heed to what I said," she yelled.

"Oh, shut the hell up, Faith! That lady ain't thinking about your dopefiend ass!" I heard a male voice shout.

I refused to turn around to see who made the comment. I figured he wasn't talking to me anyway, so why bother? As I walked farther down Dale Drive, I finally saw Seth's car. It was parked right in front of a tree, but again, he was nowhere in sight. There were at least three dozen apartments that he could have gone into. To stand there and wait for him to come out would be insane. I turned around and headed back to my car. Immediately after I got in it, I drove right back out the way I came and circled around to the other side of the horseshoe. All I wanted to see was which apartment he was in, and then I'd leave. As soon as I found a parking space with the perfect view, I parked. Then I had to sit and wait. I sat back and listened to every CD in my six-disc changer, which ran for about three hours, and still Seth remained in hiding. I called him a couple of times, hoping he would come outside to take his call, but he refused to answer, so I chalked it up as a loss.

As I was about to give up and call it a day, the guy from the white house pulled up in his Hummer and parked it right beside Seth's car. My heart jumped for joy. Hopefully, it would only be a matter of seconds before I found out where that mother-fucker was. Before I could count to ten, that guy walked right up to an apartment on the far left side of the building, carrying a brown paper bag in his right hand. Before he could reach out, someone from the inside opened the door for him. I couldn't see if it was Seth or not because of the dark screen on the door. At that point, though, it didn't matter because my mission was accomplished, and now I could carry my ass home.

Seth

I Get Money

"Ay yo, Melody, I know you fucked that coffee grinder up on purpose," Mike said the moment he stepped foot into the spot.

"Nah, Mike, it wasn't her fault," I said as I approached him.

"Where's it at? Let me see it," Mike insisted.

Melody and I both led him into the kitchen.

"See? It wasn't my fault," she pointed out. "The blade is dull now, so it isn't grinding anything anymore."

"How much shit did you lose?"

"Not much," Melody said.

"How much is not much?"

"Probably about ten pills, if that much."

"You sure you didn't stick that shit in your pocket?" Mike questioned her, giving her one serious look.

"Come on now. You know I wouldn't play with your dope like that," Melody tried to assure him.

"You better not, because if I ever find out you stealing from me, I'ma kill you, bitch!"

"Nah, dawg, I was standing around her the whole time. She didn't try to throw salt in the game," I told him.

"She better not!" Mike handed her the brown paper bag.

"Is this a new coffee grinder?"

"Yeah. So go ahead and handle your business, so I can get me some motherfucking money rolling through here. You know I hate having good dope and ain't nobody coming through to cop it."

"Oh, believe me, plenty of fiends been coming through, but we had to turn 'em away because we couldn't get the coffee grinder to mix the dope up properly," I said.

"Well, we ain't gon' worry about that anymore. That problem is solved. What I want to know is, where is everybody at?" Mike looked out the kitchen window. "I didn't see any of our runners standing at their posts when I pulled up. The only nigga standing out there is Omar, and that ain't a good look."

Wearing the surgical mask, Melody turned around and said, "I sent Ian to the store to get me some milk and a box of sandwich bags. I'm not sure where Ran is."

"Did you ask Ian or Omar?"

"Yeah, and they said they hadn't seen him since he left from around here last night," she replied.

"Well, we gon' have to recruit a couple more niggas, because I can't have y'all in the spot with all this shit and not enough niggas on the outside watching y'all's backs."

"Shit, all I need is a burner and I'll be able to hold the spot down by myself," I interjected.

Mike laughed. "Yeah, that burner will slow down a couple of cats from trying to run up in here to rob you, but it ain't gon' do shit if Narcs bust up in here."

I became defensive. "Oh, so you don't think I'd bust my gun at them crackers?"

"Come on, Seth. I was locked up with you and I know how hard you can go. But we still need more niggas outside. I can't afford to have police run up in here. I got too much shit to lose."

"You sure do," Melody spoke up.

Mike smiled at her and said, "Yeah, yeah, yeah!" He looked at me and said, "Let me holler at you for a minute."

Curious about why he wanted to speak to me in private all of a sudden, I got up from the table and followed him into Melody's bedroom. I thought he would shut the door behind us after we entered the room, but he didn't. "What's up?"

Mike said, "You know I ain't a petty-ass nigga. I am loyal to any cat that's loyal to me, and I love to see everybody eat, if they're hungry enough to go after it. I just got hit off with a huge load of raw heroin about an hour ago, and it's enough where we could build an empire with it. Niggas could get rich off this shit in a matter of months. You could walk away with a half million in profit, easy. All we got to do is get a street team of niggas who ain't scared to lock this place down, and we could be on our way."

"What about Jay?"

"I got him over in Norfolk right now, trying to recruit some go-hard niggas, so we can lock the whole Tidewater Park down."

"So, y'all are serious about this, huh?"

"Hell, yeah! This shit ain't a game! I'm trying to get rich!"

"Shit! Me too!" I said, without hesitation. The thought of making a half a million dollars in less than a month sounded real good to me. I could do a lot of shit with that dough. If I invested it right, I wouldn't have to work or hustle again.

"You sure? Because I'm gon' tell you right now, if you really want to get that type of paper in a month's time, you gon' have to work around the clock."

"What's around the clock?"

"I'm talking about you gon' have to be out this joint from sunup to sundown," he explained. "You know fiends be up searching for pills of dope early in the morning, so you gon' have to be out here at least by five AM. But as far as the time you close down, that ain't gon' change. You can still shut shop down at nine o'clock."

"Ahh man, my girl is going to kill me." I sighed, thinking about all the shade Maxine was going to throw at me.

"Just tell her how much dough you gon' make in that thirty-day period and see how she acts. I guarantee, she gon' sing another song then." Mike laughed. "Shit, bitches love money!"

"Not my girl! She'd rather have me working a nine-to-five, busting my ass for pennies, than to see me out here stacking up retirement money."

"Oh, you got one of them goody-two-shoes chicks, huh?"

"Shit, I don't know what to call her. But I do know that she's starting to get on my motherfucking nerves!"

"Come on, dawg; don't ever let a chick stress you out."

"Shit, it's too late for that."

"Well, whatchu gon' do when Samantha gets out?"

"I don't know. I've been trying to figure that shit out for the last few months."

"When she getting out, anyway?"

"She called me this morning at my mom's crib and told me she got twenty-nine days and a wake up."

"Oh shit, for real?"

"Yep."

"So, is she gon' have to go to the halfway house?"

"Yeah, but it's only going to be for a four-month stretch."

"Well, this dough you about to get is going to come in handy because by the time she gets out of the halfway house, you can set her up in a nice spot."

"Yeah, I know. She gon' be happy as hell, too. All she keeps talking about is how she can't wait until we can be together again. But it's gon' be really hard, 'cause the chick I'm fucking with now is the type that would do some underhanded shit if she found out Samantha was home and that we was back together."

"Look, dawg: don't ever let a bitch get the upper hand on you! It's too many hoes out here to be putting up with dumb shit! Look at me; I got my wife, Lacy, and two side chicks. So, if one starts giving me a motherfucking headache, I'll dip on her ass in a minute and go be with the other one. It's that simple! And I ain't gon' have it no other way," Mike said. "You see how I be handling Melody in there? I don't let her get away with shit. I come here and make my money, get some pussy, and before I go, I'll hit her off with some dough. That's the extent of it. See, she knows about Lacy and my other chick Trina, but she also knows that she can't question me about them, either. And if any one of them ever stopped by here to see me, she knows she better not open up her motherfucking mouth about shit that goes on in this house. If she ever tried that, she knows I would shut her down."

"Damn, nigga. You ain't playing, huh?"

"Hell nah, I ain't playing! I got too much shit invested out here to be letting a chick come in and fuck everything up because she's caught up in her feelings. I promise you that I ain't gon' have it!"

Once Mike touched on every issue concerning the business venture and how he wanted shit to run around there, I sealed the deal with a handshake. Before I realized what I had done, he reminded me by saying, "Nigga, you are about to be the third richest hustler in the Tidewater area!"

I laughed. "I take it you and Jay got the number one and the number two slots?"

"You sure learn quickly," he said, patting me on my shoulder before he left.

After Mike left me in Melody's bedroom, all I could do was stand there with a smile on my face and daydream about that brand-new Bentley coupe I was going to be pushing in the next thirty days. I also pictured buying myself a whole new wardrobe and going into a jewelry store to cop a couple of custom-made diamond pieces. I was going to make sure Samantha was all right too. I couldn't have her struggling like I did when I first came home. Nah, I couldn't have that. She was still my shorty, and I loved her to death. I didn't know what I was going to do for Maxine, other than give her the start-up money for her business, because she seemed to have everything. She was the most independent and controlling chick I'd ever dealt with, and most of the time we butted heads because of it. The shit I went through with her, I never had to go through any of it with Samantha. Sam was a sweetheart and would do anything I asked her to do. She'd been down for me since the first day we met, which was over seven years ago. For the first two years of our relationship, shit was beautiful. We got money together and we lived together. We did practically everything together, so when the heat fell down on us five years ago, she had no problem going down for the cause. She stayed true to a nigga, so I was going to do the same for her. That was my word!

Mike hung out at the spot with me and Melody for the rest of the night. While he was there, he recruited a handful of thoroughbred cats from around the way. Most of them were young boys around the age of seventeen and eighteen. They were known around Portsmouth for having heart, and that's what we needed for this mission. They got hired on the spot. After everybody got into position, Mike and I ended up raking in over twenty grand, and were happy because of it.

Before the young boys left, Mike hit them each off with a couple hundred dollars and promised them that he was going to arm a couple of them with burners, just in case they ran into some heat. They got all gassed up about the idea of toting a pistol around the spot, like they were in a little army. The enthusiasm in their faces made Mike's day. It made my day too, because I knew we had a ruthless set of soldiers in our midst, and it was going to be hard to break them.

As I was about to leave, Mike hit me off with my cut and gave me precise instructions about how we were going to operate our organization. "From now on, I'm gonna have the dope capped up for you before you get over on this side. All you got to do is show up at the spot out on Prentis Park and I'll have everything ready for you, including the pistols for the young'uns."

He also said he was going to have his side chick, Trina, come by twice a day to collect the dough if he or Jay weren't available to do it themselves. Also, if we ran out of product before the end of the day, he was going to have Jay drop off a small package to carry us over. I okayed this arrangement, shook on it, and headed out the door.

When I got into my car, I started to call Maxine, but decided against it. As much as I missed hearing her voice, I knew that if I got her on the phone, we would end up arguing, and I wasn't in the mood for that. It had been a long day, and the last thing

I needed was a headache. Instead, I headed on to my mother's crib.

On my way there, I made a quick stop by the Chinese place on the corner of Virginia Beach Boulevard and Newtown Road and picked up an order of General Tso Chicken. While I was there, I ran into this nigga named Monty I had beef with back in the day. He shocked me when he didn't say a word to me when I first walked into the restaurant. The way that nigga came at me when he found out I was fucking his girl, it was a wonder why I didn't end up killing him. I guess it wasn't his time to die, and since he acted like he had some sense this go-round, I spared him once more and bounced.

Maxine

Back To The Drawing Board

I tried to get Seth on the line this morning, but he elected not to answer his phone yet again. I told myself, *whatever,* and blew it off as another one of his immature tactics. All was not lost anyway, because I got all the information I needed yesterday. I wrote down the license plate number to the Hummer Seth's friend was driving and the address of the house he entered. Now that I was back at work, I was about to find out the name registered to that vehicle and who was leasing that apartment. It was going to take a couple strokes of the computer keys and one phone call, and I was going to have it all. Seth was not going to be able to hide anything from me from this point on.

Click, click, tap, tap, click, tap, tap, click was all you could hear through my silence-filled office. Right after I got into the Department of Motor Vehicles' secured information system, I typed in the license plate number of the Hummer and hit the ENTER key. The name Lacy Carrington appeared. Her address was listed as 1756 Concourse Lane in Virginia Beach. There was also a 2007 Acura RL registered in her name. From the looks of things, this woman had to either be this guy's wife or girlfriend. Of course, it didn't matter. I had her information, so it was just a matter of time before I had his.

Next, I logged onto the city of Virginia Beach's tax assessment website and found out that the residence of 1756 Concourse Lane was a home assessed at $423,000 and it belonged to Michael and Lacy Carrington. Seeing all this information put a huge smile on my face. I jotted all that information down and then called the rental office of Dale Homes and was told to fax over a release form in order for them to release the name of the person leasing the apartment. I did. Ten minutes later, I got my fax back with the lessee's name written big as day. Melody Powell was her name, and the form also stated that she was a twenty-six-year-old Section Eight applicant and mother of one school-age son. According to this document, she had never been convicted of a felony and she had sworn never to allow any drug activity inside or around the dwelling of her apartment. If she violated this, she would be arrested and evicted immediately. After reading all the content on both pages, I knew right off the bat that I could do some serious blackmailing if I wanted to. However, since I planned to handle this matter a little differently, I put the information away in a safe place.

* * *

The first half of my day in the office ended quickly. I chose to spend the second half in the field. I also chose to travel alone, since I didn't have to collect any urine samples. The first stop on my list was in the city of Chesapeake to pay a visit to my client, Sean Phillips. He was a thirty-eight-year-old, tall, lean, brown-skinned male with long dreadlocks. He was from the rough streets of Philly, which was where he caught his charge. After ten years behind bars, Sean requested to be released in the state of Virginia, where he now resided with his parents. He had been back on the streets now for two years, and so far, he had managed to comply with all the rules of his probation. If he continued to keep this up, I might release him from his probation one year early.

"How you doing today?" I asked. I looked very professional with my hair brushed back into a neat ponytail and dressed in a black Calvin Klein pantsuit and white oxford blouse. My jacket was pushed back just a little to reveal the U.S. Probation Office badge attached to the belt loop of my slacks.

"I'm fine," Sean replied, opening the front door wide enough for me to walk into the house.

"That's good to hear," I said after he closed the door behind me. "Are your parents home?"

"No, both of them are out of town visiting relatives." He escorted me to the living room area.

As soon as I walked halfway down the hallway, a funny smell of Lysol spray mixed with marijuana smoke engulfed me. I stopped in my tracks and asked, "Mr. Phillips, is that marijuana I smell?"

"Oh, nah, you know I don't mess around with that stuff," he stuttered.

"Well, why is that smell coming from down this

hall?" I pressed the issue, not moving one inch from where I was standing.

"I don't know," he said, trying to convince me. I wasn't going for it. The scent from the marijuana was strong. It didn't matter how much Lysol he sprayed to cover up the smell, because the chemical from the marijuana was overpowering it.

Irritated by his lies, I gave him a firm look and said, "Come open up this bedroom door over here to my left."

"Whatchu want to go in there for?" Sean protested. "Ain't nothing in there."

"Are you hiding something from me?" My patience was growing thin.

"Nope."

Realizing that this guy wasn't about to cooperate with me made me go into think mode. There was no doubt in my mind that I smelled marijuana, and in order for me to confirm this, I was going to have to open that first door to my left. My only problem was that I didn't think I was going to be ready to deal with what I was about to find.

"Isn't that your bedroom?" I asked.

"Yeah."

"Well, open it up."

"I can't," he replied nonchalantly.

"Why not?" I snapped.

"Because it's locked."

"Why is it locked?"

"Because I locked it."

My face turned red. "Well, unlock it," I demanded.

"I'm sorry, Ms. Shaw, but I can't do that."

Getting more and more frustrated with his lack of cooperation, I stormed toward the bedroom door, but before I could get within ten feet of it, Sean grabbed me by my arms and shoved me up against the wall, face first. The shit caught me off guard and I didn't know if I was coming or going. "What the hell are you doing?" I grunted, trying to wiggle my way from his grip.

"I'm sorry, Ms. Shaw, but I can't let you go in there."

"Sean, you better let me go right now," I screeched. "Do you know I can violate you for this?"

Instead of Sean responding to my question, he said, "Ay yo, Gee, you and Duke come on."

Less than five seconds later, the bedroom door opened and out came two men. Both of them had fair complexions and bald heads. They looked like they could be brothers, but one was short and skinny, while the other was of a medium height and medium build. The short, skinny guy was dressed in a throwback jersey, a pair of jeans, and sneakers, and looked to be in his early thirties, while the other guy was dressed in a black hoodie with the sweats to match. He looked like he was every bit of forty. As they walked by me, I noticed that they were carrying two large compressed slabs of marijuana between pieces of folded newspapers. The bottom half of the plastic bag was sticking out from underneath the newspaper. You could see the seeds from the marijuana dangling in the bottom of the bag, clear as day.

"You can hide it all you want, but I know that's got to be every bit of four pounds of marijuana y'all are carrying."

The taller guy stopped in his tracks. "Yo, Sean, whatchu gon' do with her?"

"I'm gon' tie her ass up," Sean told him.

"Sean, if you tie me up, I am going to send you

flying back to prison. And by the time you come home, you're gonna be in a fucking rocking chair!" I screamed, trying to break loose from his grip.

"You heard what she said, dawg! So, you'd be better off getting rid of her ass!" the shorter guy said.

"You shut up! Because believe it or not, I'm gonna have both of y'all asses locked up for a very long time, too!" I shouted.

"Bitch, you ain't gon' do shit to me! Because trust me, you ain't gon' ever see my face again," the short guy said.

"Mine either," the taller guy assured me.

"That's what y'all think," I snapped back.

"Ay yo, Sean, get rid of that bitch now!"

"Nah, man, let's just tie her up and gag her and stuff her in the trunk of her car."

"That's stupid. And besides, that's too much work, so just off her," the older guy insisted.

"Nah, dawg, I ain't trying to wear a murder beef," Sean protested, but it seemed like the other two guys had a little more authority. After a few more words were exchanged between the three of them, the older guy said, "Well, it's your ass, nigga, 'cause she ain't gon' ever see me and Duke's face again!"

Hearing them deliberate about whether or not to kill me sent me into panic mode. I started twisting and turning and kicking like crazy. Shit, I didn't want to die. Of course, my little antics didn't work because the older guy pulled a gun from the waist of his sweatpants and before I could figure out what was about to happen, he struck me in the back of my head with the butt of this gun. I fell out cold.

Seth

100% Raw & Uncut

Mike had just hit me off with one thousand pills of dope, which was going to bring five grand in profit. I was on my way to the spot to grind these joints out. Right when I was pulling up in front of Melody's apartment, my cell phone rang. When I looked at the CallerID and noticed that it was Samantha, I quickly answered it. Before the line was connected, I had to wait for the automated system to give me the spiel about how *an inmate was calling me from an institution and if I wanted to accept the call, I needed to press five now,* so I did.

"Hello," Samantha said, her voice sounding like a little girl's.

The sound of her voice made me smile. "What's up, baby?" I asked.

"What's up with you?"

"Nothing much. Just doing what I got to do to come up!"

"Well, I got the money you sent through Western Union last night."

"That's good."

"So, how long you gon' be out today?"

"Probably till I bang out at least thirty grand."

"Please be careful, because you know I won't be any good if something happened to you while I was in here."

"Just chill, mommie. Trust me, ain't nothing gonna happen to me. Me and my peoples got this shit on lock. Ain't nobody coming through here unless they got some dough to spend."

"A'ight, but you know I'm gonna still be worried."

"Look, I told you yesterday not to worry about me. I am straight and you are going to be straight too, as soon as you hit those bricks!"

"I know, baby, and I can't wait either, because the first thing I am going to do is jump dead on that big dick of yours and fuck you till my pussy gets raw!"

"I ain't gon' give you no dick unless you promise me you gon' give me a baby."

"Are you going to marry me?"

"Come on now, man. What kind of question is that? You know I love your pretty ass!"

"Good, because I am trying to lock shit down when I come home! I ain't trying to share you with no other bitches!"

"Samantha, you know can't none of these bitches out here hold a candle to you. That's why I don't fuck with none of them."

"So, you mean to tell me you ain't fucked nobody since you been home?"

Before I answered her question, I thought about the consequences of telling the truth. I knew that if I told her I had, she would go the hell off, and I didn't want to hurt her feelings. She really meant that much to me. I figured I'd be better off lying. I mean, it wasn't like she was going to find out about Maxine anyway. By the time Samantha came home, my relationship with Maxine was going to be over and I'd be free and clear. No drama and no worries. "Come on, now," I finally said. "Haven't we already been over this?"

"Yes, but you never give me a straight answer."

"Well, the answer is no."

"No, what?"

"No, Samantha, I haven't fucked anybody since I've been home."

"So, whatchu being doing then? Because I know how much you love pussy."

"I've been beating my meat," I lied. Somehow, I didn't sound as convincing as I would have liked.

She came back at me and said, "Seth, you are lying and you know it!"

"A'ight, a'ight! I am going to be honest. I let this one chick suck my dick one time."

"Who?" Samantha roared.

"I don't remember her name."

"So, you just let some total stranger suck your dick?"

"I wasn't alone," I said as my lies continued.

"Then who was with you?"

"It was me and my peoples chilling at his spot in

Norfolk, and he had some stripper chick come by and hit him off with some pussy. And by the end of the night, she was sucking every nigga dick in the crib."

"Oh my God! That is so nasty! Do you know you can catch a whole lot of shit letting nasty bitches like that put their mouth around your dick?"

"Sam, what kind of nigga you think I am? I didn't let that bitch suck my dick in the raw! Every nigga in the whole spot had on condoms."

"Well, it doesn't matter, because all y'all niggas are nasty!" she snapped. "I know one thing, though."

"And what's that?" I asked.

"You better not let that shit happen again! I mean, I don't ever want to hear about you fucking with no other bitches, or it's going to be some serious problems."

"Ahh, stop tripping! I am not thinking about none of these hoes out here."

"Well, you better keep it like that, because I ain't got nothing but three weeks and five days left. So I want shit to be right when I get out," she warned me.

"And it will," I assured her.

I also assured her that I would be getting her a new whip when she got out, too. I told her she was going to have to get it in her sister's name, since she wouldn't have a job coming out the gate. That was when Samantha started going on about how she had to have the new cherry M-3. I gave her the OK and got nothing but giggles for the rest of the conversation. Before we hung up, she assured me that she was going to call me back by nine-thirty. I told her that would be fine.

After I hung up my phone, I looked up and saw

Melody staring out of her window at me. I guessed that she had probably been watching me the whole time I had been sitting out here. When I walked into the house with the brown paper bag of dope in my right hand, I said, "I saw you watching me."

"And, so what," she replied with a slight grin and walked off into the direction of her bedroom.

As she walked away from me, I looked straight at her round ass. That little-ass jean skirt she had on was sticking to her butt like glue. Instead of making an issue about her response, I said, "You love wearing shit that'll get my dick hard, huh?"

Melody stopped in her tracks and slightly turned in my direction. "Seth, I've been dressing like this long before I met you."

I walked toward her. "So, who do you wear it for?"

"Myself."

"I don't believe that." I stood within one inch of her. I could have easily kissed her if I wanted to, since I was dead in her face. I held my composure and waited for her to make the first move.

"Well, believe it." She walked off once again.

"Why you keep walking away from me?" I wondered aloud and followed her.

"Whatchu want me to do? Just stand there so you can breathe in my face?"

"I want to do more than that," I replied when I entered her bedroom.

"Oh, really?"

We were both standing next to her bed. I sat the bag of dope on her dresser and shoved Melody right onto her bed. When she landed on her back, she gave me this exotic-ass look and spread her legs wide open. To see that she didn't have on a stitch of panties blew my mind. The blood flow rushed to my dick, and it swelled up instantly.

"You know you playing with fire, right?" My dick was bulging through my pants while I stared at her petite, hairy pussy. The clit on that joint was nice and plump, and my dick wanted to get next to it.

"Don't talk about it. Be about it." Melody reached down to her pussy and started rubbing it.

Watching her play with that wet thang had my dick jumping. I knew that if I didn't hurry up and slide my meat up in her and shove it in and out of her a few times, I was gon' fuck around and waste a good nut right in my motherfucking pants. Without further hesitation, I unfastened my belt, dropped my jeans and boxer shorts, and stepped right out of them both.

"Come here, girl."

I grabbed her by her ankles and pulled her to the edge of the bed. Her skirt rolled underneath her butt so that it was out of my way, so I didn't have to take it off. Right when I was about to slob homegirl down and give her a little bit of foreplay, my dick started dripping really bad with my pre-ejaculation cum. The shit was running like a faucet, so I immediately pushed all nine inches of my hard steel into her wet, juicy-looking coochie. After I pushed, pulled and gyrated my dick inside her about a good ten times in a row, I realized that I was working myself to death. Homegirl's pussy hole was big as shit. It didn't matter how much I grinded my dick in her, I wasn't hitting a single wall in that joint, and I was getting frustrated like a motherfucker.

I told her to tighten her muscles up for me and she said, "I'm trying," but that was a damn lie. All Melody did was make grunting sounds like she was doing something. It finally sunk in my head that this shit wasn't going to work, and I came up with the solution to fuck her right in her butt.

"Turn over on your stomach," I instructed her.

She did it with no problem. I pushed her skirt up a little bit more and then beat her ass cheeks with my dick. Her ass started jiggling around like a bowl of jelly. I started teasing her asshole with my tongue and then I poked my index finger in it.

"Oh my God! That shit feels soooo good!" Melody moaned, winding her ass around in a circular motion while I had her round, pretty, red ass cheeks spread apart. Juices from her ass were squirting out everywhere. The way she was bucking at me was like she was ready for me to run up in her.

I said, "You ready to take this dick in your ass?"

"Ahhhh yes, give it to me!" she begged.

I plunged my entire dick right in her ass and started going for what I knew. I pumped my shit in her for dear life and she handled it like a pro. Melody was a bonafide whore, and I believed she enjoyed that shit more than me. When it seemed like I was about to pull the head completely out, I would ram that shit right back up in her and she would scream out, "Oh yeah!" Word to life, I was ripping homegirl's asshole apart and I wasn't letting up. The way she talked shit to me while my dick slid in and out of her plump, red ass made the experience all the better, not to mention the feeling I got from all this.

What really fucked my head up, though, was

when I started jerking. Melody knew my dick was about to explode because when I pulled out of her, she turned around, grabbed my dick, and started sucking on the head of it. My joint erupted like a motherfucking volcano.

"Ughhhhhh!" I moaned.

My eyes were closed as my body jerked. When I opened them, Melody was sitting upright in the bed with a great big smile. There was no evidence of cum around her mouth, so I assumed she must've swallowed every last drop of it.

"You a'ight?" she asked me as she hopped off her bed and headed toward the bathroom.

"Yeah, I'm straight." I retrieved my boxers and jeans off the floor.

While I was putting my gear back on, she returned to the bedroom with a warm, damp washcloth and handed it to me. "Here," she said, "take care of that."

"No problem." I took the washcloth and wiped my dick off.

Meanwhile, Melody pulled a pair of pink Baby Phat sweatpants and a matching hoodie from her dresser drawer. When she was about to put it on I noticed that she wasn't going to slip on any panties. "What's up? Why you ain't putting on a pair of panties?"

She smiled at me and said, "Because I want to be good and ready when you give me some of that dick later on."

I didn't respond to her comment, and all I could do was smile. I grabbed the bag of dope from the dresser and headed into the kitchen. Before I emptied all the pills out onto the table, I sent Melody outside to round all the niggas up. When she gathered up everybody, I told all of them to come into the living room for a quick meeting. It was five young boys in all, between the ages of seventeen and nineteen, and they were high school dropouts. Now all of them were thorough as hell, but the two I figured would probably hold it down for me and be the most loyal were Hakeem and Bishop. That was why I gave them both burners and told them to guard the front and back of the apartment. I instructed the other two niggas to stand and play the watch-out while the other young'uns brought the customers to the door. I also told them that we had a lot of work to get rid of today and that it had to be gone before anybody could leave, and they understood. When I was ready to dismiss them, Hakeem's little, short, black ass had a question for me.

"Can we take these burners with us when we leave?"

I looked at that nigga with an *I can't believe you just asked me that* look and said, "Hell nah! Can't none of y'all take them joints with you. Those pistols are for protecting this spot, so you are going to only hold them while you're here."

"Can we bust a nigga in their ass if they try to run up on us?"

"You damn right! Take the motherfucker's head off if you want to," I instructed, then stopped. "Shit, I don't care what you do, just as long as you keep them from running up in here. You got it?"

"Yeah," Hakeem and Bishop said in unison.

"A'ight. Well, y'all niggas go ahead and fall out."

They walked out the crib, got into position, and everything worked out smoothly. We ran through that entire package of dope and finished selling the last pill of heroin by seven o'clock. I started to call Mike so we could re-up, but I was tired and decided to go ahead and end my day early. After I collected the burners and hit my little homeboys off with their dough, I skated out of the spot before Melody noticed. She called my cell phone the moment I sped off in my car. I answered it and gave her some bogus excuse about how I had to leave in a rush because of an emergency. She bought it and told me she could not wait until she saw me tomorrow. I got her ass off the phone because I wasn't feeling her after what had happened earlier. Granted, Melody was pretty as a motherfucker and she was a pro at taking dick in her ass, but her pussy was whack. That shit was so big and sloppy, it was pathetic.

When I thought about it some more, I couldn't believe that I fucked that bitch in the raw. What the hell was I thinking about? Was I on crack or something, because I seriously made a dummy move. I just hoped shorty didn't have that AIDS shit, because if she did, I was going to be fucked. Speaking of which, I would bet every dime in my pocket that Mike didn't touch her unless he was packing a box of Magnums. Then again, judging from how raggedy her coochie was, he probably only let her suck his dick. If in fact that was the case, the picture was becoming very clear of why he carried her the way he did. He practically looked at her like she was some ol' gutter bitch! Come to think about it, I felt the same way he did. If you want to know the truth, I was gonna have to start treating her like that too, because after what happened today, I couldn't let her think we had something going on.

Shit, I had a girl and she was a bad chick, too. As soon as Samantha got out of the joint, we were definitely going to make this thing official. Until then, I was going to continue stacking my paper and move everything out of the way that wasn't beneficial.

After I dropped Mike's dough off to him, we chopped shit up for a few minutes about what we were gon' do after we hit this lick. He told me he was going to take a trip, and I told him I'd probably do the same thing. After he ran shit down to me about how things were going to go down tomorrow, I took it all in, we shook on it, and then we parted ways.

When I got on the highway, it dawned on me that Maxine hadn't tried to call me since early this morning. I figured that maybe she got the hint that I was sick of her shit and decided to leave me alone for a while. Who knew, she might call me tonight, even though it wouldn't matter because I was not going to answer the phone. I had better things to do than to be letting her stress me out about dumb shit. From this day forward, I was going to be on some new shit. It was all about chopping niggas' heads off and getting this paper, and I would not let her stop me.

Maxine

The Domino Effect

Somehow, I regained consciousness and I slowly opened my eyes. When I realized that I was lying on the floor inside of a very dark house, I rolled over and scrambled to my feet. I staggered a bit when I stood up because I was still a little lightheaded. I held onto the wall and took a couple of steps in the direction of the living room when I noticed that everything had been turned off. The entire house was in complete silence. You could hear a pin drop, which was a clear indicator that Sean and his two co-conspirators had long been gone. I had to be sure, so I reached underneath my jacket to retrieve my nine-millimeter Glock holstered to my waist, but it wasn't there. I panicked. I snatched my suit jacket off and patted my entire upper body and waist area, but still it wasn't there. Suddenly, it came to me that one of them cowards took my gun.

"Oh shit! What am I going to do?" I asked myself as anxiety started running through me. I needed to call Karen, so I reached in my pants pocket for my cellular phone, but that was gone as well. "What the fuck!" I screamed. I had an alarming feeling that I was out of my comfort zone. I was unarmed and un-equipped. Both my firearm and my phone were gone, and I knew that I would have to answer to my supervisor because of this. A full-scale investigation would be launched, and I might be sent home or put on strict administrative duty because of it. Shit, I didn't need this type of drama in my life right now.

The only thing I could think to do was use the telephone in the house, but when I looked for one, there were none in sight. I walked through every room in the house, and all the outlets were bare. It looked as if someone disconnected every phone in there. I knew it could not have been anyone else but Sean, so believe me, that bastard was going to get his.

Running out of every option under the sun, I de-cided to get out of there and find the nearest pay phone. I looked for my car keys and they, too, were gone. *Oh shit, my car!* I thought to myself as I raced to the front door and opened it. To my relief, my car was still there, so I let out a long sigh and tried to figure out what I needed to do next. I looked down at my watch and noticed that it was a little after eight o'clock, so that meant I had been un-conscious for a little over six hours. In that time, Sean could've been on a plane, traveling to another country. He could also be hiding out somewhere in this area. I promised myself that I would find his ass, if it was the last thing I did.

After three minutes of pacing back and forth, a car drove by and pulled into the driveway of the home next door, so I sprinted over there before the driver could park the car.

"I'm so sorry for bothering you, but I was wondering if I could use your phone to call the police?" I asked.

I was out of breath as I peered into the driver's side window directly at a very young-looking black man. He had to be in his early twenties because his facial features were not fully developed and he didn't have a speck of facial hair. His ball cap was turned around backward and he was blasting the hell out of 50 Cent's new CD, *Curtis*, but when he saw how in distress I was, he immediately turned down the volume.

"You want to use my what?" he asked, as if he'd only heard bits and pieces of what I had said.

"I said, I need to call the police. I was wondering if I could use your phone," I told him.

"Yeah, sure." He handed me a cellular phone. "Is everything all right?"

I took the phone from his hand and started dialing. I attempted to answer him, but by the time I opened my mouth to speak, the 911 operator came on the line and asked me what my emergency was. I told the woman who I was and briefly explained what had just transpired between my parolee and two unknown suspects. In return, the woman told me that a police unit would be sent out to the location very shortly. I thanked the 911 dispatcher for her help, hung up, and immediately got my supervisor on the line. I knew she wouldn't be at the office at this hour, so I called her at home. She answered on the third ring.

"Hi Karen, this is Maxine."

"Hey, what happened to you? I thought you were coming back into work today."

"Karen, I am standing outside the residence of one of my parolees, and I need some help."

"What's the matter?"

I sighed. "I was struck in the back of my head with a firearm and knocked out cold for over six hours."

Shocked, she screamed through the receiver of the telephone. "What!"

"Karen, that's not it," I told her while shaking my head. "My gun was taken and so were my car keys. I'm standing outside of the residence, waiting for the police to show up."

"You're kidding me, right?"

"No, I am not."

I reiterated what happened, from beginning to end. When I was done, she told me that she was going to make a report to start an investigation. She also stressed to me about how important it was to get my government-issued firearm back.

"We can't have those guys running around in the streets with that gun," she emphasized.

I agreed to assist in this investigation in any way I could.

"Give me the address where you are, because I'm on my way," she insisted.

"Are you sure you want to come out this time of the night?"

"Of course I'm sure."

Once I had given her the address and assured her that I would watch for her, I got off the line with her and called AAA to have them let me into my vehicle and tow my car to my place. I started to call Seth so he could bring me the other set of car keys, but I knew I couldn't take the chance of having him around Karen and having her remember who he was. I figured that would be the worst thing I could ever do, so I pressed the END button on the phone and handed it back to the young man.

"Thank you so much," I said.

By then, he had gotten out of his car and sat on the hood. You could tell thoughts were running through his mind because after he stuffed his phone back into his pocket he said, "All that stuff happened to you for real?"

"What's your name?" I interjected.

"Lamont."

"OK, Lamont. Yes, it did."

"You actually saw them with drugs?"

I nodded my head.

"Man, I knew it," he said and snapped his finger.

His comment sparked my curiosity. "You knew what?"

"I knew he was doing something illegal over there."

"How did you come up with that assumption?"

"Because he was always home during the day and while he was there, I would always see at least two guys come by in expensive cars and drop off a large duffel bag."

"How did these guys look?"

"I can't tell you how they looked in the face, but the way they were dressed told it all."

"What kind of cars were they driving?"

"I remember one of them driving a black Infiniti with twenty-inch rims, and the other two cats were driving a burgundy Yukon with twenty-two-inch rims and a funny-colored green Mercedes Benz wagon."

"Was this every day?"

"Almost every day."

"How often during the course of the day?"

"Once or twice, but never more than that."

"Did you ever catch them exchanging any large sums of cash out in the open?"

"Nope. Sean never did anything with them outside. He always would let them go in the house."

"How well do you know Sean?"

"I have known him for a long time because my parents have been living here for as long as his parents lived there."

"Had y'all hung out?"

"Yeah, we used to shoot ball every Saturday, but when those guys started coming around, I started seeing less and less of him."

"Are his parents out of town?"

"Yeah, they're out of town."

"How do you know this for sure?"

"Because I seen them when they packed their luggage in their car and left."

"How long ago was that?"

"Two days ago."

"Do you have any idea where they could have gone?"

"I overheard my mom telling my dad they drove to Delaware to visit family."

"Did your mother say when they were supposed to return?"

"Nah."

I asked him a few more questions until I saw the police arrive, and then I excused myself. There were two uniformed officers and two detectives on the scene. After I gave them the required information they needed to file a report, everyone went inside Sean's residence to get more evidence of the crime that took place. While all of this was going on, Karen drove up. Her face was in disarray when she got the chance to look at me face-to-face.

"Are you OK?" she asked me the moment she came within a couple feet of me. Karen wore a sweatsuit and sneakers.

I took a deep breath and said, "I will be after all this is over."

"So, what did the police say?" she asked.

"They didn't say much. I did all the talking."

"Where are they now?"

"Inside the residence."

"Is someone in there?"

"No, but I'm assuming they are taking pictures and collecting whatever evidence they can to build this case." I rubbed the back of my head.

Karen looked at my head and said, "Was that where the guy hit you?'

"Yes," I said and frowned as if I was experiencing an excruciating pain. "I got a small knot right above my ear." I leaned my head in her direction.

She felt the small lump and said, "You need to seek some medical attention for that."

"I'm fine."

"Are you sure? Because that's a pretty big lump."

"Yes, I'm sure," I told her. "All I want to do is go home after I leave here."

"So, what are you going to do about your car?"

"I just called AAA, so I am going to have the driver tow my car to my house."

"Do you have a spare key at home?"

"Yes, I do."

"Well, how are you going to get inside your place?"

"I have a spare key hidden outside in one of my plants."

"Don't you think that could be kind of risky?"

"It is to a certain degree, but I have an alarm system and neighbors who are extremely nosey. So, if anyone wants a free go-to jail–card, they can get it."

"Well let's get you home, then," Karen said as we watched the AAA tow truck pull up.

Right before I left the scene, Karen and I both spoke with the detectives in depth about the start of this investigation. She told them that she planned to launch an investigation of her own and that it would result in criminal charges. After they handed me a copy of their report and their business cards, we all left. I jumped in the car with Karen and we both had the tow truck driver follow us to my apartment. After he released my car, Karen and I went inside my place. I tried to assure her that I would be all right, but she insisted on making sure I got into my apartment safely. When we entered the living room area, I flipped up the light switch. Karen made references about how she adored every piece of décor I had in the room, then she paused as if she had seen something really strange.

I looked in the direction in which she was staring and asked, "What's wrong?"

She walked over to the mantel right above my fireplace and picked up a wooden framed picture of Seth and me and said, "Wait a minute. Who is this guy? I swear I know him from somewhere."

"Who are you talking about?"

"The guy posing in this picture with you."

"Which picture is that?" I asked, even though I already knew what picture she was referring to.

"This one right here," she pointed out and showed me the photo.

My mouth was dry as hell and my knees were about to give way. I literally almost passed out. I mean, there I was, standing in my living room with my supervisor while she was holding a picture of me kissing Seth.

I took a deep breath and said, "Oh, you don't know him. That's my friend Alex."

"Yes, I believe I do. I never forget a face." Karen pressed the issue.

My heart pounded uncontrollably as the sweat began to seep through my pores. I honestly was at a loss for words, but I knew I had to come up with something. "You've probably seen him on television, because he plays on a minor league baseball team."

"No, that's not it." She placed the picture back down on the mantel.

"Would you like something to drink?" I tried to divert her attention away from Seth.

"No, I'm fine," she said. "I really need to be heading on home."

Karen turned around and walked to the front door. I followed her.

"Thanks again for coming to my rescue," I told her.

"No problem, but I want you to get some rest. As a matter of fact, I'm ordering you to take a leave of absence from the job. You have been through so much these past couple of days, and I feel like you'll never recover from it unless you take some time off."

I thought for a brief moment and then agreed with her. I would take the leave of absence. Karen hugged me and left. Once she was gone, it felt like a two-hundred-pound man was lifted from my shoulders. What a relief that was!

After I locked the door I raced into the kitchen, grabbed the cordless phone, and immediately called Seth's cell phone, but I didn't get an answer. I hung up and called him eight times, back to back, and he still didn't pick up. Knowing for a fact that he was still avoiding my calls had my blood boiling. What was so screwed up about this whole thing was that I couldn't do anything about it. I closed my eyes, took a deep breath, and counted to ten. When I opened my eyes again, I felt just a tad bit better. It wasn't enough to jump around with excitement, but it was enough to say *the hell with him,* and keep it moving.

I ended up calling a locksmith to change my locks. I couldn't afford to let anyone come up in my house with any surprises. Afterward, I took a long, hot bath and called it a night. Before I went to sleep, I called Heather and told her everything. She and I stayed on the phone for about an hour or so until she got a visit from a guy she used to date. I warned her not to give up the cookies, but I knew she wasn't going to listen to me. It had been a while since she'd been intimate, so I knew my words went in one ear and right out the other.

Surprisingly, a visitor came knocking on my door that next morning. The first person that popped in my head was Seth because I wasn't expecting anyone else. I jumped out of my bed with the quickness. Excitement engulfed my entire body, but when I opened the door and saw Heather standing there, every ounce of that feeling sputtered out of me like air being released from a balloon. My facial expression told it all, and Heather had a comment for it.

"I can tell you're not happy to see me this morning," she said as she forced her way past me, carrying a take-out bag from Denny's. I could only assume she stopped and picked up breakfast for the both of us, so I stood there in my satin robe and said, "I'm just surprised to see that you're not at work."

"I took the day off to spend some time with you."

"Thanks a lot," I responded with little or no enthusiasm at all. I closed the door and followed her into the kitchen.

"Did I catch you at a bad time?" she joked.

"No."

"Well, why are you looking like that?"

"It's a long story."

"What has he gotten you upset about now?" Heather asked as she took the food out of the bag and placed it on the table.

"It's nothing major. I'm just giving him a few days to cool off."

"What happened?"

"We just got into a little disagreement, but we'll be fine."

"Yeah, OK. Whatever you say." Heather took a seat.

I took a seat in a chair next to her and watched her dig her fork deep into her plate of hotcakes. She looked up at me and said with a mouthful of food, "While you're sitting there looking at me, you need to be opening up that container before your food gets cold."

I opened up the Styrofoam container and devoured my food. When it was all said and done, Heather and I had an enjoyable morning with a nice, hot breakfast and good conversation. She convinced me to take a ride out with her to the mall so I threw on a House of Deréon blue denim catsuit. It didn't fit like regular overalls; this bad boy was tight and it stuck to my body like a hand in a glove. I accessorized my attire with my favorite pair of black and gold Gucci ankle boots with a three-inch heel and the Gucci satchel handbag. I didn't know what to do with my hair, so I combed it back into a ponytail, placed my Gucci sunshades on top of my head, and called it a day.

Once we were outside, Heather volunteered to drive. We went to MacArthur Mall, located in the downtown area of Norfolk, since we wanted to do a little shopping at Nordstrom and bebe. The traffic wasn't bad at all. As a matter of fact, things were steady, and before we knew it, we were approaching our exit. Out of nowhere, a Dodge Magnum that looked just like Seth's car raced right by us at the speed of lightning. I looked down at the license plate, realized that it was his car, and immediately forgot about taking the trip to the mall.

Heather also realized that it was Seth's car. "Wasn't that your man?" she asked me.

"Yes, it sure was. And I want you to follow him, too."

Heather gave me the look of death. "For what?"

"Look, Heather, please do me this favor," I begged her.

"You are so lucky that I'm in a good mood today," she said and steered her car in the far left lane to follow him.

I sat back and watched Seth as he maneuvered his car in and out of each lane. It was apparent that he was in a rush, but I didn't know what he was rushing to. I knew I would soon find out, so I sat back and enjoyed the ride.

"I sure can't believe that I am doing this," Heather commented once more as she followed Seth inside the downtown tunnel.

"You're doing it for me, remember?" I interjected.

"Don't remind me." She pressed down harder on the accelerator.

We followed Seth as he entered into the city limits of Portsmouth and got off on Effingham Street, which was the very first exit as you came out of the tunnel.

"Where do you think he's going?" Heather asked me.

As bad as I wanted to tell her, I knew I would be

playing myself if I did. I lied and said, "I don't know, but I'm sure we're going to find out."

Heather bought it and continued to follow Seth. As we entered the neighborhood of Prentis Park, we followed Seth straight down Lincoln Street, but he didn't make the stop at the white house on the corner of Richmond Avenue. He kept driving straight down Lincoln Street, made a left on Des Moines Avenue, and took it all the way down to the end of the street. He parked directly across the street from a barbershop. Parked on the other side of him—and also directly in front of the barbershop—was the black Hummer, but the guy Mike was nowhere in sight.

"Pull over right here," I instructed Heather, pointing to a spot about a block away from Seth's car. I figured that we were in a prime location. We weren't too close and we weren't too far. The main thing was that we could see everything moving, and that was what counted most.

Heather left her car running, but that wasn't enough because she started running her mouth, too. All she wanted to know was why in the hell were we following Seth, and then she started complaining about how she had better things to do than to be sitting outside in her car spying on someone she could care less about. I ignored her because I wasn't about to feed into her nonsense. My main objective today was to find out what Seth had going on. While Heather continued to talk my head off, a brown-skinned guy of medium build, dressed in a Michael Vick football jersey and blue jeans, came storming out of the barbershop with Seth and Mike charging behind him. Seth lunged at the guy and struck him hard in the back of his head. The power behind the blow forced the guy face down to the ground. Both my mouth and Heather's mouth fell wide open. We were completely stunned, to say the least. I mean, I had never seen Seth attack anyone like that. Heather hadn't either, so she had a lot to say about it.

"Oh my God! Did you just see that?" she belted out, her eyes wide.

I was speechless. I couldn't respond as I watched both Mike and Seth beat this man with their bare hands. They literally attacked this guy like he had stolen something from them.

Upset by the whole scene, Heather shook her head in dismay and said, "So, what? You just gonna sit here and let them kill him?"

"What am I supposed to do? Go over there and break it up?" I snapped. "Shit, I just got banged up yesterday behind a couple of niggas. You think I am going to allow myself to run into some more bull-shit? Hell no! I've had my share of niggas putting their hands on me."

"Well, I am going to call the police because I can't continue to sit here and watch this madness and not do anything about it."

 While Heather dialed 911, I watched Seth and Mike repeatedly punch, kick, and stomp on that poor guy. The man looked helpless. What was so crazy was that there were a few bystanders watching the whole thing as it unfolded, like they were at a professional boxing match. From where we were parked, we could see how much blood was covering the victim's face. It became so unbearable to see, I told Heather to leave. As she was about to pull off, a dark green Impala with tinted windows came around the corner, its tires squealing, and whoever was inside opened fire on Mike and Seth. My heart immediately crashed to the floor and I envisioned Seth lying in his coffin, and that wasn't a pretty sight at all.

"We gotta get out of here," Heather said, putting her car in REVERSE and pressing down on the accelerator.

"Wait," I blurted out, "we can't leave him!"

"I am sorry, Maxine, but I am getting out of here."

My heart ached as tears started falling down my face. What was really scary was the feeling of the unknown. Not knowing what condition Seth was in really began to bother me. That changed when I wiped the tears from my eyes and saw Seth bolting down the street toward us, shooting rounds aimlessly at the Impala before it could make its getaway around the corner.

I became overjoyed. "I see him! There he is!"

Heather backed her car into the opposite corner from the Impala.

Heather refused to respond. Instead, she sped off in the direction from which we came. As soon as we made it back on the other side of the water, her mouth wouldn't stop running.

"You know what? I hope the police lock all of their asses up! Out there acting like ignorant-ass fools!" she snapped. "Do you know we could've gotten hit by one of those stray bullets?"

"Heather, you are truly overreacting, because for one, we were too far back for them to even graze your car. And two, no one was even shooting in our direction."

"Seth was."

"OK, you're right, but he was aiming at the green Impala."

"I don't give a fuck who he was aiming at, because he could've still hit us."

"All right, Heather. I see you're upset, so I am gonna let you have that one."

"What's to have, Maxine? We just witnessed a guy getting beaten to death by your boyfriend and then, on top of that, we almost fell victim to a fucking drive-by. Now, how can you justify that?"

"I am not trying to justify anything."

"Well, answer this and tell me what are you going to do about it?"

"What do you mean?"

"Come off that bullshit, Maxine. You know what the hell I'm talking about," she screamed. "I want to know if you plan on violating his ass?"

"Heather, you know I can't discuss that with you." I tried to avoid answering her question. "He's federal property and—"

"Oh, cut the bullshit!" she interjected, cutting me off in mid-sentence. "He ain't nobody's property but your own, and I've got a deep feeling that you ain't gonna do shit to him. You are just gonna let him get away with it, aren't you?"

"I don't know."

"What do you mean, you don't know? I mean, come on, you are a probation officer. You're an officer of the court who's supposed to uphold the law. What's the fucking problem?"

"Calm down!" I finally lashed out. "I don't need

you preaching to me about what I am supposed to be doing. So mind your fucking business, will ya?"

"I knew it!" Heather yelled. "I knew you weren't going to do a damn thing to that menace-ass thug of yours! But you know what? One day he's going to get his, and if you don't wake up, you're going to get caught right up in it."

"Trust me; I am not going to get caught up in anything that I don't want to."

"Don't try to convince me."

"I'm not."

Heather shook her head and chuckled. "Girl, that nigga got your silly ass wrapped around his fingers and you're too stupid to see it. I hope for your sake that you get out of that relationship with him before you fuck around and lose everything."

"Don't worry, I got everything under control."

"I find that hard to believe, because the old Maxine would've gotten that nigga arrested and violated on the spot. I remember when you used to be so hard on your parolees. You wouldn't take shit off their asses. If they acted like they were getting ready to do something wrong, you didn't hesitate to put their asses back behind bars. Now it's like you've lost all sense of who you are, and I don't like it."

"Believe me, nothing about me has changed."

Heather pulled her car in front of my house. "Yeah, tell me anything," she said and waited for me to exit her vehicle.

I saw that there was no way that I would be able to convince her that I hadn't changed, so I said goodbye and got out. Before I closed the passenger side door I said, "I'll call you later."

"No. Don't call me unless you're done dealing with that fool and he's back behind bars."

Shocked by her words and the tone in which they were delivered, I said, "Are you serious?"

"Yes, I am." Her expression was somber. "Now, close my door so I can get out of here."

Being a Gemini, I am a very proud person, so I wasn't about to let Heather see how upset she was making me. Shit, I didn't need her, for real. Besides, what kind of friend was she being by trying to tell me what to do about my man? Whether she knew it or not, I wasn't about to send him back to jail just because she said to. Not only that, but a spark inside me lit up when I saw him chasing that car down the street and firing that gun. I was literally turned on. Seeing him in action like that made me feel like I was watching an episode of *The Wire*. Believe it or not, I loved that show, and deep down inside me was a bad girl yearning to come out and do some wild shit. I guess that was why I got involved with Seth in the first place. I couldn't divulge that information to Heather. She was a goody-two-shoes type and wouldn't understand if I spelled it out for her. All she would do was judge me, and I couldn't have that. To kill two birds with one stone, I gave her what she wanted. I didn't say another word and closed her door, like she asked. She immediately drove off and didn't look back. I really didn't care how she felt about the situation, one way or another. I walked into my house.

Seth

The Belly Of The Beast

"Ay yo, nigga, you a'ight?" I asked Mike as he scrambled to his feet.

"Yeah, come on. Let's get out of here before the police come," he urged me as he rushed toward his Hummer.

I ran across the street and jumped in my car and sped out of there like lightning. Mike sped off in the opposite direction, but I knew where he was going. We did this to distract all of the nosey-ass people from pointing out to the police which way we went. When we met up on the Norfolk side, I followed him all the way down I-264 to Great Neck Road. We got off at that exit and drove another ten miles until we came to an area called Pelican Bay. The huge wall of stone with those two words engraved in it symbolized one thing, and that was that everybody who lived out here had money. As I followed Mike into this new development, I could see that there were still some houses under construction. The houses that were up were hot to death and most had families living in them. What set it off were the Porsches, Jaguars, Cadillacs, Range Rovers and Benzes that were parked in the driveways. We circled around a man-made lake and drove down Concourse Lane to a two-story, Windham-style brick home, tucked away in a cul-de-sac. The mismatched stones on this bad boy were gorgeous as hell. Plus, there was a three-car garage attached. I knew off the bat that Mike had to pay at least a mill for this joint. When I stepped out of my car, I asked him, "Ay yo, son, I know you forked out at least a mill for this joint, huh?"

Mike smiled. "Nah, but you're close."

I followed him up the driveway.

I passed this pearl white Acura RL with wood grain and a cream-colored leather interior. The shit was so plush, I did a double take. I didn't know it, but Mike saw me through his peripheral vision. He caught me off guard when he said, "That joint is hot, huh?"

I smiled, nodded my head, and followed him into his crib. Inside, we were greeted by his wife Lacy. Oh my God, homegirl was fucking beautiful. She'd put you in the mind of an Asian and black chick. Her hair was long, black, and silky and her skin was flawless. What was even more appealing about her was that her five-two frame was so tight, you couldn't even tell she was pregnant. I smiled at her and waited for Mike to introduce us.

"Baby, this is my man Seth. Seth, this is Lacy," he

finally said as he stood beside her. Looking at the both of them together was like looking at Mike Tyson and Kobe Bryant's wife. That's how pretty Lacy was and that's how big Mike was, towering over her.

She and I both said hello to each other and then Mike escorted me into the den area. "Baby, y'all want something to drink?" I heard her yell down the hall at us.

"Yeah, bring us two Coronas." She brought us two cold beers before she asked Mike, "Did you need me to do anything else before I leave?"

"You getting ready to leave?"

"Yeah."

"Where you going?"

"I'm going shopping with Megan."

"A'ight, but don't spend up all my dough." Mike smiled.

Lacy looked back at him and said, "There are not enough hours in a day to do that."

"You're right, but I'm sure it's crossed your mind."

"My mother always told me never let your right hand know what your left is doing. So, I guess it's best that I stick to that," she replied and disappeared around the corner.

"Her mother's right," I commented and took a sip of my beer.

Mike laughed and said, "To hell with her moms because she ain't nothing but a gold-digging bitch!"

After hearing him blast his wife's mother like that, I didn't know whether to laugh or act like I didn't hear him. I was saved by the bell when his cellular phone started ringing off the hook.

"Yeah, what's up?" he answered. "A'ight. Well, tell them that something came up and we ain't gon' set up shop until later." He continued talking and then ended the call.

"Niggas getting impatient about that product, huh?" I inquired.

"Yeah, that was Melody telling me that a lot of fiends keep knocking on her door trying to score. I told her to tell 'em something came up and that we'll set up shop later."

"What time you want me to go out there?"

"I want shit to cool down out there first. I would hate for you to run right back into them cats while you got my shit on you."

"Come on now, Mike. Do you honestly think I would let them niggas fuck with your shit?"

"I know you wouldn't, but those niggas are on some bitch-type shit! They would set you up to get busted by the police in a heartbeat. That's why I keep my distance from them."

"Is that what the cat back at the barbershop did?"

"Hell, nah!" Mike said. "That was Melody's baby daddy, Rick."

"Word?" I said and laughed.

"Yep, that's why I called you down there. I wanted you to see me whip his motherfucking ass for talking shit to me when he came by Melody's crib about a month ago," Mike explained. "Do you know that nigga threatened to call the police on the spot, because I had her selling drugs out of there?"

"Word?"

"Yep, he sure did."

"So, why didn't you straighten his ass then?"

"Because when I pulled out my pistol, the nigga hopped in his car and skated out of there."

"So, those cats busting rounds at us were his peoples?"

"Yeah. I heard him popping shit to them on the phone when I was sitting in the chair, getting my hair cut. From then, I knew I was going to have problems so I got on the horn and called Jay, but he didn't pick up. Then I called you, and when you told me you were on your way, a ton of adrenaline started pumping inside of me."

"Come on now, dawg, you knew I was going to come. You should've called me first."

"I know. But everything is everything. We live and learn."

"Yeah, that's true. I'm just glad I was there to have your back."

"Shit nigga, I was glad, too. I mean, you saw how those niggas came flying around that corner, emptying out their burners at us?"

"Hell yeah, I saw it. That's why I was able to dive down on the ground behind that old Honda Accord, to keep them niggas from putting holes in my ass!"

Mike took a sip of his beer and said, "Yo, those cats were amateurs. They did all that shooting and didn't hit nothing but the cars we dove on the ground behind."

"Yeah, they were kind of sloppy because if it were me, I would've killed something on the first two shots."

Mike smiled. "I would've murdered something too." He stood. "Come here and let me show you something."

I stood and followed him out of the den into a back room in the house. It was small, like a utility closet. The door to the room was made of that same kind of steel they use to create floor safes. It was at least eight inches thick. It would be very difficult for anybody to break into it, plus you could tell that it was soundproof. Mike told me the inside of it was made of solid concrete, so if anyone would ever get locked up in there he would have less than twenty-four hours to live because there was not an opening for ventilation. What was really slick about the joint was that there was another door inside of the room. As Mike led the way, I followed.

"What I am about to show you, I haven't shown no one else."

"Not even Jay?" I wondered aloud.

"Nope, not even him," he told me as he typed a code into a digital keypad mounted against the wall. The door made a clicking sound and Mike pushed it open. I saw something that didn't look real to me. I honestly thought that my mind was playing tricks on me.

"You see that shit?" Mike pointed to four piles of money stacked on top of a wooden pallet in the middle of the floor. "That's my retirement money right there. As soon as I get rid of all that shit you see right there," he pointed directly at a two-gallon, see-through plastic container filled with raw heroin, "I am going to get out of the game and take my wife on a six-month-long vacation before we settle down and make some real investments."

"If you don't mind me asking, how much is that?"

"It's two and a half mill," Mike replied with pride.

"Why would you have that much dough stashed away in your crib like this? I mean, wouldn't you feel safer with that shit in a bank somewhere?"

"Come on now, Seth, you see how this room is built. Couldn't nobody get in here if they tried."

"I see that, but don't you think it would be a little wise to have it in a bank, so you could build some interest on it?"

"Hell, nah! Fuck that! I am not letting any of them crackers get rich off my dough. It's gonna sit right here, where I can see it."

"How long did it take you to rake that shit in?"

"Probably about a year. It would've been more, but wifey's been dipping in it every chance she gets," he continued as he turned the light switch back off.

I stepped back out of the room and into the hollow area and waited for him to close the door to the safe. He opened up the second door that led back into the hallway. Once we were back in the den area, Mike took a seat.

"I just want to let you know that the reason I took you into my safe is because I wanted you to see how serious I am about getting rich. If you're serious, then you can have all of that too. Now, I don't want you to get the wrong impression that I am some ol' soft-ass nigga and I wouldn't kill you if you ever got up the nerve to run up in here and try to take my shit from me; because I would, in a heartbeat."

"Oh nah, Mike, that shit wouldn't ever cross my mind," I reassured him.

"That's a good thing, because if we're on the same page with this thing, you and I are going to be all right!" He took the last sip of his beer and sat it on the coffee table.

"Well, I'm definitely on the same page with you, because if I wasn't, I would not have gotten down with you in the first place."

"True! True!" Mike agreed. He stood up again and asked me if I wanted another beer.

"Nah, I'm straight," I told him.

We continued to kick politics to each other for another hour or so, and then we broke it off when I got a call from Samantha. Before I accepted her call, Mike handed me a Ziploc bag of two thousand caps of dope and told me to head out to the spot. I stuffed the bag in my jeans and headed out the door. As soon as Mike closed his front door behind me, I pressed the number five button on my phone before the automated system disconnected us.

"Hello," I said.

Sounding a little agitated, Samantha said, "What took you so long to accept my phone call?"

"I was taking care of some business."

"With who?"

"It doesn't matter," I cut her off. "What's good?" I hopped in my whip and headed toward the highway.

"Nothing but the fact that I'm missing the hell out of you."

"And you don't think I'm missing you?"

"I know you are, but it's just so hard being in here and you're out there."

"Sam, stop doing that. You know you're stressing yourself out when you do that."

"Baby, I can't help it."

"Look, you ain't got nothing but a few more weeks

left and you gon' be right out this joint with me, chilling. So stop tripping. Your time is almost up."

"I can't wait because I am going to show out when I see you. All those bitches out there, who've probably already fucked you or trying to fuck you right now, better recognize. When I step on the scene, they better not step out of pocket, because shit will get really ugly. Seth, you know I would kill a bitch behind you!"

"Baby, I know that. That's why I ain't fucking around with these hoes. They ain't worth it. All I'm trying to do is get money, and that's it."

"I know whatchu trying to do, but if you're out there where them hoes are, they are definitely going to try to holler at you. And you know I know, because that's how me and you met."

I laughed at Samantha after she made her point. Technically, she was right. Chicks out there had that type of radar, and they could tell if a nigga had a little bit of dough. As soon as they figured out how much you had coming in on a regular basis, they would offer their pussy up to you with the quickness. If you took them up on their offer, their next move was to lock your ass down. I couldn't have that shit. Samantha wasn't gonna have it either. I was going to continue to do me and get that cash. All that other shit wasn't relevant, so I was going to keep my distance.

After she reminded me over and over again about how much she loved and missed me, our fifteen-minute conversation was up. I blew a kiss at her through the phone before we got disconnected, but we got cut off before she could kiss me back. I stuck my phone back in my pocket and continued to make my way back to Portsmouth.

Melody was dead in my face from the second I walked into her crib. I brushed her ass off because I wasn't feeling her at that moment. Whether she knew it or not, her talk game was on zero and her pussy was whack, so all she could do for me is help me serve the customers. Now later on, I might want to fuck her in her ass, but until then, we didn't have anything to talk about unless it was about helping me collect this paper.

While I was pushing those caps off on those dopefiends out there, Maxine called my phone over a dozen times. I started to answer it a few times and tell her to leave me the fuck alone, but I knew she would have something fucked up to say, so I left well enough alone.

Samantha

Never Trust A Big Butt And A Smile

After I got off the phone with Seth, I stepped out of the phone booth and headed down the hallway toward my room.

"I've been looking for you," a male correctional officer said while my back was turned.

I didn't have to turn around to see who was asking me the question because I already recognized the voice. But to show him the respect, I turned around and smiled as hard as I could. "What, ya got something for me?" I wondered aloud and begin to walk toward him, admiring everything about him.

C.O. Rico Mendez was his name, and he was a thirty-eight-year-old, handsome brother with a caramel complexion and curly jet black hair. Plus, he had the height and body of a gladiator. His nationality was Puerto Rican. But, he said that his mother was Puerto Rican and his father was black. It wouldn't matter either way, because he had it going on, which was why I'd been fucking him the entire time I was at that prison camp. It was a lot of hoes there that were jealous of me because they knew I was fucking around with Mendez and he snuck a lot of shit in there to me from off the street and he put money in my account. So I told all of them to get a fucking life and find their own correctional officer to fuck with because they ain't gon' stop this parade. I had just a few weeks left in that hellhole, so I was going to ride that pony until the very end.

"Yeah, I sure do. And I can't wait to give it to you."

I smiled because I knew he was talking about his dick. But then he changed the subject.

"Who were you talking to?"

"My cousin," I lied.

Mendez smacked me on my ass. "You better had been!" He smiled.

"I was, sweetie."

"So, whatchu getting ready to get into now?"

"I'm going in the TV room and play a couple hands of bid wiz with my roommates."

"Well, you know my shift ends at eleven, so I wanna get with you before I leave. A'ight?"

"We can get together later, but we aren't going to be able to do anything because I'm on my period right now," I lied once more.

"Come on, mommie! Tell me it ain't so." He sounded disappointed.

Truth of the matter was, I was about to be reunited with Seth and I couldn't have him running up in me with my pussy all stretched and worn out. He'd definitely know I'd been doing something because Mendez's dick was slightly bigger than his, so between now and then I'd have to use a couple of hot feminine douches and jump into my kegel exercises so I could get my coochie tight again. I wasn't gon' let Mendez fuck it up for me.

I rubbed my hand across the crotch of his pants. His dick got rock hard that instant. "You know how I love it when you push that big dick inside of me. So, give me four or five days and we'll be right back in business."

Mendez sighed heavily. "Damn Sam, I was really looking forward to being alone with you tonight."

"You still can. We just can't do anything though."

Mendez looked like he wasn't at all happy by the fact that I just shot down his plans to fuck the hell out of me inside the counselor's office tonight. But I figured he'd be all right after he carried his ass home to his wife and two kids. Whether he realized it or not, I had a life of my own, and I planned to get on with it as soon as I got out of there. Seth was my main priority, and I refused to let another nigga come between that. Now I couldn't say the same about Seth, because he fucked around on me more times than I could count. Not to mention the fact that I was in this situation because of him. But hey, what can I say other than I forgave him and he and I were moving forward. He knew he owed me though. So, I planned to collect everything that was due to me as soon as I got my freedom. And I wasn't gonna let no nigga or ho get in my way either.

Now once I assured Mendez that I was going to make it up to him, he smacked me on my butt once again and left me standing in the hallway so he could make his rounds. Right after he walked off, I headed in the opposite direction, and as soon as I turned the corner, this bitch named Monique was posted up not too far from where Mendez and I were talking, so I knew she had been eavesdropping when she said, "I got some pads if you need some."

I stopped in my tracks and looked at this short, black, ugly-ass chick who swore up and down she was a man with her corn rows and baggy uniform.

"Bitch, don't play with me! You know I don't need none of your motherfucking pads!"

She gave me a sly little smirk. "You sure? Because I got more than I need."

I immediately became frustrated. "What's your point?"

"I don't have a point. All I'm trying to do is be nice."

"Monique, cut it out. You could care less about being nice to me, and you know it," I told her, and then I stepped away from her to leave.

But, she cut me off and blocked me from getting by her. "What's the rush?"

"Bitch, if you don't move your ass out of my way I am going to knock you the fuck out," I warned her.

"Come on now, Samantha. You know I ain't trying to get into any beef with you."

I got agitated. "Then what the fuck do you want?"

"I want to try some of what you're giving Mendez," she said.

I tried to play dumb. "And what the fuck is that?"

"Stop it, Samantha. Everybody knows you fucking Mendez. And personally, I don't care. But I am curious to find out what you're working with and why that nigga be sweating you like he does."

"First of all, Mendez doesn't sweat me. And secondly, I'm not into that bumping pussy thing, so please get the fuck back!"

"You sure? 'Cause you know I can take care of you better than that nigga can."

Refusing to stand there and listen to Monique another second, I stepped forward and forced my way by her. It felt like I almost knocked her arm out of socket because when I passed her, I hit her ass real hard with my shoulder. I thought we were going to go toe to toe with one another, but she let me ride. I guess she felt like it wouldn't be worth it because she had a girlfriend who lived in the next dorm, so how would she be able to explain to her why we were fighting? She did make a slick-ass comment as I walked away.

"Let me know if you change your mind," she yelled behind me.

I ignored her and kept it moving.

Maxine

Later That Night

I had been trying to get Seth on the phone all day long. I knew he was all right, but I just had this urge to hear his voice, especially after everything that had gone on today. The only other thing I could do was send him a text message and wait for his response. I typed in the message, I KNOW U'RE UPSET WIT ME, BUT U NEED 2 CALL ME. BCUZ I JUST GOT A CALL ABOUT A SCUFFLE YOU WERE IN EARLIER & I NEED SUM ANSWERS. I pressed the SEND button on my Blackberry and waited for him to respond. To my surprise, that stubborn bastard dialed my number. Hearing my phone ring sent my heart rate up at least fifty notches. I took a deep breath and answered.

Seth went straight into his defensive mode. I didn't get a "Hello, how are you doing?" or anything. "What altercation you talking about?"

To keep from telling him that I actually followed

him all the way to Portsmouth and watched the whole thing unfold between him, Mike, and the other guys, I came up with the most believable story of the year.

"I'm talking about the one you and some other guys got into earlier today."

"Well, whoever told you that mess lied," he yelled.

"Seth, you can tell me anything you want, but I've got a friend who works for the Portsmouth Police Department, and she said that two names, yours and an unknown name, were being thrown around her department about an assault made on a man in front of a barbershop. She also said that there were several reports about a shootout."

"Oh, nah, that's bullshit, because I don't get into shit like that."

"Seth, the guy who was beat up was the one who called your names out." I gave him no more room to lie.

"What was the other guy's name?"

"I was told that his name was Mike."

There was a moment of silence, and I knew right then and there I had his dumb ass exactly where I wanted him. He finally came out of his mouth and said, "That—that was bullshit because I don't know a guy by the name of Mike."

I knew he wasn't about to throw in the towel. I came at him even harder and said, "Well, they may have gotten the other guy's name wrong, but they definitely took down the right license plates."

Sounding a little worried, he said, "Whose license plates?"

"The license plates on your Magnum," I replied.

"And since your car is registered in my name, that's how I got the call."

"What else did your girlfriend say?"

When he asked me that question it was clear that he was beginning to become a little worried. I gave him a little assurance by saying, "All I got to do is give her the word, Seth, that it was me driving your car and she will make that tag number disappear. But I am going to need you to be honest with me and tell me what happened."

Again, Seth fell silent. I knew he was contemplating whether or not it would be in his best interest to spill his guts to me. Then again, what other choices did he have?

After about thirty seconds of him breathing through the receiver, he finally said, "A'ight listen, I was out there, but shit didn't go down like your peoples said it did."

"Then what happened?"

"I ain't really trying to talk about it over the phone."

"Well, could you come by so we can talk about it?"

"Yeah, a'ight," he sighed. "I'll be by there in a few minutes."

"Where are you now?"

"Well, I was about two blocks away from my crib, but I'm turning around now," he replied.

Hearing him tell me he was on his way to my house put a smile on my face instantly. I wanted to jump out of my seat, but I figured it would be best if I waited until I got off the phone. Immediately after we hung up, I rushed straight into the shower. It was a must that I be fresh and smelling good when he came through the door. It had been a few days since we had last seen each other, so it was important for me to show him what he had been missing.

About twenty minutes later, I was out of the shower and smelling like a bed of fresh roses. I was getting ready to slip on something sexy, but then I figured it would probably be better if I walked around with my towel on. All he had to do was snatch the towel off if he wanted some pussy, and I would happily oblige.

Not long after I lotioned my body down and sprayed on perfume, Seth was knocking on the front door. When I opened the door, he looked me up and down and said, "Why you change the locks?"

"Oh, that's a long story," I said as I closed the door and locked it behind him.

"I'm listening." He took a seat on the living room sofa.

I sat down beside him and told him about everything that went on with me the day before. He sat there in awe as I reiterated every single detail of my horrifying experience back at that house. He acted as if he couldn't believe it, so I grabbed his hand and placed it right over my right ear. "Do you feel that lump?" I asked him.

"Hell yeah, I feel that joint! And it feels like it should be still hurting you."

"It only hurts when I try to lay on that side."

"So, where are them motherfuckers now?"

"I don't know, but some detectives are handling it and so is my supervisor."

"Why is your supervisor handling it?"

"Because my gun was taken."

"Your what?" Seth screamed.

"They stole my gun."

"Ahh man, that's not good."

"I know. But that's not it."

"What else happened?"

"They also took my cell phone and my whole set of keys," I said. "That's why I had to change my locks on my door."

"Yo, them niggas got a lot of heart fucking with you like that. As a matter of fact, if I ever get a chance to run into them, I am going to murder something!"

"Seth, don't let this thing get you all upset."

"It's too late for that."

"Well, just calm down." I tried to massage his shoulder.

"Yo, I am really sick of this shit!"

"What are you talking about?"

"That job shit! Fucking with all them knuckle-head-ass niggas on your caseload."

"Look, I know you're not happy about what I do because it is dangerous. But look at the bright side; I will not be doing it too much longer, because as soon as you're done doing your thing out there, we can start up that business we were talking about," I reminded him. "Oh, speaking of which, tell me what happened earlier."

"It wasn't nothing, really."

"Well, it must've been, because I would not have gotten that phone call."

Seth sighed heavily. "Ay yo, all I got to say is that whatever that nigga said happened to him, he had it coming. End of story."

"So, you admit to attacking him?"

"I ain't going to ever admit it. But I will say that he deserved whatever he got."

"Well, were you a part of the shootout?"

"Like I said, I would never admit to doing a damned thing. I wouldn't care if you caught me on camera, because I am going to still say it wasn't me."

"I understand all of that, but I am your woman. So why are you trying to keep shit from me?"

"Because at the end of the day, you're still my probation officer."

"So what, you think I am going to have you locked up?"

"I don't know what you would do anymore."

"Come on now, Seth. You know that if I wanted you back in jail, I would have done it a long time ago."

"Like I said, I don't know what you would do anymore."

This conversation wasn't going anywhere, so I changed the subject. "So, how much money have you saved thus far?"

"A couple of grand. Why?"

"I was just wondering how far you had to go to get to your goal."

"I ain't got far."

"Do you think you can still do it in a week's time?"

Seth hesitated a bit. "Nah, a week ain't gon' be enough time."

"So, how much time are you gonna need?"

"I'm not sure, but I'll let you know."

What I had gathered so far from his responses was that it wouldn't matter what I said, because he had already made up his mind how this situation was going to play out. I didn't say anything. The last thing I wanted was to start another argument, so he could run out on me while I was trying to make my point. Instead of giving him an extension with restrictions, I'd take a step back and let him use his own discretion on how long he needed to be out there on his hustle.

I said, "OK, take as long as you like."

Seth looked at me like I was speaking a foreign language.

"Whatchu just say?" he asked.

I smiled. "I said, take as long as you like."

"What, is this a joke or something?"

"No," I answered him, still smiling.

"Why are you smiling, then?"

"Because I am happy to see you." I hugged his neck.

I leaned over and started kissing the side of his face, too. As I moved my lips toward his, he pulled back from me and said, "Nah, I ain't in the mood for that right now." He stood.

The feeling of rejection shot through me like an injection and it didn't feel good, either, so I stood up as well and asked, "What's wrong with you?"

"Ain't nothing wrong with me," he said. "I'm just tired, and I want to get some sleep."

"Well, go in the bedroom and lay down," I insisted as I tightened the towel around me.

"Nah, I'd rather crash out here on the sofa. That way, I could still sleep in my clothes."

Hearing Seth tell me that he would rather sleep on a fucking sofa than lay in the bed next to me was beginning to wear me down. I wanted so badly to curse his ass out and ask him if he'd been out there fucking around on me, but what good would that do? All that would do is start an argument and give him a reason to leave. Besides, I wouldn't get the truth out of him anyway. He would definitely deny fucking another woman, and he would take it to his grave.

I sighed heavily and said, "All right. If that's what you want, let me go and get you some covers." I went to the linen closet.

While I was gone, Seth took off his sneakers and set them side-by-side at the end of the sofa. He took off his New York Yankees ball cap and set it on the coffee table. By the time I got back in the living room, he was lying on his stomach with his face facing the back of the sofa. I laid a bed sheet across him first, then placed a blanket on top of that.

"Good night," I said.

"Good night," he replied without even looking my way.

Since I knew the night was definitely over for us, I went into my bedroom disappointed as hell because I wanted some dick so bad. Not only that but the feeling I got when he held me in his arms after he fucked me to death was the most powerful aphrodisiac of them all. Too bad I wouldn't be experiencing that tonight.

That next morning, Seth got up before I did. I heard him messing around in the kitchen so I automatically assumed that he was fixing me some breakfast. To avoid spoiling the surprise, I continued to lie in the bed and waited for him to come strolling in my room with my tray of food. But for some unknown reason, Seth had other plans and it didn't include preparing breakfast for me. As a matter of fact, he showed up in my bedroom fifteen minutes later, empty-handed, talking about he had to leave. I sat up in the bed with an expression of disappointment and asked him where he was going.

"I got to take care of some business," he replied.

"Right now?" I looked over at the alarm clock on my dresser. Eight-thirty AM.

"Yeah, I got to head out to the spot. But I got to run home first."

"Am I going to see you later?"

"I'll let you know."

Frustrated by his lack of consideration for my feelings, I asked, "What's wrong with you?"

"Ain't nothing wrong with me."

"Then why are you being so standoffish toward me?"

"I'm not being standoffish."

"I can't tell, especially when I tried to kiss you in the mouth last night and you pushed me away. And then on top of that, you wouldn't even sleep in the same bed with me. So, my thing is this: If you didn't want to be bothered with me, then why did you come over here?"

"Because you told me to, so we could talk about that shit with those people taking down my license plate number."

"OK, true enough, I did. But are you going to stand here and act like you would not have come unless I called you about that incident?"

"Ay yo, Maxine, I am not trying to get into a heated debate with you." Seth began to back out of the room. It was clear that he was trying to leave, so I got up from the bed.

"I am not trying to start a heated discussion with you, so why are you trying to leave?"

"'Cause I got shit to do, and I ain't trying to leave out of here with a headache."

I sighed, because by now I was consumed with frustration. Seth wasn't trying to hear one thing I had to say. If I continued to walk behind him like I was forcing him to hear what I had to say, I knew he wouldn't be trying to come back to see me no time soon. I toned down my approach and asked him if I would be seeing him later.

"I'm not sure. But, I'll let you know," he told me again and walked out the door.

Shocked by the way he handled me, I stood there in the doorway with the dumbest expression I could muster up and watched him get in his car and drive off. There was no mistake about it: I was heartbroken like a bitch when he uttered those words out of his mouth. I honestly wanted to tell him to kiss my ass and never come back. I mean, who the hell did he think he was, parading around here like he was fucking King Tut or somebody? Well, let me be the first to say he wasn't, and if he kept that bullshit up, I was going to shut him down. And I meant that.

Seth

Another One Bites The Dust

Mike changed shit up on me this morning. At the last minute, he called me and told me that I wouldn't be meeting up with him to get the product because he was tied up doing other shit. He did say he was sending his chick Trina with it, and that I needed to be at the spot out in Dales Homes within the next thirty minutes. After I told him that I was already in P-Town, he asked me where I was exactly.

"I'm at the 7-Eleven on the corner of Effingham and London Boulevard, getting me some gas."

"A'ight. Well, go out to Dales Homes right after you leave there."

"A'ight," I said.

Once my tank was full, I hopped back on the road and headed out to the spot. As soon as I got to the entrance, where you saw the sign WELCOME TO DALES HOMES, fiends started coming out from everywhere.

Some of them acted like they wanted to jump on the hood of my car when I started driving around the horseshoe. I had to roll down my window and threaten a few of them not to touch my motherfucking whip, or I was going to put a bullet in their asses. They backed off and let me go on about my business. When I drove up to Melody's building and got out, some bold-ass fiend walked up to me and said, "You that nigga with the Black Label dope, huh?"

"Why, you the police or something?" I asked.

"Hell, nah, do I look like the police?"

"Well, are you a snitch?"

"Hell, nah, I ain't no snitch! But I'll be your personal dick sucker if you let me hold something!" she said.

I burst into laughter and said, "Ay yo, bitch, get the fuck out here witcha nasty ass! I wouldn't let you suck my dick if my life depended on it."

"First off, my name is Faith, not bitch!"

"I don't give a fuck whatcho name is. Now, whatchu need to do is get the fuck out of here before I smack the hell out of you for disrespecting me!" I stood there and waited for her to leave.

"Y'all big-time-ass niggas love to talk shit to women when y'all get a dope package and a little bit of money in your pocket. But believe me when I tell you that your little world is gon' come crashing down on you when you least expect it. Every nigga who came out here and sold heroin didn't last a month. They either got locked up, or the young boys from 'round here ran their asses out. So you better watch your back, young blood. These streets are treacherous! And the ones that's close to you are gon' be the ones that's gon' getcha!"

"Oh shut the hell up, Faith! Ain't nobody trying to hear that shit you talking," Melody interjected from behind the screen door. "Now carry your ass before you get hurt!" Melody unlocked her door and came out on the porch.

"Yeah, whatever," Faith said. She turned around and left.

After the dopefiend-ass bitch walked off I looked at Melody, dressed in her famous booty shorts and wife-beater and said, "I take it that you know her."

"Yeah, she's been hanging out here for a while now."

"Well, she don't know who the hell she's fucking with because if you would not have come outside, I would've smacked the shit out of her."

Melody laughed at me. "Yeah, she's got plenty of mouth, but she's harmless."

"Well, she better keep her motherfucking distance from me, because I ain't gonna tolerate her shit like everybody else."

"Trust me, she got the picture," Melody assured me and then we both went into the house.

What was crazy was that as soon as she locked the door behind us, she pushed my back against the wall and started rubbing her hand all over the crotch of my jeans. Before I allowed my dick to swell up, I grabbed her hand and pushed her back.

"Nah, we ain't got time for that right now," I told her.

She started whining. "But, why, Seth? I'm horny as hell, and I want you to fuck me!"

"Not now," I told her and pushed her completely away from me.

"What's wrong with you?"

"Ain't nothing wrong with me. Do you know that you are the second person who asked me that same question today?"

"Well, that should tell you something," Melody commented as she threw her hand on her hip and walked off into the kitchen.

I started to respond to her comment, but I figured that wouldn't be necessary. I let her silly ass go on about her business. A few minutes later, she strutted her ass back in the living room while I was sitting on the couch in deep thought with my eyes closed. When I heard her take her last step, I opened my eyes to see what the hell she was doing. Before I could utter a single word, she stood over me like she had an attitude.

"Are you going to open up shop or what?"

"Yeah, as soon as the dope gets here."

"What happened to you bringing it here?"

"Mike called me and said he wasn't going to be able to get up with me, so he's sending a chick name Trina over here."

"Oh, that's a motherfucking lie! That bitch ain't coming over here, and I mean that shit!" Melody protested.

"Well, call Mike and tell him, because I ain't trying to get involved with that bullshit!" Before she could get further in the conversation, someone knocked on the door.

"Who is it?" Melody yelled.

"It's Trina," I heard a squeaky voice say.

I stood and waited for Melody to open the front door. When she finally did, this pretty, Amazon-looking chick walked inside. She nearly took my breath away. Her body was built just like Tyra Banks, and her facial features were identical to that actress Meagan Goode, who played opposite Tyrese in the movie *Waist Deep*. Trust me, the chick was gorgeous. Trina approached me with her long, blond-streaked, copper-colored hair flowing down her shoulders, styled in a silk wrap. She was rocking a blue and white Christian Dior denim dress, C.D. high-heeled sandals, and the matching C.D. denim duffel handbag, and I knew she was about her business. She only sported one diamond ring on the right hand, but it was a canary diamond, and it was beautiful. What really set it off was the diamond bezel watch and the canary diamond earrings in her ears. All that shit together had to be at least ten carats, and if it wasn't, then it was real close.

On some real shit, homegirl walked up in this spot like she was a model for real, and Melody couldn't fuck with her. Granted, both of these women looked good as hell. Mike really knew how to pick them. However, if you stood Melody next to this chick, there was no comparison because you could tell that Trina was about her money. Now that I think about it, this chick right here was hotter than Mike's wife Lacy. The fragrance from her perfume was light and sweet and it complemented the hell out of her swagger. I wished I could spend some quiet time with her, but since I knew that would be a long shot, I snapped back into reality and focused on the business at hand.

"How you doing, Ms. Trina?" I finally asked.

She smiled. "You must be Seth."

"I sure am, if you got something for me." I smiled back at her.

Becoming a little animated, Trina said, "You trying to make some money?"

"Oh, most definitely!"

Melody wanted her presence to be known so she interjected by saying, "Hi, Trina."

Trina looked at Melody with the most unconcerned expression she could give her and said, "Oh, hi." Without skipping a beat, she immediately went into her duffel handbag. She pulled out a huge Ziploc bag with a minimum of two thousand pills of dope inside it and handed it to me.

"Did he tell you how many were in here?" I asked.

"Yeah, he said it was twenty-five hundred of them in there."

"A'ight. Well, that should be enough," I said.

Trina zipped her handbag back up and turned to leave. "Well, OK. If you need something, call Mike and he'll probably have me come back."

"A'ight. I sure will," I assured her after taking a quick glimpse of her ass. I did it so fast, I don't even think Melody caught it.

"OK. Well, take care."

"You do the same."

Trina walked out of the door.

Melody slammed the front door immediately after Trina let the screen door close behind her. She turned back around and looked at me with a look of hate all over her face.

"Can you believe that shit?" she screeched.

I played dumb. "Whatchu talking about?"

"It just came to me that if I would not have spoken to that bitch first, she would not have spoken to me. But the fucked up part about it was the fact that she walked into my house. Now what kind of game was that?" she roared. "I mean, who goes in a person's house and doesn't speak when they walk through the door?"

"Well, she just did it."

"My point exactly, and that's one of the reasons why I can't stand her ass! Ol' disrespectful bitch!"

"Come on now, Melody. Don't let that shit get to you. It's a beautiful day outside, so don't let her ruin it for you."

"It's too late. The bitch already got me," she commented and stormed off in the direction of her bedroom.

As soon as she left, I rushed to the living room window to see if Trina had pulled off. It was killing me to see what kind of whip she was pushing. I looked through the mini blinds and caught her backing a two-door, money green, G37 Infiniti out of the parking spot. I knew shorty was about her work, and if any nigga wanted to take her from Mike, they were going to have to be raking in some serious paper. And I could just be the man to do it.

Right after I closed down the shop, I met Mike in the parking lot of this strip club called Magic City so I could pay him his dough. When I tried to leave after the exchange, Mike asked me if I would stay awhile and go inside the club with him. I figured that since I didn't have shit to do, I might as well.

The whole time I was in there, Maxine blew my phone off the hook. When I didn't answer her, she sent me a text message, begging me to call because she missed me. I texted her back and told her I was taking care of business and that I would call her when I was done. Her reply to me was, OK, BABY! I LOVE YOU!

I didn't respond to her last message because the texting back and forth was beginning to get on my nerves. I just stuck my phone back in my pocket and leaned back in my chair so I could enjoy the scenery.

Mike ordered two bottles of Moët while we watched a couple of chicks shake their asses across the stage. Both of the broads looked average in the face, but their bodies were right. Their titties weren't hanging, and there wasn't a stretch mark in sight.

"Who that chick right there?" I asked Mike, pointing to the light-skinned, big booty chick with blonde hair who was dancing upside down on the pole.

Smiling, he said, "Oh, that's Blondie!"

"So, you know her?"

"Everybody knows Blondie." He smirked.

I focused right back on Ms. Blondie. This bitch had me in a deep trance and Mike noticed it, so he tapped me on my shoulder and said, "Why don't you call her over here after she gets off the stage?"

I nodded to let Mike know that I intended to do just that. While I was thinking about how I would love to bend Blondie over, my attention was diverted when I heard a familiar voice come up on the right side of Mike.

"Hi baby," I heard the voice say and then the sound of a loud kiss. I turned and saw Mike's girl Trina, dressed in a gold shimmery thong, with her ass hanging out. She had a set of gold shimmery adhesive pasties covering her nipples and a pair of five-inch stilettos, and it blew my damn mind. It was evident that she was working there, but I would not have ever believed it if somebody had told me. Nevertheless, she was sexy as a motherfucker, and I would have loved to lay my body next to hers.

I didn't want to disrespect Mike by staring at his girl, so I turned my head and looked back toward the stage, but after seeing Trina's bad-ass body, I was no longer interested in looking at Blondie.

"I see you brought company with you tonight?" I heard her comment over the loud music. It almost sounded like she was yelling.

"Yeah, I figured since we make money together, why not get a drink together?"

"Want me to give him the royal treatment?" Trina asked Mike.

"Yeah, go ahead," he insisted and pushed her in my direction.

I didn't know what the hell was going on, but when I realized that Trina was coming toward me, I got nervous as a motherfucker.

"You ready for me to show you a good time?" she asked with a smile.

Not knowing how to respond, I formed the dumbest expression I could and then I looked over at Mike who was, by this time, laughing his ass off. "Man, what's up?" I yelled over the music.

"Just sit back and enjoy yourself," I heard him say.

Before I could shoot a rebuttal back at him, Trina turned her ass around toward me, sat right down on my lap and started grinding all her ass on my dick. And, boy did my joint swell up. The feeling I was getting almost made me pass out because I was having difficulty trying to enjoy it. Having Mike three feet away from me, watching my every move, made me uncomfortable like a motherfucker. My dick was telling me to close my eyes and enjoy the feeling, but my mind was telling me that all this shit was a setup. When I was getting ready to push Trina away, she grabbed both of my hands and placed them across her hips, then she leaned back into my chest.

Oh my God! Why did she do that?

She was torturing the hell out of me. I looked over at Mike again and he waved his hand at me and yelled, "Relax, man! Enjoy yourself!" I got the reassurance I needed. He was fine with the situation. I didn't let loose like I wanted to, but I took the edge off enough to get into the mood. I even closed my eyes and began to fantasize how I would flip her around in my bed.

"How does it feel?" Trina whispered in my ear as her moves got a little slower.

"You feel my dick, don't you?"

"Yeah, and it feels like it's big, too."

"Oh, really?"

"Yeah. I bet you be having chicks going crazy off it, too."

"I don't know about that."

"Stop trying to be modest. I know good dick when I feel it."

"So you think it's good?"

"Yeah. You look like you'd fuck the shit out of somebody."

I laughed.

"What's so funny?"

"I'm just tripping off this whole shit."

"What?"

"You and Mike."

"What about it?"

"I can't believe he's letting you give me a lap dance."

"Oh, this is nothing. He lets me do this all the time. It's my job. And plus, it gets his dick hard to see me riding another nigga's dick."

"Word?"

"Yep." Trina grabbed my hands and placed them across her titties.

"Hold up! Whatchu doing?" I snatched my hands back.

"It's fine. See? Look at him. He's enjoying it." She pointed to Mike. Sure enough, Mike was sitting back, sipping on his glass of champagne and enjoying the scenery. I wondered if this nigga was bugged out or what. I mean, I could never have my girl grinding on another cat's dick and sit back and watch it like it was OK. He had to be some kind of sicko! But hey, what could I say other than if he liked it, I loved it. I placed my hand right back on Trina's soft-ass titties and started massaging and squeezing them. They felt so good, I wanted to scream!

"You are about to blow off some steam, huh?"

"Nah, but I want to."

"Well, I see your eyes were closed, so what were you thinking about?"

"I was thinking about you."

"What about?"

"I was thinking about how I would make love to you if we were somewhere else other than here."

"Care to share those details?"

"Not really."

"Why not?"

"Because Mike is my boy, and I don't want to overstep my boundaries."

"I understand that, but will you give me just a teaser?"

I laughed. "I'll just say that I would make you feel real good."

"Shit! You're making me feel good now," she said. "Feel how wet you got my pussy." She rubbed my right hand over the crotch area of her thong. When I felt the warmness of her pussy, I knew that she was serious. Instead of moving my hand, I left it there and started rubbing my fingers back and forth across her pussy. I could feel that her pussy lips were nice and plump, just like I liked them.

"Hmmmm," Trina moaned. "That feels so good!"

"Just imagine how it would feel if it was my dick."

"Owwww," she moaned again, bucking at my hand. "I bet it will feel real good."

"You getting ready to cum, ain'tcha?"

"Yes!" Trina suppressed a scream by biting down on her bottom lip.

Without even thinking about the repercussions I would get from Mike, I slipped my hand inside her thong and fingered her clit and her vagina until my fingers were soaking wet. Within seconds, homegirl released a puddle of her juices and then she let out a long sigh.

"Damn, that felt good!" she whispered in my ear and then she slowly kissed it. I slid my hand out of her thong and placed it on the armrest of my chair. I wanted so badly to smell it, but I knew Mike was looking at me, so I didn't want to play myself.

"I owe you for that one." Trina smiled and sat up.

"Yeah, you sure do."

She got up from my lap and stood up in front of me and fixed her thong. When I saw that she was taking her time to do it, I remembered that she was at work so I needed to fork over a few dollars to her. As I went into my pockets to get my dough, I wondered how much would be appropriate to give her. OK, granted, she was definitely an ordinary stripper and they normally charge ten dollars for a lap dance. But this was my boss's girl, so I knew I was going to have to step my game up and give her at least one hundred dollars. I mean, that would be the noble thing to do since he bought us a couple of bottles of champagne. I pulled two fifty-dollar bills from my roll of money and handed them to her.

Trina took the bills without hesitation and folded them both together in the palm of her hand. "Hope to see you again," she said.

"At these prices, you probably won't," I muttered under my breath.

"What did you say?" she yelled.

"Nothing. I'll holler at you later." I waved my hand, hoping she would get the hint.

Finally she did. When she carried her ass back over to where Mike was, she took him by the hand

and led him into this back room. I followed them with my eyes, but after they went behind the curtain, I immediately lost eye contact. There was this big, ugly nigga standing outside that room with his arms folded, wearing all black. I knew he had to be one of the club's bouncers, so I got up from my chair and approached him.

"Ay yo, dawg, what's this room for?"

"It's a private room for the strippers and VIP guests."

"Is it an open room?"

"Nah, it's five small rooms back there with couches in them. The owner got it set up back there like that to give cats a little more privacy."

"So, you're telling me he could go back there and do whatever he wanted to do?"

"Yeah, he could because he's the owner."

Shocked by his response, I said, "Word?"

The bouncer smiled and said, "Yep, he's the big dawg around here."

"Well, I bet he's paying you real good to protect him and all these chicks 'round here."

"Yeah, I get my just due."

"Well, homegirl with the pasties does too, because she just hit me up for a hundred dollars for a lap dance."

"Just for a lap dance?" He was shocked.

"Yep. She stuck me up without a pistol."

He shook his head. "Oh yeah, she got you good and now she's getting ready to give him the real thing."

"Oh, but it's all right. Because sooner or later, I am going to get the real thing, too," I assured him and then went to the bathroom. It was mandatory that I wash my hands and try to dry the wet spot on my boxers. When I got inside the bathroom and saw how filthy it was and that there were no paper towels or toilet tissue, I knew it was time for me to get the hell out of there. After I washed my hands, I dried them off on my jeans and walked out of there. I didn't even let Mike know I had left. I just got in my car and headed back to the beach.

On my way down the highway, I called Maxine and told her I was on my way. After she told me that she would wait up for me, I put the pedal to the metal because all I could think about was how I was going to blow her back out. The way Trina had my dick throbbing, I knew I wasn't going to be able to go to my mom's crib without busting that nut off in somebody. And since Maxine had been begging for it the past couple of days, I figured she was worthy enough to get it.

After I got my rocks off, I laid in the bed and re-played that whole scene with Mike and Trina at the club. I began to wonder why he didn't tell me that he was the owner of the club. I mean, what was the point in that? Did he have something to hide? Well, whatever it was, it could not have been that serious, because I could have really cared less. One of these days, I was gonna bring it to his attention, too.

Maxine

My Second Mistake

I was so happy when my baby came over and gave me some dick. I think if I had to go at least another day, I probably would have gone crazy. So far, everything had been going smoothly. I got up around six o'clock the next morning and fixed him breakfast because he told me that he was going to have to head out to the spot early. I didn't gripe about it one bit. I figured arguing with him about him hustling would only send him farther and farther away from me, and I couldn't have that. I loved him too much for him to leave, so I'd already drilled it in my head to just deal with whatever he had going on since it was only going to be temporary.

While he was eating, I suggested that we go on a vacation together. I figured this would be a good way for us to spend more time together, and perhaps bring us back closer. For some reason, this idea didn't sit right with him, so I asked him what was wrong.

"Ain't nothing wrong."

"Well, why don't you want to go out of town?"

"It's not that I don't want to go out of town," he said, stuffing bacon into his mouth. "The timing just isn't right."

"Then when would be a good time for you? Because I am going to be off at least two or three more weeks."

"I'll let you know."

"Is it going to be within the next month or so?" I pressed the issue, hoping he would give me a straight answer.

"Nah, I don't think it's going to be that soon."

Not at all happy by his response, I sighed. But I didn't complain about it. I just sucked it all in and said, "Well, just let me know when it would be OK for me to call my travel agent."

"A'ight," he said and continued to eat.

After he ate, he hopped in the shower and was out in less than five minutes. He threw his clothes on in about the same amount of time it took him to bathe, kissed me, and headed back out the door.

"Call me, OK?" I yelled out the door.

"A'ight," he said and then drove off.

After he left, I sat down on my living room sofa and wondered what the hell could be going on with Seth. He'd been so distant from me lately, and I knew that argument he and I had over four days ago couldn't have had anything to do with it. Not only that, the time that he'd been spending at Melody's house was a bit too much, which made me wonder if he was fucking her. I mean, something had to be going on because he loved sex and he had to have it at least twice a day, so who was he getting it from? It sure wasn't from me. I swore that if I found out he was getting it from her, then there was definitely going to be a lot of problems. There was going to be problems that she and Seth weren't going to be able to handle. Now that I thought about it, I was going to have to take a trip out there to find out how this young girl looked so that I would know if she was Seth's type or not. From there, I could draw my own conclusions. I just hoped for their sakes that the conclusions I drew fell in their favor because if they didn't, then all hell was going to break loose.

I got dressed and was on my way out of my apartment when I heard something vibrating. When I turned around to see what the hell it was, it stopped. I stood still and waited to see if I would hear it again and sure enough, I did. *It is coming from my kitchen,* I thought and dashed off in that direction. When I turned the corner and saw Seth's BlackBerry on my countertop buzzing around, I was completely shocked. Seth never went anywhere without his phone. That thing stuck to him like glue. I moved closer to pick it up, but it stopped vibrating again. I went into the call log to display the number when the thing started vibrating again. I noticed that another call was trying to come through but when I saw that the number came up PRIVATE, I immediately answered the call.

"You have a pre-paid call from an inmate at a federal correctional facility," the recording said. "If you do not wish to accept this call, please dial ZERO or hang up. To block future calls from this inmate, please press the POUND key now. If you wish to accept the call from SAMANTHA, please press FIVE now."

"Samantha," I said to myself. My heart pounded rapidly inside my chest when it dawned on me that she was his co-defendant and ex-lover. "What the hell is she calling him for?" I screamed, but it all registered very quickly. If I wanted the answer to that question, she would be able to give it to me. I pressed FIVE.

"Hello," I said.

There was a long pause before she responded. I guess she was trying to figure out who could be answering Seth's phone. When she couldn't come up with the answer, she got up the gumption to ask, "Who is this?"

"Who are you?" I asked back.

"I'm Samantha. Seth's fiancée."

"Oh, really? Well that's strange because I'm his fiancée, we live together, and I'm pregnant with his child." I couldn't help but say that, even though I knew that part of it was a lie. Seth and I didn't live together and I wasn't pregnant, but she didn't know that.

"What the fuck you just say?" Samantha screamed.

"Sweetie, now I know you heard me and I refuse to repeat myself," I replied sarcastically.

"Bitch, don't be getting smart with me! Do you know who the fuck I am? I will kill you and that motherfucking baby in your stomach!"

"I want to see you try it," I dared her, chuckling a bit.

"You can laugh now, bitch, but it ain't gon' be funny when I get out! Believe me, I've only got three weeks left, so go ahead and finish playing house. All that's gonna come to an end when I become a free woman. Now, watch what I tell you."

"Sweetie, I applaud you for your confidence but right now, you are dealing with an illusion," I told her. "Because you see, Seth and I have been together for almost a year now and he tells me constantly how much he loves me. So I don't believe I am going anywhere, especially since I'm carrying his baby."

"Oh trust me, bitch, when I come home, you and that baby will be history!" Samantha roared.

"Wait a minute, sweetie. Please calm down! Am I upsetting you?" I snickered.

"Keep laughing, bitch! Remember, your days are numbered, so enjoy them while you can because I am wifey, and when I show up, all the hoes and tricks scatter."

"Well first off, I am not a ho! And I am definitely not a trick. I am an educated woman with class and my own money, unlike you."

"Bitch, I don't care how educated you are. That shit ain't gon' work for you when I get home. Now watch and see."

"Whatever you say, Ms. Samantha."

"Don't feed me that shit!" She was getting irritated. "What's your name anyway?"

"I don't think you need to know all of that. But I will tell you that I control a lot of shit and I've got a lot of clout, so if you try to come near me or Seth,

I will have your ass back in prison so fast, you will feel your head spin!"

"You ain't gon' do shit to me," Samantha retaliated.

"Well, try me and see!" I warned her.

Before Samantha could get another word in, I disconnected the call and right when I was about to let out a loud scream of frustration, Seth startled me. He'd come from out of nowhere. "Who were you just talking to?"

My heart fell down in the pit of my stomach when I turned around and saw Seth standing there with the most livid expression possible. From his tone, I could tell that he wanted an answer that instant. I took a deep breath and said, "I was talking to Samantha."

"Who?" he asked, even though I knew he had already heard me the first time.

"I said, Samantha," I repeated.

He walked toward me. "What the fuck did you have to say to her?" He snatched his BlackBerry out of my hand.

"I had a lot to say to her, especially after she told me y'all are going to be together when she gets out in three weeks," I snapped.

"So, what did you say?" he snapped back, not at all concerned about how I put emphasis on the part that Samantha was coming home in three weeks. It should have been apparent that I was upset and a little intimidated about her homecoming, but Seth wasn't fazed by that. All he wanted to know was what I said to her. I let his ass have it. "I told her that we were together! Why?"

"Ay yo, you are real foul! You know that?"

Ignoring his insult, I went straight into question mode. "What is going on with you and her, Seth? Why did she tell me that y'all were going to be together when she came home?"

Refusing to answer my question, he fired back at me with a question of his own. "Why the hell you answered my phone? That's my personal shit! You know how I am about my privacy."

"Fuck your privacy!" I smacked him. "You fucking betrayed me." Then I got in his face. "All this time, I've been wondering why the hell you were being so distant and now I know. It's her. You are trying to brush me off so you can go off and be with her, but it ain't gonna happen. And I can promise you that one!"

Seth stood there with a red handprint across his right cheek. "Whatchu gon' do?"

I stood my ground. "Try me. You'll see."

"A'ight." He went into my bedroom.

I had no idea what he was about to do, so I followed him. When I saw him storm over toward my closet and grab everything that was his, I went crazy. "What you think you're doing?" I yelled, trying to snatch clothes out of his hands.

"Maxine, you better move out my way," he growled.

"I'm not going anywhere. And you ain't going anywhere, either," I protested.

"You are a motherfucking lie! I'm getting away from your crazy ass!" He continued to try and force his way by me, but I tried to hold him back with my weight. It didn't work, though. He used his 185 pounds to move me right out of the way. I stumbled and almost fell to the floor.

"You are not leaving me!" I ranted and raved after I caught my balance and charged behind him.

Clothes were falling out of his arms as he made his way down the hallway of my apartment. He was able to recover a few pieces along the way but there were others that I wouldn't let him touch. "You ain't taking this," I blurted out as we played tug-of-war with a mink coat I purchased for him on our first Christmas together.

"Well, keep it! I don't give a fuck about that shit!"

"You ain't taking this either," I roared once again, snatching a pair of tailor-made slacks that were thrown across his shoulder. At that instant, Seth became infuriated. He stopped in his tracks and dropped every article of clothing in the middle of the floor. "You know what? Keep all this shit!" he yelled. He stormed outside and slammed the front door behind him.

At that very moment, I knew Seth was gone and that he wasn't coming back. Samantha told me out of her own mouth that they were going to be together when she got out of prison. What was hurting my heart so badly was that when I asked him about it, he didn't deny it. But I had a trick for the both of their asses if they thought that I was going to let them be together. Especially after all the shit I had invested in his sorry ass! Not in a million years.

The very next morning, which was a Friday, I got up, got dressed, and headed to the office. I wasn't going in to perform my regular duties. I was simply going in to do some more research. I ran into that bitch, Carolyn Granger, on the way in. Dressed in one of her usual black or navy blue suits, she sparked up a conversation with me the second I stepped into the elevator. "I thought you were off for a couple of weeks."

I cringed at the sound of her voice but instead of showing her my true emotions, I smiled. "I am, but I'm working on a few things at home so I needed to come into my office and get a file."

"Does Karen know you're here?" she asked.

"No, but I am sure you will tell her," I replied sarcastically and stepped off the elevator the moment the door opened.

I knew she was shocked at my response, but evidently it didn't faze her because she fired right back at me and hit my ass right below the belt. "Did Karen tell you that personnel gave me her position?"

I gritted my teeth really hard because I'm sure Karen already told her that I knew about her getting the position over me. Instead of dignifying her question with a response, simply because it was a rhetorical question, I only gave her a nod.

"Well, you know that means I am going to be your boss?"

"I'm sure you're looking forward to that."

"You know I am." She smiled. "I can't wait to turn things around in this office."

"I'm sure you can't," I said.

"Oh, but it's gonna be for the best," she belted out while the elevator door opened.

"Yes, I'm sure," I commented and then I stepped off the elevator and didn't look back.

When I got to my office, I felt a sense of emptiness when I opened the door. Everything was in place but, for some reason, it felt like something was missing. When I rummaged through my things and realized that everything was still in place, I sat down behind my desk. It dawned on me that I was the one who was missing from the equation. It also dawned on me that my job was my life before I got turned down for the promotion, and to make matters worse, the fact that Seth was taking my love for granted really had me pissed. But before I allowed my emotions to get the best of me, I grabbed his file from my file cabinet and booted up my computer. I already knew Samantha's full name, but in order for me to locate her in our database and find out her exact release date, I needed other pertinent information like her date of birth and her social security number. I opened up the file and searched through every court document until I ran across the section where it had her listed as his co-defendant. My eyes lit up because I knew I was one step closer to finding out when she was becoming a free woman.

I keyed all of her information into the system and instantly, her whole file appeared right before my eyes. In bold letters her release date read: NOVEMBER 21, 2007. I almost passed out when I saw it. That was near the Thanksgiving holiday. As I continued to read, I discovered that she would be released to the halfway house on 20th Street in Norfolk to serve a four-month term and complete a drug rehabilitation program. Her release date from the halfway house was MARCH 17, 2008. Then she would be released to 509 Middle Town Arch in Norfolk, which was listed as her parents' address. As I read farther down, I came across some information that I wasn't quite ready for. There, posted right before my eyes, was Carolyn Granger's name listed as her probation officer. I knew that this was not going to be good. If Samantha ever found out that I was the one that went back and forth with her on the phone about Seth, and that Carolyn and I couldn't stand one another, she would have a field day and try to bury my ass. So, what the hell was I going to do? How was I going to get her out of the way without implicating myself? That was something I needed to think about hard and long. I pushed my keyboard to the side, leaned my head back against the headrest of my chair, and closed my eyes in deep thought. Just as I was about to channel my thoughts into creative mode, there was a knock on my door.

"Come in," I said.

Karen opened my door and popped her head around it. "Got a minute?" she asked.

"Yeah, sure. What's up?"

Karen came inside and took a seat. "I've got good news."

"What about?"

"I just got a call from one of the detectives investigating your assault, and he informed me that they have Sean Phillips in custody."

My face lit up. "When did they get him?"

"Earlier this morning. He was stopped in a road block that five state troopers had set up to sift out drunk drivers near Richmond. After the state troopers instructed him to pull over, they noticed that the decals on the license plates had expired and when they asked him for his license and registration, he tried to drive off and make a run for it but the other troopers blocked him off and shut him down immediately."

"You've got to be kidding!"

"No, I'm not."

"Was he traveling alone?"

"No, he had a female companion with him. The officers said that they planned to detain her for a couple of hours and hoped that she'd have some information that could lead to the whereabouts of the other two."

"Well, did they at least find my weapon?" I asked with desperation.

Karen paused for a second and then she said, "Well, they weren't sure because the weapon they found had most of the serial numbers scratched off, but the detective assured me that Mr. Phillip's fingerprints were all over it. He is going to have that weapon sent to Forensics to see if they can recover what was left of the numbers and see if they come up with a match."

I let out a sigh of relief. "So, what's gonna happen next?"

"Well, the charges have already been filed, so all we'd have to do is go through the process of waiting on his conviction in state court. Then we could violate his federal probation and send his butt back to prison."

"Where exactly is he now?"

"Richmond city police have him in custody, but

the detectives from Chesapeake assured me that he would be back in their jurisdiction by the end of business."

"Well, I sure hope they find out whether that's my weapon or not."

"Oh, they will," she assured me, and then abruptly changed the subject. "So, how is everything with you?"

I smiled with confidence. "Everything is fine."

"Come off that, Maxine. You know I know when something is bothering you. Now, tell me what's wrong."

"Nothing is wrong. I am fine, Karen."

"So tell me why you're back at work."

"Because I was bored sitting at home," I lied.

"Where is your male companion?"

"I'm sure he's probably at work."

"Well, why don't you go out and pamper yourself? Get a full body massage or something. Take a trip to the Poconos with your male companion."

"All that sounds good but at the end of the day, I am going to still feel that void of wanting to be here at work. Karen, you know I hate sitting around doing nothing. I've got to keep busy or else I'm gonna go crazy!"

"Well, you need to get over it," Karen insisted as she stood and started to gather up the loose documents of Seth's file. My instincts stopped her plans to grab his folder. I blocked her hand and insisted that I put the file back myself. She refused to let go of the few pieces of documents she had, so I literally snatched them away from her and accidentally tore all four papers in half. Karen was appalled by my actions and I couldn't say anything in my defense. "What's the matter with you?" she asked.

Standing there with the other half of the torn documents in my hand, I looked at Karen with a dumb expression on my face. I knew that I had to come up with a good enough excuse of why I was acting this way, so I quickly gathered my thoughts. I said, "Karen, I am so sorry. I guess being away from work is starting to get to me."

Karen took the torn pieces of paper out of my hands and laid them on top of the other files. "Go home, please. Take that vacation, like I told you," she encouraged me.

"All right. Well, just let me shut down my computer," I said.

She became adamant. "No, I will do it."

I sighed heavily. "OK."

Karen watched me closely as I grabbed my handbag and car keys and casually walked around to the other side of my desk. As I made my way toward my office door, she shuffled all the paperwork around in order to get it back in one neat pile. When my hand was on the doorknob, Karen said, "What's going on with this female offender?"

"Who?" I asked, even though I knew who she was talking about.

"Samantha Mitchell."

I turned around to face Karen and said, "Oh, I was checking on the status of her release."

"Why would you do that, when she's not one of your case files?" Karen asked with suspicion.

I caught a knot in my throat that instant. I knew I had to come up with something very clever because she was waiting for a convincing answer. I couldn't come out and tell her I was checking up on Ms. Mitchell because she was gonna take my man when she came home. Karen would look at me like I was crazy. I had to come up with something more substantial. Then it came to me out of the blue. "Because she's a co-defendant of one of my parolees, and I wanted to make sure I stayed on top of her release, since they are not supposed to have any verbal or physical contact with each other."

Karen took a seat behind my desk so she could get a closer look at my monitor. "Well, it says that she is going to be assigned to Carolyn's caseload. Well, that is until she takes over my position, so just get with her if you think that there's gonna be a problem."

"Well, I don't want to jump the gun because she is going into the halfway house upon her release from prison."

"Call the director and let them know that your client is on supervised probation and that it's a condition of his probation that he is not to have any contact with Ms. Mitchell. If he goes up there, then he will automatically get violated. As a matter of fact, . . ." Karen's voice faded as she began to sift through the stack of papers.

"What are you looking for?"

"I am looking for your client's photo, so I can make a photocopy of it and hand it to Carolyn. She can attach it to this lady's file when she sends it over to the halfway house."

"Oh no, you don't have to do all of that." I rushed back to my desk.

"Wait, I got it." Karen paused and pulled the picture closer to her face. You could tell by her expression that she was in really deep thought. It was obvious that she'd recognized Seth's face from the photo back at my apartment. I believed she was beginning to think that her mind was playing tricks on her, but then again she wasn't quite sure. If that was the case, I wanted to play along. "What's wrong?" I asked, trying to play it cool.

"This isn't the guy in that photo back at your apartment, is it?"

I laughed hysterically. "You must be kidding, right?"

"I know that sounded crazy, but this looks just like that guy."

"Well, believe you me, it's not."

Karen took another look at Seth's picture and then she shook her head. "I swear this guy looks just like your friend."

"You think so?" I asked.

Karen put the photo aside. "Well, kind of," she replied in a way that said she was unsure. Then she pressed a couple of keys and used the mouse to shut down my computer.

I stood there in amazement and wondered how I was able to persuade her to believe that Seth was not the man in my picture back at my place. That was truly a close call, and I would never put myself in that predicament again. From that point on, I was gonna have to keep all my personal shit at home and keep Karen's ass out of there. Simple as that!

Karen killed herself to shut down my computer and put Seth's file back in my file cabinet. She grabbed his photo and attached a sticky note to it, to remind herself to make a copy of it and leave it on Carolyn's desk. I wasn't too happy about her decision to do that, but there was absolutely nothing I could do about it. If Carolyn ever got wind of what was going on between Seth and me, I knew that I was going to be in for it. I even thought about slipping into Carolyn's office and snatching the picture off her desk before she saw it. But as thorough as Karen was, she would definitely make it her business to check back with Carolyn to make sure she got it. Now I had to come up with a plan B.

It had been a week since I had last spoken to Seth. I had left him messages on his voice mail and sent him text messages, but he refused to respond. I even sat in my car and watched him run in and out of Melody's apartment to service the different drug addicts. Melody came outside a couple of times herself, so I got a really good look at her. She was definitely Seth's type, which made me wonder what they could be doing behind those closed doors. For her sake, she'd better keep her pussy to herself because if I ever got a feeling that shit wasn't looking right between those two, I was going to go the fuck off and she was going to lose her little-ass project house. I meant that shit from the bottom of my heart.

Seth

Never Mix Business With Pleasure

Melody had been trying to get me to fuck her on an everyday basis. I kept telling that ho that it wasn't like that between us, but she wasn't trying to hear me. First off, her pussy was on zero and her mouth game wasn't much better. The only thing I got pleasure from was when I was fucking her in her ass. I loved that shit! It got addicting at times, and I found myself wanting it every time my dick got hard. I believed she knew that shit too, and tried to use it to her advantage. I wasn't stupid. I was hip to her game and I think she knew that, too. What really got me was when she tried to walk around there like we were a couple. She fucked my head up yesterday when she asked me if I could take her ass shopping. I looked at that bitch like she was crazy, handed her ass twenty dollars and told her she'd better call Mike, because I was not the one. She got mad as hell with me when I told her that shit, but that shit didn't bother me. I had other shit to worry about, and I intended to handle it.

Everything was running smoothly; the boys were outside watching out for the Narcs and keeping the money coming steady with the dopefiends, and I was chilling in the kitchen, tearing into a plate of oxtails and white rice with a side of plantains I picked up from M.P.'s Island Café on the way there. The food was good as a motherfucker and I was into it, too. Then my cell phone rang. When I saw that it was my baby Samantha trying to get through, I answered it on the spot.

"What's good, baby?" I said through a mouthful of food.

"Nothing much. Whatchu doing?" she asked.

"Just chilling at the spot, eating these big-ass oxtails."

"Awwww man, I ain't had none of them joints in years. Damn, I bet they are good!"

"They are," I replied between chews.

"Where did you get them from?"

"From this spot off Virginia Beach Boulevard in Norfolk, called M.P.'s Island Café."

"How long have you been at the spot?"

As I was about to answer Samantha's question, Melody brought her silly ass in the kitchen and asked me if I was on the phone talking to Mike. Now, I knew that bitch knew I wasn't talking to Mike. She just wanted Samantha to hear her voice in the background so I'd have to explain to Samantha who she was. See, that's what these sideline hoes do. They had to keep unnecessary shit going so they could make your main girl feel a little insecure. It worked every single time. In fact, Samantha fed right into it. "Who the hell is that bitch?" she screamed.

"It's my peoples' girl."

"What's her name?"

"Her name is Melody."

"Seth, don't lie to me! That bitch in the background sounds just like the chick that answered your phone last week and popped all that shit to me."

Hearing the rage in Samantha's voice, I knew she was about to blow her top. That conversation she had with Maxine last week took her over the edge. Maxine really had Sam believing that she was pregnant and that we lived together. I broke it down to Samantha and told her who Maxine really was, and that what she told her was a lie. She had a fit when I told her that Maxine was my P.O. and that I'd fucked her. In the same sentence, I lied and told her that when I fucked her, it was a one-night stand and I ain't fucked with her since. Unfortunately, Samantha didn't go for it. She wanted to know why Maxine had my cell phone and why she would make up all that shit if it wasn't true. I kicked it to her like Maxine was on some fatal attraction type of shit but I shut her down, once and for all. Samantha wasn't too happy at all about everything I had just laid down on the table, but the damage was already done. What could she say?

"Sam, Melody is not the same chick you talked to; that was Maxine," I tried to explain.

"Maxine, Melody. Both of those bitches' names sound just alike."

"Yeah, you're right, but that's not her."

"Well, why is Melody all in your face?" she asked me, still heated.

"Mommie, she just walked in the spot and asked me if I was talking to her man on the phone."

"Well, tell her ass nah, so she can keep it moving."

"I just did," I lied.

"Well, did she carry her ass?"

"Yes, she did," I said, simultaneously waving Melody out of the kitchen so I could have some privacy. When she left, I was able to calm Samantha a little more. After I told her that I loved her about five consecutive times, she felt a lot better. If you want to know my honest opinion, telling your girl you loved her over the phone while you were in the company of another woman was some powerful shit. Chicks fed off stuff like that. It made them feel superior because they figured that if you came out your mouth and expressed your feelings to them while you were standing next to another chick, then that chick didn't mean shit to you. In this case, Samantha happened to be right.

"Can I ask you a question?" she asked. "Why is that chick hanging out with you while her man is somewhere else?"

"She's not hanging out with me. This is her crib and I make moves for her man."

"That doesn't make sense," Samantha said. "What kind of man would let another nigga come up in his girl's spot to work?"

"Samantha, trust me. It ain't even that type of party."

"Whatchu mean by that?"

"Believe me, that nigga don't give a fuck about

this shit around here. He's got a wife and a baby on the way, so this is only a temporary arrangement."

"So, what you are saying is that he's basically using her?"

"Exactly," I agreed.

Sam laughed. "Yo, y'all niggas got plenty of shit with y'all!"

"Not me," I denied.

"Oh yes, you do." She started laughing again. "'Cause if you didn't, you would not have fucked your probation officer and led her on believing that y'all were going to be together."

"Come on, Sam, I already told you that it wasn't like that."

"I know what you told me, but what would possess you to fuck your P.O.? I mean, what were you thinking about?"

"Do we have to go through this again?"

"You damn right! Because you got out of answering me the last time."

I sighed heavily. "Look, Sam, it was a bad judgment call and it won't happen again."

"I know that much," she said, cutting me off. "I want to know why you did it. Because there has to be a reason."

"I don't know why I did it. It just happened."

"Now I know it didn't just happen. You probably got it in your head that if you gave her some dick, she'd go easy on you with your time on paper. But let me tell you something right now; she knows that I'm about to come home, so I know some shit is going to go down. Now, I don't know how you are going to do it, but you better step to her and tell her that I ain't for no drama, so she better stay away from me."

"I gotcha! Trust me, she ain't gonna fuck with you."

"Come on now, Seth. Who do you think you're talking to? That bitch has it out for me already. I know she's gonna want to get me violated."

"She could only do it if she was your P.O., and I know that ain't gonna happen because she's already mine and that would be a conflict of interest."

"Not being my P.O. isn't gonna stop her. I am quite sure she has friends who work with her that could do as much damage as she would."

"Yeah, you're probably right, but why are you racking your brain behind this shit? She isn't gonna do shit to you. I told you I was going to take care of it."

"You better, because if I get any flack behind your wandering dick, I am gonna cut the shit off myself. You understand?"

I laughed, even though I knew Samantha was serious. "Mommie, don't act like that," I said in a subtle tone. "You know I am going to take care of you, right?"

"You better, because remember—I'm doing this bid for your ass!"

"I know, Ma. That's why you ain't gonna have to worry about shit when you come home," I assured her.

Our conversation lasted for another three or four minutes and then we were cut off. Before we got disconnected, I reassured Samantha that everything would be taken care of and she would not have any problems. I sealed my promise with a kiss, and from where I was sitting, I think she bought it.

After I hung up with Samantha, I called Melody back into the kitchen and cursed her ass out behind that stunt she had just pulled. She acted as if it was just a misunderstanding, but I knew how cunning bitches could be, so I wasn't trying to hear that bullshit.

"Look, Melody, don't run up on me like that anymore. When you see me on the phone, I want you to turn around and leave so I can have some privacy. You understand?"

"Yeah, I understand, but it's not my fault you're fucking with someone who is insecure!" she replied sarcastically and stormed back out of the kitchen.

"You would know something about that, wouldn't you?" I yelled, but she didn't respond. I was glad because I had a headache and I wasn't trying to add any more pressure to it.

As the day went on, Melody stayed out of my way. She acted like she had an attitude, but I didn't give a damn. I preferred her to be this way so she could keep her ass out of my face. I could handle my business better that way, which was always a good thing.

At the end of the day, me and my street team raked in eighteen grand. It was a little less than normal, but it was only because the police kept riding through and scaring the fiends off. I had to end up taking the rest of the dope with me. I normally wouldn't ride home dirty, but I figured since heroin mixed with baby laxative goes bad after a day or two, it would be a waste of time for me to give the shit back to Mike. I could just get up early in the morning and come back out and get rid of it then. Mike agreed with me when I met him and gave him his dough, so it was a done deal.

Samantha

Sideline Chick

I walked straight to my room after I got off the phone with Seth. And even though we didn't end our conversation on a bad note, I was still a bit ticked off. My intuition was fucking with me, and I needed somebody to vent to so I was glad my roommate Ms. Blair was in the room when I got there.

"Girl, that nigga is about to drive me fucking crazy!" I screamed.

"Who?" she wanted to know.

"Seth."

Ms. Blair sat up on her bunk and sighed. "What did he do now?"

See Ms. Blair was not only my roommate, but also my homegirl. And even though she was West Indian and ten years older than I was, she knew what time it was when it came to men. She was full of wisdom, so I always looked to her for advice. "Besides talking me into taking his gun charge, I think he's cheating on me again."

Ms. Blair cracked a smile. "What gave you that impression, honey?"

"Because when I was just on the phone with him, I heard a woman's voice come out of nowhere. And do you know she questioned him and asked him if he was talking to some guy named Mike? But, I'm not stupid. I knew she did that so I could hear her voice and then start questioning him about who she was. And guess what? It worked."

"What did he say about it?"

"He told her to chill and sent her on her way. But he said it in a way like he was trying to hide something."

"Well, did you ask him who she was?"

"Yeah. But, he lied and told me she was his homeboy's girlfriend. So, my thing was why is she there with you and not with him? And that's when he told me that he was at her house waiting on the guy Mike to get there."

"Did you believe him?"

"Not really."

"Well, let me say this," Ms. Blair began. "Because you are here you have no way of finding out whether or not he's telling you the truth. So, take his word for it until you find out otherwise."

"But, what if he is cheating on me with her?"

"Sweetheart, he's a man. And men cheat all the time. So, that's why it's important for a woman to get everything she possibly can from him while you have 'em. Because as soon as they think they've found someone else better, they will leave you at the drop of a dime. So, take my advice and live for today and save for tomorrow."

"All that sounds good, Ms. Blair, but what I really want to do is kill him sometimes."

"Nah, love! The best way to get a man back is by taking him for everything he's got. I mean, take him for all he's worth. And if you feel like that's still not enough, then go ahead and kill 'em! But, just make sure you don't leave any witnesses around or any evidence that would lead the police back to you." She smiled. But, deep down inside I knew she was serious as hell.

See, Ms. Blair was there for attempted murder on her husband. She got a twenty-year sentence. She said her husband was a big time drug dealer from Trinidad and they had a beautiful home in south Florida but the feds confiscated it along with their construction business and all their possessions. Her husband got twenty-five years because he got caught with several kilos of cocaine in his possession while he was entertaining his mistress in an expensive hotel suite thirty miles from their home. Ms. Blair said she had no idea the feds had his hotel room under surveillance because if she did, she would not have gone there to kill him. She said she wished she would've gotten someone else to do it because she wouldn't be in this predicament. I told her to stop crying over spilt milk because her time was almost up. With only two years left, she could start over and find herself a new man. She laughed at me and said, "Samantha, I am fifty-three years old. Who in their right mind is going to want me?" I smiled back at her and told her that there are plenty of men looking for a beautiful woman such as herself. Too bad for her though, Immigration was sending her back home to Trinidad, so she was gonna have to go back there with nothing but the clothes on her back. Hopefully when I got out and got on my feet I'd be able to give her a nice piece of change to go back home with because she was a good woman and she didn't deserve that.

After our conversation, we headed down to the TV room to play a few games of bid wiz. We stayed down there until it was time to go to the dining room for chow.

Maxine

He's Sticking It To Me Hard

Another week had passed, and I had yet to salvage my relationship with Seth. He still refused to accept my calls or return any of my text messages. I even made a couple of trips to his mother's house early in the morning, like around six AM, but I could never seem to catch him there. The only thing that came to mind was that he'd spent the night out and that thought turned my stomach upside down. Who could he be staying out all night with? I knew Samantha hadn't come out of prison yet, because November 21 was eight days away. Who could it be other than that chick Melody? I mean, he did spend an awful lot of time selling drugs out of her house. I knew it had been a lot because he was practically there from sunup to sundown, and I knew they had fucked each other. What kind of role she played in his life was another issue, and I intended on getting the answer to that as well. I needed to see if Seth's car was parked outside her apartment and I would be able to make that happen as soon as I got this slow-ass car from in front of me.

Beep, beep! "Could you please move the hell out of my way?" I screamed, right after I honked my car horn.

The driver in front of me finally got the message and pulled his 1995 Toyota Corolla to the side of the road so I could get by. When I passed the car, I noticed it was an old man behind the wheel and he looked terrified. I graciously smiled at him with an apologetic expression and kept it moving. I knew he probably thought I was crazy but I also thought the same damn thing about him, especially at the speed he was moving. Once he was out of my way, I proceeded with my mission, which was less than a mile away.

As I drove, I thought of what I was going to do when I arrived in Dales Homes. I also wondered about whether or not it would be feasible for me to go up to Melody's front door if I saw Seth's car parked outside. I mean, would that be a smart thing on my part, or would it be very foolish? I wondered how Seth would react. Would he go off on me? Or would he just simply brush me off and close the door in my face, like he did at his mother's house? In this situation, it would be very hard to tell but at this point, but it really didn't matter because I didn't care how he reacted. I wanted to see her reaction. With that attitude, I parked my car about a half a block before her apartment building and started walking in that direction.

Now, it was still kind of dark outside and the fact that it was cloudy wasn't gonna bring the sunlight into the sky any sooner. However, the streetlights gave me a little something to work with as I navigated down the narrow street. Dressed in my hooded sweatsuit and sneakers, I pulled my hood farther down over the top of my face and walked with my head down as I made my way toward Melody's apartment. I found myself walking over dozens of syringes and broken needles. The sight of it was scary. I wondered how in the hell the children played out there. It was too dangerous, if you asked me. Someone definitely needed to clean up these streets.

"Got them yellow bags," I heard a guy's voice yell, but I didn't look up to see if he was talking to me. I figured whatever it was he was trying to sell wouldn't do me any good. First of all, I didn't have a habit, and second, it wasn't gonna get me closer to my man so I kept it moving. I took a few more steps and ran into two women who were standing in the walkway. To keep from moving out of their comfort zone, so to speak, I walked around them. When I passed them I noticed one of the chicks pushing a needle into the other woman's neck. The shit terrified the hell out of me, so I jumped.

"Yeah, yeah, push all that shit up in me." The woman smiled as she instructed the chick with the syringe. Then in the blink of an eye, her smile wasted away and was replaced with an expression of fury. "Bitch, you tricked me up again!" I heard her yell. She snatched the syringe out of the other chick's hand. "This shit ain't nothing but cold-ass tap water!"

"Whatchu talking about?" the other woman asked.

"You know what the fuck I'm talking about! Don't just stand there and act like you didn't switch the shit up."

"I didn't!" the woman fired back. "I put every last bit of dope I had left in there, so the dope must've been bad."

"Come on, now. What kind of game you playing? That heroin came from the nigga that be in Melody's house and his shit is always good, so you got one over on me this time. But that's all right 'cause I'm gonna get your trifling ass back!" She threw the syringe on the ground and stormed off in the direction I was walking.

"Yeah, whatever," the other chick said and walked off in the opposite direction.

I continued to walk forward, leaving them behind, but somehow one of them managed to catch up with me. "You got to watch out for these conniving-ass bitches out here. They will steal from you in a heartbeat, and the fucked-up shit about it is that they'll do it right in your face and make you think they're doing something else."

Instead of responding to her comment, I ignored her and started walking faster. She noticed me trying to be evasive and said, "Hey, what's up? You holding?"

With my head down, I said, "Nope."

"Whatchu trying to score?" she pressed.

"Nothing," I sighed.

"What, you the police or something?" she asked, then stopped in her tracks.

"No, I am not," I replied, aggravated and disgusted.

"Well, if you ain't, then you better pull off that

hood 'cause if you don't, niggas around here are going to think that you're either the police or a stick-up kid, and they'll start shooting at you."

Alarmed by what this woman had just said, I stopped in my tracks and immediately pulled my hood off my head. At that very moment, we recognized each other.

"Wait a minute, you're that same lady I seen out here about two weeks ago, aren't cha?"

I nodded.

She walked a little closer to me. "But I thought you said you didn't get high?"

"I don't."

"Then what are you doing out here this time of the morning?"

I sighed. "It's a long story."

"Well, whatever kind of story it is, it couldn't be worth you running behind it."

"What do you mean by that?"

"Listen honey, these streets aren't no joke. They will swallow your ass right up if you let them, and then you're gonna be walking around here looking just like me. And I'm sure you don't want that."

"Look, ma'am," I said, but was abruptly cut off.

"My name is Faith."

"Well, Faith, like I was saying, I am not out here looking for drugs. I am out here looking for my man."

"What's your man's name?"

"His name is Seth and he drives a green Magnum."

"Oh, I know who you're talking about. That's the guy who hustles out of Melody's spot."

"Yeah, that's him," I replied eagerly, hoping that she would take the bait.

"Well, he's sitting down in her house as we speak."

"Do you know if he's been down there all night?"

"Oh nah, he never stays out here all night. He always closes down shop like about nine or ten o'clock, and then he turns right back around and comes back around this time."

"I wonder why he comes back out here so early?"

"Shit, you don't know?" Faith chuckled.

"Know what?"

"That's when you make the most money. Dope-fiends like me wander all over the city this time of the morning, looking for a pill of good dope. To us, it's like waking up and going out for breakfast. We have to have at least one or two pills of some good heroin to get our day started. As soon as we run across some dope that'll knock your socks off, we'll tell everybody we know. Believe me, word of mouth around here will either kill ya or make you rich."

"Well, let me ask you this." I pulled her to the side when I saw a guy walking in our direction. After he passed us, I said, "Have you dealt with him directly?"

"What do you mean by that?"

"Have you bought heroin directly from him?"

"A couple of times. Why?"

"Have you ever been into the house?"

"Oh nah, he won't let anybody in the house except for his little street crew."

"So, how do y'all make the trade off?"

"Early in the morning, we got to go to the back door and hand our money through the window. But during the day time, we got to go through one of the little watch-out boys he has standing outside of the apartment."

"How well do you know Melody?"

"Well enough. Why?"

"Would you know if they were fucking around with each other?"

"If they are, no one knows about it because she supposed to be messing with the big guy, Mike."

"Well, have you noticed anything between them two?"

"No, but that still doesn't mean they aren't. Like I said, if they are sneaking around, they are keeping it on the D.L."

"Well listen, I want you to do me a favor."

"What's up?"

"Would you walk with me down to Melody's place, so it won't look suspicious when I try to look through her window?"

"I'll walk with you down there, but I know you ain't going to be able to peep in her windows because she has black curtains covering every single window."

"Damn! What am I going to do now?"

"I'll tell you what: if you give me ten dollars, I'll have a reason to knock on her door and look and see if I can see something."

I reached inside my sweatpants, pulled out the only twenty-dollar bill I had to my name, and handed it to Faith. "I want my change back," I told her.

"All right," she replied and we started walking.

My heart started beating like crazy. "So, what do you want me to do while you go up to the house?"

"Just stand back a couple of feet and act like you're watching my back or something."

"But what if he sees me?"

"If you stand around the other side of the building, he won't."

"All right," I said again because at last, it seemed like a plan was coming together.

When we got up to Melody's apartment Seth's car was, indeed, parked out front. I walked by it and rubbed my hand across the hood to feel if it was still warm, and it was. "You weren't lying," I said to Faith.

"What are you talking about?"

"The hood of his car is still warm so you were right; he did just get here."

Faith smiled, revealing her yellow-stained teeth, and turned to walk toward the back of the building. I followed her to the edge of the building and stopped. Faith tapped on the window, told Seth what she wanted, handed him the money and got her drugs in her hands in less than sixty seconds flat. I was truly amazed at how their transaction went so smoothly. When Faith walked back around the building, I held out my hand for my change and asked her if she was able to get a look into the house.

"Nah, I couldn't see shit because he turned off the kitchen light when he came back to the window with the dope."

"What about before? Did you get to look inside when he first took your money?"

"Nope, because he only cracked the window just enough so that he would be able to take the money out of my hands."

"Damn!" I said as we walked back down the street toward my car.

"What's wrong?" Faith asked me.

"I am so frustrated right now, I could scream."

"Well, don't do that," she warned me.

I sighed heavily and was about to say something when I got sidetracked by someone's screen door closing. When I turned around and saw Seth walking outside toward his car, my face lit up. Instead of bringing attention to myself by standing in the middle of the sidewalk, I pulled Faith over to a car parked a couple feet from where we were. I took a seat on the hood and acted as if we were talking. Faith stumbled a bit but she caught her balance. "Whatchu doing?" she wondered, and before I could answer her, Melody came storming out the front door behind Seth, with bare feet and wearing a skimpy-looking nightgown.

"Wait, Seth! I am so sorry! Please let me make this right. I will do anything," she begged.

Seth hit the alarm on his car to unlock the door. "You better get the fuck away from me before I smack the hell out of you."

Melody grabbed his shirt. "Please let me make this right!" she said again.

"Didn't I tell you to get the fuck away from me?" he snapped.

"Please don't go. I am sorry. I promise I won't do it anymore." She began to cry.

"I know you won't, because after Mike gets through with your ass, you're gonna be sorry for real!"

Melody literally got down on her knees and started

sobbing uncontrollably. "Seth, please don't tell Mike. He will kill me!"

Seth burst into laughter. "Yeah, I know he will, and that's probably what your silly ass needs. Now, get your dumb ass off the ground and get back in the house."

Melody got off her knees and before she turned around to go back into the house, she looked at Seth and said, "Please give me another chance."

"Come on now, how many chances do you want? This was my second time catching you sniffing that shit, so I ain't gon' let it slide this time."

Melody stood there in silence for about ten seconds and then I heard her say, "You know what? You can go right ahead and tell him but just know that when you do, I'm gon' come right behind you and tell him me and you been fucking."

Hearing her come out of her mouth and say that they had been intimate gave me a queasy feeling in my stomach. I almost threw up, but I held my composure long enough to see Seth smack the shit out of her. He hit her so hard, I heard her ass slide across the rocks.

"Yeah, and while you're at it, tell him I smacked the hell out of you, too."

Melody gave him a look of disbelief as she held the side of her face with her hand. I thought she was going to get up and charge at him, but she didn't. Seth got into his car and flew out of there like a bat out of hell. I started to get into my car and follow him, but I decided against it when I saw Melody trying to stand to her feet.

"Where you going?" Faith asked me when I began to walk toward Melody.

"I am going to go and talk to her."

"Well, I'm gone. I'll be around here somewhere if you need me," she said and walked in the opposite direction.

By the time I got within a couple feet of Melody, she stood to her feet and began to brush the small fragments of dirt off her butt. "You all right?" I asked her.

Startled by my sudden appearance, she looked at me and said, "Oh shit, you scared me."

"I'm sorry. But are you all right?"

"I think I got a couple of scrapes and bruises on my ass, but I'll be all right." She limped toward her front door.

I started walking alongside of her. "Need some help?"

"Nah, I'm all right."

"Hey, wait. Can I ask you something?"

Melody stopped and turned around. "What is it?"

I took a couple of steps closer to her, so I could get a better look at her face. "I just want to let you know that I saw what happened to you. Now, I don't know what made him smack you like he did, but I just want to let you know that you shouldn't tolerate a man putting his hands on you."

Melody smiled. "Girl, that wasn't nothing. Me and him just had a misunderstanding. Trust me, he'll be back after he calms down."

"Is he your man?" I asked, hoping she would give me the information I'd been searching for.

"Nah, but we're close friends, though."

"What do you mean by 'close friends'?"

"See, me and him got a thing where he's got his girl and I got my man, but we still find the time to spend together while he's here."

"It doesn't bother you that he has a girlfriend?"

"No."

"Why not?"

"Because from what he tells me, she's in jail. And what can she possibly do for him while she's in there? Nothing. So that's why I'm keeping her spot warm."

Listening to this fucking slut tell me that she and Seth had been fucking, and that she was keeping Samantha's spot warm until she came out of prison, sent me a clear message that I must've been out of the equation, for real. What really made me nauseous was the fact that I was standing directly in front of a Section Eight bitch who got to fuck my man more than I did. Now, what part of the game was that? I mean, what did I have to do to get this man to see that I had more to offer than Samantha and this low-class whore right here? Did I have to lose everything I had worked so hard for just to get down to his level? I mean, come on. What was this world coming to?

After going back and forth with this dingbat about her drama-filled life, I ended our conversation with my "I wish you the best" spiel and got the hell out of Dodge. Believe you me, I wanted to burst her bubble and tell her who the hell I really was, but I figured if I had, I probably would not have gotten as much information out of her stupid ass. So in a way, I was kind of happy that I did the right thing . . . even though I would have liked to see her expression when I let the cat out of the bag that I was his woman, for real. Anyway, all was not lost. I got what I came out there for. Now, I could move forward with my plans to shut all this shit down.

Seth

You Gotta Watch Your Own Back

Melody was one sneaky-ass bitch! I couldn't believe she stole another pill of dope from me and tried to push the shit up her nose while I was in the next room. Was she crazy, or was she fucking stupid? Whatever the hell she was, I knew she'd better not try that bullshit again, because if she did, I was going to definitely have to tell Mike. Now, I knew he was not gonna be too happy about it but hey, what could I say? His bitch was a fiend and I was not gonna take the fall for her ass. It was not gonna happen. The best thing for me was to keep the dope on me at all times and make sure she stayed the hell away from me. I was not trying to fuck her no more, and I was not really trying to have too much talk for her, either. According to Mike, we only had about three more weeks' worth of dope and we were done. That meant that we were going to close down the shop for good and I could take my money and get as far away as I could from Melody's dumb ass. Me and my baby Samantha could go live big and do whatever the fuck we wanted to; that was, if Maxine didn't decide to wreck our plans. She did have the power to throw a monkey wrench at any given moment, so I was going to have to think of something to prevent her from doing it. Shit, I might have to start giving her the dick again and make her think that everything was OK between us. Knowing her, though, she'd probably see right through it. I just hoped she didn't fuck with Samantha because she was the type of chick that would go upside Maxine's head and wouldn't think about the repercussions until later. I mean, Samantha would hurt her real bad. I didn't want my baby going back to prison behind some shit I could have handled, so I was going to have to think of something real fast. Whether I wanted to believe it or not, Maxine hadn't talked to me for over two weeks so I knew she was really upset with me and was plotting on a way to get me back. I was gonna have to put on my thinking cap as well.

Mike and I hooked up at a nearby gas station so he could furnish me with another batch of dope. He handed me a Ziploc bag of twenty-five hundred pills. I looked at the motherfucker like he was crazy.

"Man, we ain't gon' be able to get rid of all this shit by nightfall," I told him.

"Yo, I just heard it's a drought out there, so trust me, dopefiends from all over are going to be coming at you."

"You know the police been riding real hard these last few days."

"That's because niggas is running their mouths. But don't sweat it. Remember, you got some thorough-ass young'uns out there with you, and the way I see it, they ain't gon' let the police kick up in that spot."

What Mike said kind of made sense, but if those narcs wanted to run up in Melody's crib bad enough, they'd find a way. I knew from experience how they operated. They'd send two undercover police, looking just like dopefiends, to the spot and would have those young boys down on their faces before they saw it coming. I listened to Mike run his mouth about how we had shit around the way locked down, but like I said before, anything you built up could be knocked down. In other words, I was gonna need to be on my p's and q's from this point on. After our conversation was over, Mike asked me if I would do a job for him. I looked at him with a curious expression and asked him what kind of job did he want me to do. When he told me that he wanted me to get rid of Jay, I was at a loss for words.

"Whatchu mean, you want me to get rid of him?" I asked.

"I want you to kill him."

Caught off guard by his abrupt decision to end Jay's life, I hesitated for a moment and then I looked at him in a bizarre kind of way. "Damn, son, what's going on? You and that nigga beefing or something?"

"Nah, we ain't been beefing but for the last week or so, my dough has been coming up short. And when I asked that nigga where my money was, he gave me some ol' bogus-ass excuse about how he had to take a lot of shorts off each pill of dope, so that's why the count was off. But I know that's bullshit because I've got this young nigga over there at the spot telling me that Jay is taking straight money and he's beating the head off every pill he sells."

"Word?"

"Come on now, son, you know I don't play about shit like that."

"How much did he say he was losing off every pill?"

"He told me he was taking two-dollar shorts."

"Damn! That's a lot of dough to be losing on a daily basis, especially if you're giving him two to three thousand pills. Shit, that nigga got to be pocketing anywhere between four to six grand, plus whatever he's making from the dope he's taking out of the pills you give him."

"I know, and the thought of it makes me wanna put a bullet right in that motherfucker's dome!"

"So, why don't you just step to him and tell him to give you your motherfucking dough?"

"Because I know the nigga is going to stand right in my face and lie to me."

"But what if he doesn't, and fucks around and gives you your dough?"

"It still isn't going to matter. I can't have that nigga on my payroll anymore. Once you betray my trust, I can't have you around me anymore. That's why if you hurry up and get rid of his ass for me, I'll give you a third of everything he took from me."

"When do you want this done?"

"The sooner the better."

"A'ight. Well, give me a couple of days and I'll have it done."

"You think you're gonna need a couple of burners?"

"Nah, I'm straight. I do need to know where you want me to clip him. I mean, I know you don't want me bringing any heat to the spot."

"Yeah, I was going to tell you that the best way to get him is when he leaves the spot because he always stops by the smoke spot on Reservoir Avenue before he goes to the crib. Out there it is very dark because the niggas 'round there knocked out all the street-lights to keep the narcs from running up on them at any given moment. So if you can run up on him and put a couple slugs in his head right after he comes back out of the spot, niggas is going to think that he's either getting robbed or he's got beef, so they're gonna run for cover and you ain't gonna have to worry about any witnesses."

"What about the dough he's going to have after he closes down the shop?"

"Don't worry about that because I am going to get Trina to pick it up before he leaves."

"Well, have you thought about how you are going to get your other dough back?"

"Yeah, I've got that covered. I'm gonna have somebody kick up in his girl's spot where he keeps his stash, while you got him trapped on Reservoir."

I took a deep breath after Mike laid down his plans to have Jay robbed and killed. It was obvious that his mind was made up, so I didn't question him any further. After I gave him a nod to indicate that I was down for whatever, he ran down a few more details about what time I could be expecting Jay to leave the spot. He gave me some vital information about Jay's most vulnerable spot on his body. I took mental notes of everything, and afterwards gave Mike the proper handshake and hopped back into my whip. As I was about to leave Mike said, "Ay yo, is everything a'ight over at the spot?"

I hesitated for a minute because I was beginning to think that this nigga was asking me a trick question. But then it dawned on me that if Melody had already called him and told him about that little altercation we had this morning, that would have probably been the first thing he wanted to talk about. Then again, this nigga was kind of strange, so you couldn't ever tell with him. I mean, look at the situation with Jay beating Mike for his dough. Now, Mike was walking around and acting like everything was OK around Jay. Jay was walking around, going on about his business, not even knowing that tomorrow night was going to be his last night getting a piece of pussy. After I ran that whole scenario through my mind I took a deep breath and said, "Everything is cool! Why? What's up?"

"Nothing. I was just asking since I hadn't been over there in a few days."

"Oh yeah, everything is straight."

"A'ight. Well, hit me up later after you shut the shop down."

"A'ight," I said and pulled off.

I headed back over to Melody's crib. She was in her bedroom when I walked in the house, so I went straight into the kitchen and broke down the package into bundles of one hundred pills. After I did that, I called my street team and told them to come to the spot. They got there in less than thirty minutes, so we suited up and got busy. Everything was going good until I heard one of the fiends standing outside of the spot complaining that we sold her some bad dope. I opened up the front door and stepped outside on the porch. The young'un Bishop stood before the old-looking fiend with his burner pointed directly at her head. "Didn't I tell your motherfucking ass not to come back 'round here with that bullshit? Do you want me to blow your motherfucking head off right now?" he roared at her.

"Come on now, Bishop, let her go," I yelled from where I stood.

"Nah, son, this bitch has been trying to get over on us for these past couple of days. And she just threatened to call the police on us, too!"

"Let her go, dawg! You know we don't need no heat 'round here, especially with all this shit we got to move," I reminded him.

Bishop hesitated for a moment, as if he had to contemplate on whether or not it would be beneficial to take my advice. I became angry and wasted no time in showing it. "What the fuck you doing, thinking about it or something?" I snapped.

"Nah," he said and pulled the gun back from the lady's head and released his grip from around her neck.

"Well, what the fuck were you waiting for?" Frustration and rage were written all over my face.

"I was just waiting for her ass to say something else," Bishop explained.

Meanwhile, the woman had walked away, but before she got too far, I sent Hakeem behind her so he could hand her another pill of dope. I did this to keep her mouth closed. I didn't need the police running up on us right now. We had too much dope we had to get rid of. Not only that, my baby Samantha was coming home in less than a week, so I definitely wanted to be out there to see her. Shit, we had too much stuff we had to catch up on, and I wasn't gonna let no knucklehead-ass nigga fuck that up for me. And I meant that shit from the bottom of my heart.

Once Hakeem straightened the lady out and blessed her with a freebie, I laid a few words of wisdom on Bishop. "Yo, man, what the fuck is wrong with you? You can't be sticking burners in mother-fucker's heads like that. Whatchu trying to do, set it off 'round here or something?"

"Nah, dawg," Bishop sighed. "See, that bitch been popping shit to me and Hakeem for the last couple of days, talking about we keep selling her bad dope and that if we don't give her a refund or another pill, she was gon' call the police on us. I got tired of her running her fucking mouth, and that's why I pulled my burner out and buried it in her head."

"Look, I understand all of that, but you can't be walking around here pulling out your piece every time one of these motherfucker's threatens to call the police."

"All I was trying to do was scare her stupid ass!"

"I know that, but this is not the place or the time to be doing that. Mike hit me off with a huge bundle of dope, so he expects us to get rid of that shit without any interruptions. You got me?"

"Yeah, I gotcha," Bishop assured me.

"A'ight. Well, get back to work. And if you have

any more problems with these fiends, just come and get me so I can handle it."

"A'ight," he replied and headed back to his post, which was the front right side of the apartment building. When I looked around for my other three street soldiers, they were standing at their assigned spots too. I looked at every last one of them and asked them if they were all right and they all nodded their heads or said, "Yeah, I'm straight."

"A'ight. Well, keep y'all's heads up, because we gon' have a long day." I went back inside.

"What the hell was all the commotion about out there?" Melody asked the moment I stepped back into the house. Dressed in her usual booty shorts and T-shirt, she stood in the entranceway of the living room and waited for me to answer her.

I was short and to the point. "One of the young'uns had some problems with one of your dopefiend friends, but I straightened everything out." I walked right by her.

"What dopefiend friends? I don't fuck with none of these motherfuckers out here, and you know that!" she yelled, walking behind me.

"If you keep trying to get high, then there's no doubt in my mind that you and all them fiends out there are going to start hanging out and getting high together."

"Shit, no, I'm not! Trust me, I can control this shit."

"Yeah, a'ight." I brushed her ass off. After I grabbed my bottle of sweet tea out of the refrigerator, I walked right by her ass again and went back into the living room. I guess Melody got the hint that I didn't want to be bothered because it sounded like she was going to come behind me but once she got into the hallway, she turned right and headed back into her bedroom. Thank God. Now I could get a little *me time*. Block out all this bullshit and think about what I was gonna do when my baby came home and how we were going to spend all that dough I was stacking. Good times were definitely ahead. Too bad Maxine wasn't going to be a part of that equation. She'd be all right, though. I was gonna make sure of that.

Seth

Killing Two Birds With One Stone

It was unbelievable, but me and my soldiers got rid of every pill of dope Mike laid on us. We didn't finish until after midnight, but hey, we got it done. Soon afterward, I headed on over to meet Mike so I could give him his dough. He was happy as hell to know that I had gotten rid of all that dope. It seemed like that was all he talked about throughout our entire conversation. It felt good to know that I did my thing and that he recognized it. Right before I hopped back into my whip, he asked me had I thought about how I was going to execute Jay. I told him that a few things had ran though my mind, but I wasn't quite sure about how I was going to get it done. "I'll let you know either way I go," I assured him.

"Well, you know he's still at his spot, just in case you want to scope him out," Mike said.

"A'ight," I replied and then I pulled off.

As soon as I got through the downtown Portsmouth tunnel and back onto the Norfolk side, I drove across the Berkley Bridge. Instead of taking Highway I-264 so I could head on down to my mother's crib, I made a detour and jumped off the Tidewater Drive exit. It only took me two minutes from the exit to get to Jay's spot in Tidewater Park. That part of Norfolk was known for niggas getting murdered. The last time I heard, at least ten niggas got shot out there every week. If Jay became one of those statistics, the Chief of Police would probably write it off as another nigga involved in a drug deal gone bad.

"Got them red tops!" I heard a young boy yell toward my car as I cruised down Golf Street.

I ignored homeboy and kept it moving. I drove into the next block and made a right onto Church Street. By the time I got close enough to get a good look at Jay's spot, and the surrounding area, he was standing next to his car, talking to some skeezer-looking chick. I tried to speed up to avoid being seen, but it was too late. My cover was blown. Jay's full attention was off homegirl and he turned to face my car.

"Ay yo, Seth," I heard him yell.

I pumped my brakes, rolled down my window, and poked my head out. "Who that?" I asked, as if I wasn't sure who had called my name.

"It's me, Jay, nigga," he announced and walked toward my car.

While I watched him approach me, I didn't know what the fuck to do. I knew right off the jump he was going to ask me why I was out there, so I knew I was going to have to have something convincing to tell him. I mean, I couldn't tell him that I came out there to check him, because then he would know that that was a lie. I had never come out there before, so why now? Besides, we weren't like that, so there was no reason for me to be coming out there. As a matter of fact, we didn't fuck with each other at all. Some of it had to do with Melody, and the other part had something to do with me getting real close to Mike. Yeah, I knew Jay didn't like that shit, especially since Mike put me in charge of the whole scene out in Dales Homes. But in this game, rules changed all the time. The moment you thought everything was lovely and money was rolling in and you had plenty of bitches you could fuck, another nigga was going to come right behind you. In a split second, they could take it all away from your dumb ass. I knew this because I was just the nigga who'd do it to you. Then when it was my time, a nigga was going to do it to me. That was just how the dice rolled.

"What's good, son?" Jay asked as he shook my hand.

"Everything is lovely. I'm out here looking for this bitch named Dana," I told him before he made an attempt to ask.

"Dana," Jay said, as if he was trying to figure out who I was talking about. "How does she look?"

"She's a brown-skinned, short, thick chick with a big-ass mole over her lip. The shit is so big, you can't miss it." I laughed.

"Did she tell you where she lived at?"

"Nah. She told me she was going to be standing out on Washington Street, but I don't see her ass 'round here nowhere." I turned my head around to look at the other side of the street, as if I was looking for her.

Jay stood back from my car and glanced down both ends of the street. "Shit, I don't see her either."

"She told me she was wearing a red and white vest jacket, but I didn't see nobody out here with that shit on."

"Me either," Jay said.

"I know one thing, she better bring her ass out here in the next ten seconds because if she doesn't, I'm gone and I ain't coming back."

"Call her."

"I just tried to, but she didn't answer her phone," I lied.

"You sure that bitch is on the up and up? 'Cause it sounds like she's trying to set your ass up to get robbed or something."

"A bitch ain't got enough heart to set me up." I laughed, but I was dead serious.

"Well, these bitches out here got plenty of heart, so you better watch your back."

"Oh, I'm straight! But, I'm gon' holler at you!" I eased my foot off the brake. My car started rolling away real slow.

"A'ight," Jay said and stepped back from my car.

The moment I pulled off, it felt like a burden was lifted from my shoulders. I laughed out loud as I thought about how predictable Jay was. He was also very vulnerable when it came to chicks. I saw that he let his guard down when he was entertaining one of his whores. If I wanted to, I could've lit his ass up while he was talking to homegirl, but I knew that would not have been the right move and besides, it was too many motherfuckers out on the streets, which meant a whole lot of witnesses. I saw what I needed to see, so I was straight, and now I was gonna carry my ass to the crib. I'd think about how I was gonna run up on Jay's ass after I got me a good night's sleep.

The next morning I got up with a clear head. My moms made me a BLT, and after I chased the sandwich down with a cold glass of orange juice, I grabbed my car keys off the kitchen table. When I attempted to leave the kitchen, my mother sparked up a conversation about Maxine.

"What's going on with you and Maxine?" she asked.

"What do you mean, Ma?"

"She's been ringing this phone off the hook, and I am sick and tired of it."

"Tell her to stop calling here!"

"Why don't you tell her?"

"I ain't got nothing to say. I'm done with her."

"Does she know that?" My mom stood with her back against the countertop, sipping on a cup of hot tea.

"Yeah, she knows it."

"Well, I find that hard to believe because I had a long talk with her today, and she gave me an earful."

"What did she say?" I couldn't wait to hear what Maxine said to my mother.

My mother sighed heavily. "I think she's going to violate you."

"What makes you say that?"

"Well first off, she doesn't like the fact that you're spending a lot of time away from her, and second, you won't return any of her calls. Now, you know how crazy that girl is, so why are you playing with her emotions? Don't you know that woman has your life in the palm of her hands? She can send your butt back to prison in a heartbeat and there won't be nothing you could do about it."

I was frustrated. "Momma, don't you think I already know all that?"

"So what's the problem, then? I know you've got at least an ounce of common sense left in your brain somewhere!"

I chuckled and shook my head. "Momma, you are something else!" I walked over to her and kissed her on her forehead. "But don't worry about me. I am going to call Maxine and straighten out everything. All right?"

"I hope so, because I done already endured one of your long prison sentences and I don't think I can go through another one."

"Momma, I promise you that I am not going back to prison," I tried to assure her.

"I sure hope not," she muttered and then walked me to the front door. "You know, you wouldn't be going through this nonsense if you would've listened to me when I told you not to mess with that lady in the first place. I knew it was a bad idea from the very beginning. But no, you didn't want to listen."

"Momma, don't let this mess get you all bent out of shape. I told you I was going to handle it, so stop worrying." I kissed her forehead once more.

"The day I stop worrying will be the day you start living right."

"Give me two weeks and your prayers will be answered." I smiled and walked away.

"Be careful," she said and watched me as I walked toward my car.

"I will," I told her.

The moment I got into my car, I pulled out my cell phone and dialed Maxine's home number. She didn't answer the phone so I dialed her cell phone number. She answered it on the second ring.

"What's up with you?" I asked her.

"Don't you think I need to be the one asking that question?"

"Well, go 'head," I responded nonchalantly.

"Seth, please don't be a smart ass! You know you've got a lot of explaining to do."

"About what?" I asked.

"For starters, how come you haven't been answering my phone calls?"

"Because I wasn't trying to get in an argument with you."

"That's a lame-ass excuse. Now, I know you could've come up with something better than that."

Frustration began to consume me. "Look Maxine, what's up? Whatchu gon' do?"

"Whatchu mean, what I'm gon' do?"

"Are you getting ready to send me back to jail, or what?"

"If I were, don't you think I would have done it by now?"

"Well, why the fuck you keep calling my mother with that bullshit, then?"

"All I did was call her and tell her that I had been trying to contact you on your cell phone, but you hadn't been answering my calls. I just asked her to get a message to you, and that was it."

"My mother ain't no young girl, so her heart can't take all that shit you keeping throwing at her."

"So, what you're trying to say is that I offended your mother?" she asked sarcastically.

"Nah, I didn't say that."

"So, what are you saying?"

"Listen Maxine, just stop calling the house. Point blank! If you want to holler at me, call my cell phone, but if I don't answer, then you'll just have to talk to me later. It's just that simple."

"So, it's like that, huh?" She sounded irritated.

"Look, Maxine, I don't want no beef with you, a'ight? All I want is for shit to be easy. I just want to make this money and hit you off with the dough you need so you can open up that business you've been talking about."

"You think I give a damn about the money?" she screamed. "I want you, but lately you've been acting like that's a problem. And I know Samantha is the main reason why you've been giving me the cold shoulder. But let me tell you this: if you think you and her are going to be together when she gets out of prison, then you've got another thing coming."

"Is that a threat?"

"Call it whatever you want, because I can promise you that if I see you and her together, both of y'all's asses are going right back behind bars. You can mark my word on that one."

"So, it's gonna be like that?"

"You damn right, because I have done nothing but have your back from day one, and everything had been going good. Then all of a fucking sudden, when you find out that your gangsta bitch is on her way out of the system, you start flipping the script on me. Do you honestly think that I am going to sit back and just let you toy with my feelings? Hell no! I swear on everything I love that if you don't wise up and get your priorities back in order, I am gonna let the fucking cat out the bag! And I don't care if I get pulled in all this madness too, because at this point, my life means absolutely nothing since I can't have you in it. So, if this whole conversation doesn't get us to come to a compromise, then you might as well say goodbye right now and hang up the fucking phone."

As I listened to Maxine go on and on about how I'd made her feel since we separated, I realized that this bitch had become a serious nut case. She was seriously contemplating getting all of us locked up if I didn't come back to her. I mean, how deranged did that sound? My moms was right about this chick, and I was at a loss for words and didn't know how to handle her ass. I wanted so badly to curse her ass out and tell her to kiss my ass and do what she had to do because I was sick of the threats. But I knew that would be a dummy move on my part, so I did the opposite and told her some shit I knew she wanted to hear.

"Ay yo, look," I said, trying to get my thoughts together, "let's get together later on at your place, so we can talk about this further."

"There's nothing to talk about. Either you're

gonna do what you're supposed to do by me, or I am going to have to do what I got to do," she replied sternly.

I sighed heavily and then I said, "Can you please cut me some slack? You acting like a nigga done did you grimy or something."

"You have," she said without hesitation.

"All right, check this out. After I finish taking care of my business, I'm gonna come by your crib so we can lay everything out on the table."

"What time will that be?"

"I'm not sure. But it won't be too late," I told her.

"Do you think you'd be able to get over here before midnight?"

"Yeah, I'm sure I could do that."

"All right. Well, can you do something else for me?"

"Yeah, what's that?"

"Can you keep your dick in your pants?"

I was at a loss for words again and did not know how to respond when Maxine threw that request out like that. My curiosity got the best of me because I wanted so badly to ask her where the hell that came from. I mean, for her to come out of the blue and tell me to keep my dick in my pants only meant that she knew something. But then again, she could just be playing me to see if I'd volunteer some information. And I wasn't gon' do that. Shit, I'm the type of cat you'd have to catch in the act before I'd confess, and since it wasn't that type of party, I was gonna play dumb and act like I didn't know what she was talking about.

"Whatchu mean by that?"

"Come on now, Seth. You know what I'm talking about."

"No, I don't."

"Yes, you do."

"No, I don't. So tell me."

"Seth, just cut it out! I know you've been fucking one of them project chicks out there where you be hustling. But, I'm telling you now that it better stop."

"Where the hell is this shit coming from?" I wanted to make a statement, but I knew that would be the wrong thing to do, especially since Maxine seemed like she knew what she was talking about. I refused to get myself caught up in a lie.

"Don't worry about all of that! Just tell me you aren't going to fuck that ho anymore!"

Damn! She definitely put me between a rock and a hard place with that one. How was I going to answer that? Because if I told her yes, then she was going to know that I had been fucking someone other than her. But if I continued to act like I didn't know what she was talking about, she'd probably blow off the handle and do something really crazy. But hey, I guess I was gonna have to take my chances.

"Hey look Maxine, can we talk about this some other time? I just pulled up at the spot and niggas are standing outside my car waiting for me," I said.

"Do you think I give a fuck about those mother-fuckers out there?" she screamed. "Right now, my main concern is getting our business in order. All that other shit you're talking about is irrelevant. So you tell them niggas to wait."

"You're right! You're right!" I said, trying to avoid an argument.

"OK. Well, answer my question then, Seth."

I sighed again because the pressure was mounting. It had become obvious that she wasn't gonna let up off this subject, so I knew I had to either come clean or deny this thing to the bitter end. And guess what? I did the latter. "A'ight, listen, because I'm about be honest with you," I said, trying to choose my words carefully. "There was a chick out the way that was trying to holler at me, but I shut the whole shit down."

"So, you're saying y'all never fucked?"

"Nah, we didn't. But I did kiss her once."

"Why are you lying, Seth?"

"What am I lying about?"

"You know what? You've got to be one of the stupidest niggas I know. Don't you know that when women ask their man if they'd been cheating, they already know the answer? We just want to see if y'all niggas would come clean with us. Now as far as this chickenhead is concerned, I already know it's more than what you're telling me. As a matter of fact, I know how she looks and I know y'all been fucking."

"Well, tell me how she looks then." I hoped this would put her on the spot and then she would shut the fuck up.

"I can do more than that," she chuckled, "because not only do I know how the bitch looks, I can tell you her name."

"Go ahead then." I encouraged her because I knew she was pulling my leg. She was stalling too much. I leaned my head back against the headrest of the driver's seat and waited patiently for Maxine to give it up and stop wasting my time. As soon as I began to get too relaxed, she threw a bomb at me when she uttered Melody's name. My mouth fell wide open and my heart fell in the pit of my stomach. All I could think was, *How the hell does she know about her?*

"Don't get quiet now, nigga! I know you hear me."

"Yeah, I hear you," I said and took a deep breath.

"Well, I want you to hear this too, because I am going to say it only once."

"Go ahead, I'm listening."

"Well, for starters, I know about her little Puerto Rican ass! And I know y'all be fucking on a regular basis too. That's why I ain't been able to get me some dick. But when I say the motherfucking buck stops here, it stops here! And not only that, you've got until the end of this month to make all the money you can because I am shutting your operation down. There will not be any more of the hustling thing going on after that point. You need to get it out of your system now and get in the mode of opening and operating the business we are going to build together. And as far as your hood friends are concerned, you are going to cut them off too. There will be no room for them when you and I start over and build our new life. Now, I know I am throwing a lot on you at once, but I know what's best for you, so this is the way it has to be."

"So, you mean to tell me that there's no room for compromise?"

"Nope. I gave you enough freedom; now it's time to come on home."

"So, it's just like that?"

"Yep," she replied point blank.

"A'ight then. I guess I'll see you later."

"So that's it?"

"What do you want me to say? I mean, you pretty much laid everything down on the line."

"So, you're not gonna give me any feedback?"

"What do you want me to say, Maxine?"

"I want you to tell me that I'm right and that things are going to roll just like I just laid them out."

"I ain't gotta tell you all that. Because at the end of the day, my actions are what counts, right?"

"Yes, but it wouldn't hurt to acknowledge the fact that I'm only doing this because I love you."

"Maxine, it's not a secret. I know you love me. That's why I am going to repay you for everything you've done for me."

"So, you're not mad because I gave you an ultimatum?"

"Nah, I'm cool." I lied because truth be told, if I was in front of her silly ass right now, I probably would have smacked her in her fucking face. How dare she continue to threaten me like she did? Then to say that if it meant bringing herself down she'd do that, too. I mean, how stupid was that? Man, this chick had serious self-esteem issues, and I saw that I was going to have to find a way to get as far as I could from her ass! I didn't care if I had to dip on her and leave the state. Whatever it took was what I was going to do. In the meantime, I was going to have to play her game.

After I reassured Maxine at least two more times that I was all right with the chokehold she was about to put on me, I blew a couple of kisses at her through the phone and told her I would get with her later.

When I arrived at Melody's crib she was standing

outside on her porch, dressed in a red, tight-fitting sundress with spaghetti straps. She had her hair combed back into a ponytail. I can't lie, she was looking sexy as hell. Then reality snapped back into play when she opened up her mouth.

"Hakeem, could you run to the corner store and get me a pack of cigarettes and a box of tampons?"

"I'll get you a pack of cigarettes but I ain't picking up a box of tampons," Hakeem protested.

"Boy, stop acting like a pussy! You know you can get my tampons. Now, take this money and carry your ass on down the street before I start bleeding all over the place."

Listening to this chick degrade herself in public sent a clear message to me that she was, and would always be, gutter trash. After Hakeem took the money from her, I shook my head and got out of my car.

As soon as Melody saw me, she smiled and said, "Hey baby!"

Instead of greeting her back, I told her we needed to talk. I grabbed her arm and pulled her into the house.

"What did I do now?" she whined.

"Who the fuck you been talking to about us?"

"What are you talking about?"

"Stop acting stupid! You know what the fuck I'm talking about."

"No, I don't," she said, puzzled.

"Come on now, Melody, you've been talking to somebody because I just got off the phone with my peoples and they told me that you've been running your mouth, telling people we fucking around.

Now that shit ain't cool, especially when I've got a lot invested right now."

"Who was I supposed to have been talking to?"

"So you're telling me you don't remember?"

Melody stood there in silence and thought to herself for a moment. Then she said, "The only two people I remember talking to about you are my homegirl and some lady that walked up to me yesterday after she saw you smack me and leave."

"What did she look like?"

"She was a brown-skinned lady, about my height, maybe an inch or two taller. She reminded me of Nia Long because of her facial features and the way she wore her hair. But her style in clothing was different."

"What did she have on?" My heart raced.

"I think she had on a sweatsuit."

"And what did she say? I mean, how did she approach you?"

"Well, wherever she was standing, she had to see you hit me because as soon as you pulled off, she walked right up to me and asked if I was all right. When I told her yeah, she started preaching to me about how I shouldn't tolerate a man putting his hands on me and then after that she asked if you were my man."

"And what did you tell her?"

"I told her nah. But I did tell her we were close friends. Then she asked me how close of friends we were, and that's when I told her that you and I both had somebody else but we still found the time to spend together while we were here."

"Why the fuck you tell her all that?"

"I don't know," Melody replied, knowing she had talked too much and to the wrong person.

I let her have it. "What the hell you mean, you don't know?" I yelled. "You got to be the stupidest chick I know because I don't know nobody else who would tell a complete stranger all of their damn business, and especially the part about us fucking."

"But I didn't say we were fucking," she stated, attempting to correct me.

"You didn't have to; she ain't stupid! Trust me, she read between the lines."

"Well, since you're so bent out of shape behind this, who was she?"

"Don't worry about who she was!" I snapped. "From now on, keep your business to your mother-fucking self."

After I scolded Melody for running her mouth to Maxine, I told her that we were done. No more of that sneaking around and fucking. That chapter was closed. I also told her that shit would be run differently around there, too. She was going to stay far away from the dope and I didn't need her collecting the money anymore, either. After I laid down the new laws, I left her ass standing in the living room looking stupid. I couldn't stomach her ass anymore. She was a fucking waste, if you asked me. Now I saw why Mike wasn't thinking about her dumb ass! I wasn't gonna be thinking about her ass either. After I left this spot for good, trust me, I wasn't gonna look back.

Samantha

Playing With Fire

Mendez and his partner in crime C.O. Clayton walked around all the units and did the four o'clock head count. When they were done he came strolling back by my room and signaled me to come meet him at our usual spot, which was the supply room near our visiting room. I was dreading to go because I knew he was going to stress me out about why I'd been avoiding him. The truth of the matter was I wasn't trying to give him any more of my pussy. I was tired of that nigga jumping up and down on me like I was his girl or something. It wasn't like he was taking care of me for real. The lingerie and the food he snuck up in there wasn't enough for me to be fucking him on a regular basis. OK, granted he put a couple hundred dollars in my account every month for the last six months, but if you looked at it, that wasn't nothing but $1,200, and my pussy was worth more than that. As far as I could see it, his coochie coupon had expired, and I had to tell him.

As soon as we entered the supply room, he closed the door and flipped the light switch. We were in a room full of cleaning supplies, and the smell of the ammonia, bleach, and disinfectant permeated the entire room. It wasn't too bad where we couldn't breathe, but I knew we weren't going to be in there long, so I was happy. Now Mendez didn't waste any time to pull me into his arms. Immediately after I fell into his embrace, I stiffened up.

"What's wrong with you?" he asked.

"I'm just not in the mood right now."

"What is it going to take for you to get in the mood?"

"Nothing."

"What do you mean 'nothing'?"

"Want me to be honest? I'm just not feeling you anymore."

He released me from his embrace. "What the fuck you mean by that?"

I stood there with my arms folded near my breasts and sighed heavily. "Do I need to spell it out for you? I don't want to do this shit with you anymore!" I snapped.

Mendez snapped too. He became so angry, he grabbed me by my neck and forced my back up against the wall with his right hand. His actions took me by surprise. "Bitch, do you know who the fuck you talking to like that? I don't let my wife disrespect me, so I damn sure ain't gon' let you do it."

"You better let me go before I scream!" I threatened him.

"Go ahead and scream. Ain't nobody gonna hear you," he dared me with a psychotic expression plastered all over his face.

"Let me go!" I screamed.

He added more pressure around my neck and then he pressed his body against mine. "Bitch, you owe me! So, I'm about to collect!"

"So, what, you about to rape me or something?" I roared.

Before he could answer me, someone knocked on the door and startled the hell out of us. He released me from his grip and immediately walked over to the door. "Who is it?" he whispered.

"It's me, Clayton," his friend said.

Mendez opened up the supply room door. "What's up, man?" He smiled.

"Yo, man, you need to wrap that up. I can hear you out here."

"All right. I'm coming," Mendez assured him and began to shut the door.

"A'ight, well I'ma stay out here just in case some inmate tries to come around this door and snoop around."

"All right." Mendez sighed with frustration and then he closed the door shut. And before my heart could skip a beat his body was pressed against me again, but this time he had his mouth pressed to my ear and the words he whispered made my skin crawl. "You better thank God Clayton saved your ass! But just remember that this shit ain't over. I'm gonna get what's mine."

When he took a step back from me I stood there and looked at him like he was fucking insane. It was

obvious this man wasn't dealing with a full deck, so
I wanted him to get the hell away from me as soon
as possible. As he moved toward the door, I followed
suit. But he made it clear that he wasn't through
with me, because right before he grabbed a hold of
the doorknob, he grabbed me by my arm, swung
me around, and forced my face against the wall like
a police officer would do someone resisting arrest.

"What are you doing?" I snapped.

"Shut up!" he demanded.

Next thing I knew, this motherfucker had pressed
his dick and started grinding on me while he un-
zipped my pants and slid my right hand down inside
of them. At that moment, I started bucking at him
by trying to elbow him in his side, simultaneously
tugging on his hands because at that point, this
nigga had my entire coochie in the palm of his
hands. He was literally trying to get an arousal out
of me.

"Get off me!" I screamed once more.

He tried to muffle my mouth to keep Clayton
from hearing me, but it didn't work. Clayton jig-
gled the doorknob and said, "Come on Mendez, we
gotta go, man."

Hearing Clayton's voice gave me the notion that I
was safe and that Mendez's spree of sexual favors was
over. When he finally let me go, which was about three
seconds later, I gathered as much saliva to the front
my mouth as I could and abruptly turned around and
spit every drop of it right in his face. And when it hit
him, the shit fell slowly down his left cheek. Lucky
for me, it caught him off guard, so before he could get

his thoughts together and react, I flew out of the supply room with my pants unbuttoned.

"I'ma get you, bitch!" I heard him yell from behind.

But I ignored him and kept it moving. Thankfully, Clayton was back there with him, because I truly believed that motherfucker would have tried to run me down and kill me. Lately he had gotten so possessive, and I couldn't get with that shit. Other inmates had noticed it too, which was one of the reasons why rumors had been circulating about our relationship. Mendez's lieutenant pulled me in his office and questioned me about my relationship with Mendez not too long ago, but I told him there wasn't one. Since he didn't have any hardcore evidence, he had to leave us alone. Boy, was Mendez lucky. He just didn't know how heartless I could get. Because if I really wanted to bury his sorry ass, I could set him up and get his dumb ass fired. But the warden would launch a full investigation on our asses that would surely prevent these assholes from releasing me to go to the halfway house. They would make me do the six months' halfway house time right there, and I couldn't have that. No way. The best thing for me was to stay away from his ass and that's exactly what I intended on doing.

Seth

Putting One In The Head

Later that night, I was able to close the shop down early because we got rid of every pill of dope Mike packed inside the Ziploc bag. On my way out, Melody asked me for ten dollars so she could order a pizza for her son. Her mother was bringing him over in the next half hour, so I handed her the dough and bounced.

Mike met me in our usual spot, but this time, he wasn't alone. He had a couple of niggas posted up in his whip with him. One nigga was sitting beside him in the passenger seat, and the other cat was posted up in the back seat. It was too dark to see their faces, but I said, "What's up?" to them anyway.

"You ready?" Mike asked me after I handed him the dough.

"As I will ever be." I smiled and looked down at my watch; it was ten minutes after nine. That meant

I had a couple of hours to play around with before I made my move on Jay. Since I knew that Jay wouldn't be leaving his spot until sometime after midnight, I told Mike I was going to make a quick run and then call him when I was ready. After he said OK, I hopped back into my car.

Before I pulled off, Mike instructed me to call him from a pay phone before I made my move. "Remember, you gotta give Trina enough time to run over there and pick up my dough first, a'ight?"

"A'ight," I said, and then we parted ways.

Once I was back on the road, two things popped in my mind. The first was that I knew I had to stash my dough at my mom's crib. I also knew I had to make a trip over to Maxine's crib so I could do some making up. As much as it was killing me to give into that bitch, she had me by the balls. I figured I was going to have to do what I had to until I could come up with another plan to get from under her paws. I mean, that bitch was psycho, and I felt it in her voice that she wasn't playing any more games with me, so I was going to have to lay down for a few. But as soon as I got a plan together, I was going to be ghost and it wasn't gon' be shit she could do about it. That's my word!

When I arrived at my mom's house she was up watching television, so I kissed her on her forehead and went to my bedroom. I had this little storage compartment right over my bed in the air conditioning vent. I grabbed the screwdriver from the toolbox in my closet and loosened the screws on the metal plate to the vent. Once the plate was finally off, I reached inside and grabbed the small metal box that was attached to the wall with two magnets.

"Seth, I'm getting ready to go to bed now so if you need me, I'll be in my room," my mother informed me from the other side of my bedroom door.

"OK." I snatched the box from the vent before she decided to be nosey and come into my room to see what I was doing. As I was about to lock my door, I heard her footsteps as she walked away. When I heard her close the door to her room, I sat on the edge of my bed and emptied out all the dough I had stashed away in the box. When I added the money I'd earned that night, I came up with a sum total of sixty-seven grand. And from the looks of things by the time I ran through Mike's whole package, I was going to be at least three to four hundred thousand dollars strong. Just the thought of it began to get my dick hard. Not to mention the ideas that were going through my mind about how I was going to spend it. Shit, a nigga like me was going to be straight for a very long time. If I played my cards right, me and Samantha could escape from this bitch and head out to Mexico. Maxine's dumb ass wouldn't be able to stop our show then. Freedom from her would be a beautiful thing.

As I was packing all my dough back into the box, my cell phone rang. When I looked down at the Caller-ID screen and saw a number I didn't recognize, I elected not to answer it and pressed the IGNORE button. As soon as I stuck my phone back into the holster, it rang again. When I looked down at the screen once more, the same number popped up. I figured that whoever was calling me had to be important, so I answered it.

"Hello," I said.

"Hey Seth, this is Trina."

"What's up?"

"I'm just calling to tell you it's about to go down, so meet me at the spot."

"A'ight," I said and hung up.

From that moment, I knew that my actions were going to change my life forever. If I had an ounce of guilt in my heart for what I was about to do to Jay, it really didn't matter at that point because I had already given my word to Mike. I told him I was going to take care of it, and in this game, you couldn't give a man your word and go back on it. Actions like that would cause you to get killed. So I stuck an "H" on my chest, put my money box back into place, tightened the screws on the vent, and grabbed my keys to head back onto the streets. Before I exited my mom's crib, I changed into a pair of dark blue overalls and slipped on a pair of old run-down Timbs I had in the back of my closet. I didn't have a ski mask at my disposal, so I decided to do without.

The whole time I was driving, my heart was beating one hundred miles per hour. It wasn't like I was scared to do this nigga in because that wasn't the case. What was fucking me up on the inside was that I was having an adrenaline rush. Picturing myself splattering this nigga's brains all over the pavement for a large sum of cash put a huge smile on my face. I pressed down on the accelerator because I figured the quicker I got over there and got the job done, the sooner I got my money. And guess what? That was what I did. Judging from my watch, it only took me approximately fifteen minutes to get out there.

I had surveyed the area the day before, so I knew which position I would take to do Jay in. I parked my whip two blocks away from the spot, but before I got out of my car, I dialed Trina back at the number she used earlier.

"Hello," she said.

"Ay yo, Trina, this is Seth. Where you at?"

"I'm about to pull up to the spot right now. Why? Where you at?"

"I'm walking up the block."

"All right. Well, give me a few minutes to get in and out and then you can do your thing."

"A'ight."

I sat my phone down on the passenger seat of my car, pulled out my .50 caliber Desert Eagle from underneath the driver's seat, and made sure the joint was fully loaded with hollow points. I cocked it back, loading one in the chamber, and stuffed the pistol inside the pocket of my overalls.

I paced myself as I moved toward Jay's spot. My heart was still pumping mighty fast, but it wasn't like before. I knew I would be able to function properly while I executed my mission. When I got there, I noticed Trina's Infiniti parked on the opposite side of the street from Jay's spot. When I didn't see her in the car, I took a couple steps backward and knelt by a tree. Thankfully, the tree was big enough to hide my entire body, plus it gave me a helluva view to check out my surroundings. While I was back there, I was able to see everything moving. So far, I could see only one person hanging out on the streets. It looked like a fiend was searching for something on the ground, but after he found what he was looking for, he grabbed it up and scattered like a roach. About five more minutes had passed and Trina still hadn't come out of the house, and I was getting tired of kneeling down on the ground. When I stood up to stretch, I heard their voices echoing from around the building. It sounded like they were both laughing at a joke Jay told her, so I knew this would be the perfect time to knock him.

When they came from around the building, Jay was standing about five feet away with his back facing me. When I took the first step and aimed my pistol at him, Trina fucked around and looked into my direction, which caused this nigga to turn around and look over his shoulder. When Jay turned around and saw me aiming my pistol at him, he tried to make a run for it but I started busting my shit off at him. *Boom! Boom! Boom! Boom!* My burner roared like a cannon when the bullets exploded from the barrel. I knew Jay didn't have a chance of escaping. When I looked down on the ground at him, I knew he was gone when I saw two of the four bullets had struck him in his head. Homeboy was laid out, his head surrounded by a puddle of his own blood, with his eyes open as if he was still alive.

Trina was struggling with her keys, trying to get into her car. All of a sudden, bullets started ringing out again. Two niggas dressed in black ran up on the scene and started firing shots. Bullets were flying everywhere, so I dove back behind the tree to take cover. When I felt like I was in a good position, I started busting my gun right back at them. Those niggas didn't know what to do because they couldn't see me, so they decided to retreat. I was glad, too, because I didn't have enough ammo on me to keep those niggas off of me. I guess I did a good thing by diving back behind the tree, or else my ass would've been lying next to Jay. I didn't make a move until I heard car tires squeal down the street in the opposite direction. I rushed over to Trina to see if she was all right, but she was slumped over on the ground. When I turned her over, I saw that she had been shot twice. I also noticed that she was drifting in and out of consciousness, so I grabbed her into my arms.

"Hold on shorty, don't die on me. I'm gon' get you out of here."

"Awwww, I'm in so much pain and my skin is burning so bad."

"Wait, Trina, don't panic. Calm down, I'ma get you some help." I lifted her from the ground.

"I d-d-don't think I am going to make it," Trina said, her words slurring.

"Yes, you are. Stop talking like that, shorty. I'ma get you some help, and then me and Mike are going to get the niggas who did this to you."

I continued to reassure her and carried her down toward my car. People started pouring out of their houses to see what was going on, but I tuned their asses out after Trina said, "Mike is the one who did it."

"He what?" I stopped in my tracks.

"Mike set this whole thing up so you and Jay could get killed."

"But why? I mean, what did I do? I ain't been nothing but loyal to that nigga."

"What I am about to tell you, I want you to keep

to yourself," Trina began. "And the only reason why I am telling you is because I want to clear my conscience and do what's good before I leave this world."

"Whatchu talking about? I'm not gonna let you die."

Trina started coughing up blood, so I lifted her head up. She said, "Mike owes two brothers from New Orleans, named Bruce and Scottie, millions of dollars. And if he doesn't pay them back by the end of the month, they told him they were going to kill him and his wife. So all the money you and Jay made for him, he needs that back so he can pay the people he owes. And to do that, he had to get rid of y'all."

"So, who are these niggas?"

"His cousins. I'm sure you saw them earlier tonight when they were with him."

"Ahh shit! That was them?"

"Yep. Mike only had them in the truck with him so they could see how you looked."

"A'ight, but why didn't he get his cousins to kill Jay, and then kill me next?"

"Because he didn't want to make it look like two isolated incidents. He wanted it to look like you and Jay were having a shootout, so he could kill two birds with one stone. Luckily for you, Jay forgot to bring his gun outside with him. So you better watch your back."

Bugged out by all the shit Trina was telling me, all I could do was shake my head. And right before I tried to ask her another question, she closed her eyes and took her last breath. I panicked and laid her back down on the ground and as soon as I stood back up to make a run for it, I remembered that she had Mike's profits on her. I dug inside of the purse she had strapped around her neck and pulled out four stacks of money wrapped up in rubber bands, and a plastic bag. I snatched her BlackBerry and the holster from her pants and made a run for it.

Seth

Trying To Figure Shit Out

Since the whole thing with Jay and Trina went down the way it did, I decided to lay low at Maxine's crib. I had been chilling with her for the past four days, and believe me, life there hadn't been a bowl of cherries. She had been on my ass the last few days because she knew Samantha was coming home today. I couldn't get out of the bed this morning without her saying something in reference to Sam. "Today is the big day for your girlfriend, huh?" she asked.

I ignored her and headed to the shower. But that didn't stop her, though. Before I could even blink my eyes good, she was on my heels, rubbing the shit in my face. I guess she wanted to get a reaction out of me.

"I know you heard me," she said as soon as she entered the bathroom.

"Yeah, I heard you, but what do you want me to say?"

"I want to hear you say that you ain't gonna go try and see her," she replied, standing before me with her chest poked out.

"Look, I told you I wasn't, so why are we going through this again?"

"Because I don't believe you."

I turned the shower water on. "Well, you're just gonna have to." I slid my boxer shorts off and stepped into the shower.

I thought Maxine was going to give me some more lip service, but she didn't. I guess it sunk in her head that she could do nothing else but trust me. I mean, what other choices did she have? Whatever they were, it wouldn't have mattered because I was going to see my baby today if it killed me.

"What time are you leaving?" I heard her yell from the hallway.

"After I get out of the shower. Why?"

"Because I was hoping we could go out for breakfast."

"I thought you were going to work this morning."

"I don't have my first case until one o'clock, so I'm not going in until then."

"Well, I ain't going to be able to go to breakfast because I've got a few things to do."

Her pressure must've risen after I uttered my last words, because she stormed back into the bathroom with the quickness, snatched the shower curtain back and said, "Like what?"

There I was, standing butterball naked, dick hanging with soapsuds running down my body, and she wanted to ask me a whole bunch of unnecessary questions. I looked at her and said that I had a few things to do for my mother. I also told her I needed to run by the spot and check things out since I hadn't been there for a few days.

"But I thought you said that there was no need for you to go out there if you didn't have any work?"

"Maxine, I am just going out there to check the scenery out and to see if Mike got a hold of some new shit." I was lying through my teeth because, truth be told, I didn't want no parts of that spot anymore. Especially now that I knew Mike wanted me dead. If I told her that, she would lose her motherfucking mind and would surely call a couple of her U.S. Marshal buddies to protect us. The best thing for me to do was to keep her nosey ass as far away from the truth as long as I possibly could.

"Why can't you call him and ask him all that?"

"Come on now, you know that ain't how we get down. What niggas you know talk about drug deals over the phone?"

"Oh, there are still some out there who do."

"Well, believe me, it ain't many," I commented as I rinsed off.

"So when do you think you'll be done?"

"I'm not sure, but I can try to be done with everything by the time you come home from work."

Maxine looked at me suspiciously and then she chuckled a bit. "Yeah, OK. Whatever you say," she commented. "Just keep your phone on, because I might be getting off work early today." She walked out of the bathroom.

"Yeah, a'ight." But quiet as it's kept, I wasn't paying

her ass any mind because I wasn't gonna do anything but wait on my baby Samantha. As soon as I got my phone call from her oldest sister Paulette to let me know that they were on their way from Alderson, West Virginia, I was going to be straight. I knew it was going to take them at least five hours to get here. In the meantime, I was going to handle some business. Mike was first on my list. I had to keep that nigga at bay. I had to let that motherfucker think that I didn't have the slightest idea that he intended to have my head on the same platter as Jay's. I couldn't give him any reason to suspect that I took the dough Trina had collected from Jay before the hit. As long as I kept making him think that the police had confiscated his dough, the better my chances would be in getting close enough to kill him.

Since the shootout, I had only spoken with Mike twice. After I told him what happened and that Tina got caught up in the crossfire, I said it would be best if I laid low for a few days until the shit blew over. He agreed and told me to get with him later. I never did ask him for the money he promised to give me after I knocked Jay off, but I was going to mention it the next time I talked to him. I could not give this nigga the slightest inclination that I walked off with his dough. Knowing the way he was, he would put two and two together, if he hadn't already. God forbid, though, because he would definitely go after my moms, and I couldn't have that. Lucky for me, I never showed him where she laid her head because shit would really hit the fan then. I wouldn't allow anybody to touch a hair on my mother's head. If that meant I would have to die for her, then so be it.

She didn't ask for the lifestyle I chose for myself, so I had to protect her to the end. And that's my word!

Right after I got dressed, I kissed Maxine on the lips and promised her that we would get together and do dinner later.

"Don't stand me up," she said.

"I won't," I replied and left.

To kill a little bit of time, I went by my mom's crib just to make sure my dough was still in its safe spot. Once I unscrewed the door to the vent, retrieved the box from inside and opened it, my eyes lit up like lights on a Christmas tree. I counted every single bill and the count was still $317,000. I wrapped it up, placed it in the box, and put it back into the vent. Immediately after I put the screws back in, my Black-Berry rang. I looked down at the CallerID and saw that it was Paulette's number. I answered it because I knew Samantha had to be in the car with her.

"Sam, baby, this better be you," I said with excitement.

"You know it is!" she replied with the same amount of excitement.

"Where y'all at?"

"We just got out of West Virginia."

"How far are you now?"

"Well, we've been on the road for about an hour and a half, so we probably got about four hours left."

"If you've been on the road for an hour and a half, then why are you just now calling me?"

"I tried calling you a few times, but Paulette's cell phone didn't get a signal until we got out of them damn mountains."

"A'ight, y'all go ahead and drive safe and I'll see you in about four hours."

"Where we gon' meet at?"

"Paulette is going to bring you to the Marriott hotel in downtown Norfolk, so you ain't gon' be too far from the halfway house."

"By the time we get there, we ain't gon' have nothing but two hours to spend together."

"Trust me, Ma, that's plenty of time."

"Seth, have me something hot waiting for me, because I am starving."

"Whatchu want?"

"A nice T-bone steak with a baked potato and some jumbo shrimps."

"Whatchu want to drink?"

"It doesn't matter. Just something really cold."

"A'ight, I'm on it," I assured her.

"I love you," Samantha said.

"I love you too, Ma. Can't wait to see you."

"I can't either. So get your dick ready, 'cause I'ma fuck you real hard."

I laughed. "Yeah, a'ight. We'll see." Within minutes, my phone started ringing again. This time, it was Maxine. What a fucking coincidence. To avoid any drama from her silly ass, I answered my phone to see what she wanted.

"Where you at?" she asked.

"I'm at my mom's house, why?"

"I was just checking because my sources tell me that your co-defendant was just released from Alderson not even two hours ago."

"So whatchu telling me that for? You know I

could not have been with her, because I just left you less than thirty minutes ago."

"I'm just calling you to warn you that I am not playing with your ass! I also want to tell you that I may not be able to follow you around and watch every move that you make, but trust me when I tell you, I got other people watching you for me."

I took a deep breath. "Are you trying to start an argument?"

"No, I'm not. I just wanted to warn you."

"A'ight. Now, are you finished?"

"Yep."

"A'ight, well I'll holler at you later," I replied, gritting my teeth. On some real shit, I wanted to tell that bitch that I didn't care who she had watching me because I was going to see my girl today if it killed me. Then I figured, since she got motherfuckers spying on us, let them tell her. This bitch was making shit really easy for me to just walk away from her ass and not bless her with shit. The last few days this ho had been carrying me like I was the bitch, and that shit was getting old like a motherfucker! Whether she knew it or not, I was getting ready to make a power move, and neither she nor Mike was going to see it coming.

As soon as I hung up with Maxine, I hopped on the highway and drove to Portsmouth. I had no intention of stopping, and all I wanted to do was ride by the spot to see what was going on. Mike had already schooled me and told me that he had niggas pushing dope for me until I came out of hiding.

Supposedly it was the same two niggas he had riding shotgun in the truck with him the night of the shootout. It had been killing me to see how they were handling things out there. I knew they still had Hakeem and Bishop on the payroll and the other two young'uns as lookouts, so to prevent any of them niggas from seeing me, I parked on the other side of the horseshoe and traveled on foot.

The block was packed, like I thought it would be. Fiends were lined up all the way around one side of Melody's building. I didn't see Bishop nor the other two young boys I had watching the spot for me, but I saw Hakeem and one of the niggas who tried to murder me that night. At one point, Melody stepped outside to empty her trash can and as she entered back into the crib, I noticed the other nigga step to the front door without a shirt on, so I knew he had already made himself at home. From the look of it, the nigga looked like he had been living there for years. He also looked like he just came home from doing a bid. The nigga's guns were huge as a motherfucker, so I knew he'd bench press every bit of three hundred pounds. He was the type of cat Melody liked, so I knew right off the bat that her trifling ass had already fucked him. He just didn't know that she was probably about to set his dumb ass up too.

After I sat out at Dales Homes and watched these clown-ass niggas parade around like they owned the projects, I turned around to leave. On the way to my car, I ran into that fiend chick named Faith that always harassed me about sucking my dick for a pill of dope. I thought I was going to have to curse her ass out before I dipped out, but she came at me with a different approach and I was stunned like a motherfucker.

"I told you they were going to replace you, didn't I?" she said.

"Yeah, you did," I said and chuckled. "But, how did you know?"

"I know a lot of shit, but a lot of these niggas out here don't be trying to listen to me. They think I'm crazy as hell! But I'm not. I've got plenty of sense."

"Well, tell me what you know." I stepped just a little bit closer to her.

"Information doesn't come free," she told me.

I reached into my pants pockets and pulled out twenty dollars. "What can I get for this?" I asked her.

"I can tell you a lot for that," she insisted and snatched the twenty-dollar bill out of my hand.

"Well, start talking," I demanded. Instead, she walked in the direction of my car and gave me an earful. She told me that Melody was an informant for the police; that was why a lot of the niggas that sold out of her house didn't last more than two months.

"Does Mike know this shit?" I wondered aloud.

"Yeah, he knows it. That's why he keeps sending niggas over there to her."

"But I don't get it. Why is he doing it? He can lose a lot of product and dough setting niggas up to get busted by the police."

"See, they got this pact where he'd send different niggas over there for about a month or so to get rid of about $100,000 worth of dope. When he gets low, he gives Melody the cue to hand the nigga over to the police, in exchange for his own freedom."

Shocked as hell by what this chick was telling me I said, "You are bullshitting me! You mean to tell me this nigga uses motherfuckers to sell off all his dope, and then sets them up to get busted with the last bit of his dope, just so he can keep his own ass from going to jail?"

"Yep."

"Come on now, you've got to be kidding me! This has got to be a joke."

"I don't do no joking. Melody and that nigga Mike have been doing this shit for some time now. I mean, I know I have seen at least ten different niggas selling dope out her spot and all of them either get knocked off by the police or shot because somebody tried to rob them."

I shook my head in disbelief. The shit this lady was telling me was crazy like a motherfucker. Who would've thought that both of them were snitches? They had intentions on having my ass done in either way, and that was some foul shit. Now it all made sense. Trina wasn't lying; Mike wanted Jay's murder to look like a robbery so he could get all his earnings before the police had a chance to get it themselves. Too bad I intercepted those fake gun-toting-ass niggas, or else they would've gotten me, too.

After Faith gave me all the information I needed, I hauled out of there and never looked back. I figured I was going to have to come at this nigga Mike another way since he had the police on his side.

Seth

Welcome Home

I was bugging out while I headed back over to Norfolk, thinking about all the shit Faith told me. My mind was clouded like a motherfucker, trying to figure out how I was going to handle this situation. Whatever I came up with, I knew it wouldn't be a cut-and-dry solution because these motherfuckers I was dealing with were a new breed. And that was some ill shit.

I bullshitted around at MacArthur Mall for another couple of hours, trying to get Samantha some things I knew she would need. I remembered that about a month ago, she told me she had put on a few pounds so now she wore a size twelve jeans and a medium shirt. With that much information I was able to pick her up a few things I knew she would love. After I went into all the hot female clothing, lingerie, and shoe stores, I packed all the shopping bags in the trunk of my whip and headed straight to the hotel.

Earlier that morning, I made the reservations over the phone, so all I had to do was pay for the room when I got there. As soon as I paid in cash, the clerk behind the desk handed me a room key, and the bellboy escorted me on up to the Executive Suite, which was on the top floor. The inside of this motherfucker was plush as hell. For a whopping five hundred a night I had a king-sized bed with a Sleep Number mattress. The room also came with a kitchenette, a living room, and an eating area. The bathroom was even hotter, with a Jacuzzi bathtub big enough for four people. I mean, the shit was huge. I knew one thing, and that was if I wasn't getting this room for me and Samantha, I sure could've called in about two or three other chicks and would have had plenty of room to get buck fucking wild.

While I was getting everything organized, I remembered that I had to get Samantha's food. I called Guest Services and ordered us both steaks with baked potatoes and one side order of fried jumbo shrimps.

"How long will it take for y'all to bring this order up to the room?" I asked the man.

"It shouldn't take more than twenty to twenty-five minutes," he replied.

"A'ight. Well, that's cool," I assured him.

"Are we billing this to the room?" he asked.

"Nah, I'm paying cash," I told him.

"OK, we will see you in a bit."

"A'ight."

In a bit was exactly how long it took for the room service guy to bring the food, which was perfectly timed because less than five minutes later, Samantha was calling to tell me she was downstairs in the lobby of the hotel.

"Come on up. I'm on the top floor in the Executive Suite," I told her.

Moments later, my baby was getting off the elevator. I stood there in the entranceway of the door to my room, ready to take her right into my arms. As soon as she rushed toward me, that's exactly what I did. After I hugged her for a good three minutes straight, I pushed her away from me so I could get a good look at her.

I smiled and grabbed her into my arms and escorted her into the room. "Damn, Ma, you look real good."

"You look good too baby."

Admiring every inch of the room, Samantha said, "Ahhh man, I like this. This shit is nice as hell!"

"Good. I'm glad because this motherfucker cost me an arm and a leg."

"How much was it?"

"Don't worry about it. Just get on over here and eat your food before it gets cold."

"Fuck that food! I want you!" She started tugging at my clothes.

"Come on, let's get in the shower," I suggested.

"A'ight, come on."

When I saw Samantha's body hit that water, my dick got hard in an instant. The way her ass looked after all these years brought back some serious memories. I grabbed her into my arms and pulled her body into mine. Then we started kissing like our minds were going bad. Sam started grinding her pussy against my meat, and I had to admit that the shit was driving me crazy.

"Pick me up," she demanded.

I did and she wrapped her legs around my waist. That left enough room for me to slide my dick right into her pussy.

"Ooooh, yeaaaaah!" she said the second I pushed my joint inside of her. I started stroking my dick in and out of her like I was searching for something really nice.

"Yeah baby, fuck me harder!" she demanded. I grabbed her around her waist real tight and brought her body down on me real hard. Her pussy and my dick collided into each other like a train wreck. *Boom!* Then, her body jerked.

"Ahhhh yes, baby, do it harder," she moaned.

"You love this dick, don't you?" I asked as I pushed my dick up in her harder. The feelings inside of me were indescribable. I didn't know if I was coming or going, but I did know that after pounding her pussy real good and consistently for about seven minutes, I was ready to bust off. But being the man I was, I knew I couldn't. I knew it would have only been proper to wait for her to get her shit off first, so I held my nut back by thinking of other shit. Then after two more minutes passed, I heard her say, "Ahhhh baby, I'm about to cum!" I knew it was on then. While Samantha spilled her juices out on my dick, I ejected some of my own. When it was all said and done, both of us collapsed inside the bathtub until the water started getting cold on us.

Back in the room, we climbed into bed and talked about old times, since she had about an hour left to kill. We talked about everything under the sun. We even talked about how we first met. Then somehow the subject came up about how she caught me cheating on her with her sister and how they got into a fight over me. I didn't really want to talk about that bullshit, but Samantha wouldn't let it go for nothing in the world.

"Remember how I popped her ass in her face when I saw y'all walking out of the hotel?"

"Nah, I don't," I said nonchalantly, hoping she would shut the fuck up. Shit, I wasn't trying to relive that bullshit! It was bad enough I got caught, and I felt stupid about it. Did she think I wanted to sit back and talk about it all over again?

"Come on now, Seth. You remember when I bashed her fucking face in."

"Samantha, why you trying to start an argument?"

"I'm not trying to start an argument."

"So, what kind of point are you trying to make?"

"I'm not trying to make a point at all. But I am trying to show you where we came from, and look at us now."

"Yeah, yeah, yeah!" I said and got out of the bed. Because on some real shit, I wasn't trying to feed into that. OK, I was wrong for fucking her baby sister but, hey, the bitch was hounding me and she had been doing it for months. She practically begged me to fuck her. Since she looked good, I couldn't refuse. What fucked the whole thing up was that I kept going back for more. I think I probably fucked Tammy about a dozen times. Then she started catching feelings and doing stupid shit like leaving me voice mail messages about how she missed me and she couldn't live without me. So one particular day, I took her to a hotel in Chesapeake and she decided she wanted to call Samantha on her cell phone and lay the phone down on the night stand so that Samantha could hear our entire conversation. That bitch called out the name of the hotel we were in, then she made her move on me and we started fucking. When I tell you Samantha got an earful, believe me she did. All I knew was that after we got our rocks off, I was ready to go. When I opened up the door to the room, I wasn't expecting to see Samantha standing there, and believe me, my heart wasn't prepared either. When Samantha lunged back and threw a power punch into Tammy's face, I knew it was over. I think it took about three people to break them up. When it was all said and done, Tammy got her ass kicked. Of course, Samantha left me alone, but I begged and pleaded for about three months until she took me back. Now here we were, going through the same shit, just with a different chick.

Before I dropped Samantha off at the halfway house, she asked me to take her by her mom's crib since we had about thirty minutes to waste. It seemed like everybody, including her aunts and uncles, were there. The house was packed with every family member who lived in the area. As soon as I walked into the front door, I greeted everybody, hugged her mother, and eased my way into the living room. I got bombarded by Sam's uncle

Reggie. He was the family crackhead and always wanted to borrow money, knowing good and well he wasn't gonna be able to pay you back.

He sat on the seat beside me, smiled and said, "Let me hold something."

"Reggie, I ain't working with nothing right now," I replied.

"Come on now, nephew, I know you got at least ten dollars." At this point, he usually began to beg.

"I told you I wasn't working with nothing."

"Nigga, who you think you talking to? I see that brand new whip you pushing outside, and I know my niece ain't gon' fuck with you unless you got something in your pockets, so you can tell somebody else that lie."

"Listen, man, I told you I ain't have no dough. Now, if I had some, I'd slide you about twenty dollars. But right now, I'm fucked up."

"A'ight, well let me wash your car for you."

"Reggie, didn't I say I didn't have shit?"

"Yeah, but I know I'd probably find some change or something inside your cup holders."

I laughed and shook my head. This nigga wasn't hearing me at all. But, I couldn't knock his hustle. Instead of sitting there and continuing to listen to his bullshit, I got up and walked into the kitchen to where Sam was. On my way, I happened to pass right by Samantha's sister, Tammy. As soon as she saw me, her eyes locked onto mine. I guessed she was shocked to see me. It had been a few years since the last time we saw each other, so I did the polite thing by speaking. After she spoke back, she strutted her pretty ass right by me. When I turned around to take a look to see if her ass was still fat, Samantha came from out of nowhere and smacked me right in the back of my head.

"You are so fucking disrespectful," she snapped.

Caught off guard, I rubbed my head, trying to ease the sting from the blow and then turned around toward Samantha with a stupid expression on my face. "Whatchu talking about?" I asked her.

"Don't act stupid, Seth! I saw you looking at Tammy's ass!" she yelled. "What, you want to fuck her again?"

"Hell, nah! Are you crazy?" I snapped back.

"I couldn't tell, especially after the way you were all up on her." I tried to reach for her but she knocked my hands out of the way. "Don't touch me, because you know you are wrong." I looked around the living room and everybody and their mother was watching us. I tried to defuse the situation by grabbing Sam's arm and escorting her into a nearby bedroom.

"Why you had to make a big-ass scene in front of your family?" I asked her as soon as I closed the door behind us.

"Why the fuck you got to be so damn disrespectful?"

"Sam, all I did was turn around and look at her."

"No, liar, you turned around and looked down at her ass!"

"OK, I did and so what? I mean, why you gotta make a big fuss about it! All I was doing was looking. There ain't no harm in that, is it?"

Sam punched me in the arm. "Fuck you, Seth!" she said. "Take me to the halfway house right now."

She walked out of the bedroom and slammed the door behind her. I walked out of the room a few minutes later so it wouldn't look like we were still beefing. It didn't work because she was running her mouth to everybody on her way to the front door. But before she got there, her uncle Reggie stopped her in her tracks.

"Hey Sam, somebody is on the phone for you."

"Who is it?" She sounded irritated as she reached for the cordless phone.

"He didn't give me his name," Reggie told her.

Now I'm standing there in front of her wondering to myself who in the hell could be calling her? And to know it was a nigga really threw me for a loop. But what was really messing my head up was the fact that he knew she was here. I waited to hear what she had to say.

"Hello," she said with an attitude. And then she frowned her face up and said, "How did you get this number?" And when she said that, a red flag went up in my head and I flipped out.

"Who the fuck is that?" I asked her, my veins on the verge of popping out of my forehead.

But Samantha ignored me and continued with her conversation. "Don't worry about who that was," she yelled.

"Tell that mutherfucker I'm your man!" I demanded.

All her family members were standing around waiting to see how she was going to handle this, but she ignored me once again. "Look, don't call my damn house anymore and I mean it!" she told him and then she pressed down on the END button and disconnected the call.

Immediately after she hung up with homeboy, I stood there and waited for her to tell me who the fuck he was but she didn't. Instead, she handed the phone back to her uncle and walked out of the house, so you know I followed behind her like a pimp who walks down on the heels of his hoes. And when I got outside I let her ass have it.

"Who the fuck was that nigga you were on the phone with?"

"Why the fuck you worrying about it? I'm sure you've got your share of hoes out here."

"Sam, don't play with me!" I warned her as we both got into my car.

She closed the passenger side door and looked straight head. "I'm not playing with you," she replied sarcastically.

"I think you are. And I am not taking you to the halfway house until you tell me who the fuck you was on the phone with."

Samantha hesitated and then she said, "It was some nigga named Mendez."

My patience was about to run out. "Who the fuck is he?" I screamed.

"Somebody I use to know back in the day."

"Well, how the fuck he knew you were home? What, you were writing that nigga when you were locked up?"

"Hell nah!"

"Well, how he knew you were home?"

"I don't know."

"Well, that nigga better not call you again," I

warned her and then I started my whip up and squealed my tires as I pulled off.

Instead of responding, Samantha folded her arms and turned her face toward the window. We rode to the halfway house in complete silence. But, I knew we would be all right by tomorrow. That's how shit was with us. We'd fight one day, and then we're cool the next. Besides, she couldn't get enough of me. Nor could Maxine, which was why they were gonna always come back, no matter how much I fucked up.

Maxine

Back In The Office

I didn't know what Karen's problem was, but she had been riding my ass about my caseload. Since I had been away from the office she had been all in my files and shit, and checking behind me to see if I was doing all the follow-up meetings with my second-time-loser clients.

"What's up with this guy? When is the last time you scheduled a home visit with him?" she asked, showing me the file that belonged to a Mr. Omar Clarke.

"Lately he hasn't complied with any of my letters to come in and do a urine screen, and when I tried to pay him a surprise visit at his residence about three weeks ago, he was nowhere to be found."

"Does he work?"

"No. His former employer told me he fired him over a month ago."

"I am going to take his file with me because he

needs Form 21-B filed on him immediately. I've got to have him off the streets in the next forty-eight hours, because this guy is hazardous to society."

"I would've filed the paperwork a long time ago, but you forced me to take leave right after I had those two incidents back-to-back, remember?"

"Yeah, I realize that, but this individual should not have been overlooked. If you were having problems locating him before you took off, you should've taken the file home and worked on it from there. You could have attached an urgent memo and stuck it on my desk or e-mailed me so I could've dealt with it. There's no reason why this individual should still be walking the streets."

"You're right, but—"

"No, Maxine, there's no room for the word *but* in this situation," she interjected. She went on to say that she had noticed by the reports in my files that I had become a little slack with my clients. Of course I tried to refute that, but again, she cut me off. Karen had me cornered in my office for at least two hours, going over my clients' files. After she indicated the cases she wanted me to take immediate action on, she gave me a forty-eight-hour deadline to have all eleven of the men and women back behind bars. But that wasn't it, because as soon as she began to put the files back into the cabinet, she stumbled across Seth's file again. Once more, she had my heart about to burst right out of my chest.

"I swear, every time I see this man, he looks just like the guy posing in the picture with you at your apartment."

I chuckled again, but I was fearful as hell. "You know what? He does kind of look like him, now that you've mentioned it." I agreed, hoping it would throw her off.

Guess what? My magic worked. Karen nodded her head in agreement and stuck his file right in the cabinet with the others. Boy, I'll tell you that was a heart attack just waiting to happen.

"Keep me abreast of what's going on, and have a full report on my desk by morning, OK?"

"OK," I said and watched her leave my office.

I looked down at my watch and noticed that it was a little after four. My heart rate increased because my gut feeling was telling me that I needed to call the halfway house and see if Ms. Samantha had already checked in, and if she had, I wanted to know who dropped her off. I picked up line two on my office phone and dialed the direct line to the halfway house. On the third ring, a woman picked up.

"Thanks for calling Rehabilitation Services. This is Sonya. How can I help you?"

"Hi Sonya, my name is Maxine, and I am a United States Federal Probation Officer. I was calling to check on the arrival of a Samantha Mitchell, who should have been admitted into your facility by now."

"Yes, as a matter of fact, she has," Sonya said. "I checked her in myself about an hour ago."

"Oh, OK, good. By any chance would you know who dropped her off?"

"No ma'am. I'm sorry, but we don't ask the residents those kind of questions unless they have been restricted from being around certain individuals."

"I'm sorry if you hadn't been informed, but she has certain restrictions."

"Is this information in her file?"

"My duty officer said that she faxed over a photo

and an F-17 form about three weeks ago, so it should be there."

"OK, hold on a minute and let me check," she said and then I heard her lay the phone down.

I listened to complete silence for about three minutes and then I heard her pick the phone up again. "I have her file here," she informed me. "Let me take a look while I have you on the phone."

After a few seconds passed Sonya said, "OK, I see the F-17 form and the photo of a black male by the name of Seth Richardson."

"Yes, that's it."

"I will let Ms. Mitchell's case manager and the house monitors know what's going on, so everyone will be aware of the situation."

I sighed with relief. "Thank you so much, Sonya."

"You are so welcome," she said.

"Hey, Sonya, can I ask you one more thing?"

"Sure."

"What is normal protocol for the new residents?"

"What do you mean?"

"I was wondering about the rules and regulations for earning passes and how long they get to go out?"

"Well, in Ms. Mitchell's case, she won't be able to leave this building for weekend passes until she has secured a job and has been working for at least two weeks. Once she can pay her housing fee, she'll earn passes weekly."

"How is she able to find a job?"

"After she goes through orientation, which will be tomorrow, she will be given a pass to go out every day from eight AM to three PM to submit applications to employers who hire ex-offenders."

"Will she be monitored while she's out and about?"

"No ma'am, I'm afraid not."

"So, she could just go anywhere she wants and be with whomever, and y'all won't know about it?"

"Technically, she could because we don't have the manpower to follow every one of our residents. All we can do is monitor her while she is on or around our property."

Not at all happy by her response, I quickly thanked her for her time and patience and got the hell off the phone. I pulled out my cell phone and dialed Seth's number.

"Hello," he said.

"How are you doing?" I asked him as nicely as I could.

"I'm cool. What about you?"

"I'm OK now that I'm finally getting ready to leave out of these doors, so I can see you."

"Whatchu trying to get into?"

"I don't know. Maybe we can go to dinner or a movie or something. I mean, it really doesn't matter to me."

"A'ight. Well, let's see a movie because I just ate a plate of leftovers I found in my mom's refrigerator."

"Did you take care of all of your business?"

"Yep."

"How long have you been back at her house?"

"Probably about two hours. Why?"

"Oh nothing, really. I was just being curious."

"Well, what time do you want me to meet you at your place?"

"Go there now, because you know it's gonna take me twenty minutes to get there."

"A'ight, so I'll see you there."

"I love you."

"I love you too," he told me and then we hung up.

Hearing him tell me he had been at his mother's house for over two hours and that he loved me put a huge smile on my face. Nothing in the world could upset me right now. After I shut my computer down and grabbed my handbag and car keys, I walked out of my office and didn't look back. I didn't have to look back because my stalker friend and colleague, Mr. Marcus Finley, was having a heavy conversation with my hating-ass colleague, Carolyn Granger, right at the exit. As badly as I wanted to turn around to avoid running into both of these idiots, I psyched myself into believing that this was only a dream and that it would be over as soon as I got out of the building. As I approached them I said, "Excuse me. Coming through." That wasn't enough for Marcus. He had to turn all the way around and give me his undivided attention.

"Hey wait a minute, what's the rush?" he asked and grabbed at my jacket.

"I'm late for a dinner engagement," I told him while simultaneously trying to pry his fingers from my clothing.

"Carolyn and I were just talking about how she would testify on your behalf in your upcoming hearing against Dwayne Harris, that character who head-butted you."

I looked over at Carolyn's pale face and said, "Oh that's sweet! To what do I owe the favor?"

"You don't owe me anything," she said sympathetically. "I figured that was the least I could do, considering we're colleagues and all."

Bullshit! I thought to myself.

"Yeah, and I agree," Marcus added.

"Well, that's sincerely a nice gesture on your part. Get with me in the AM, and we'll go over the specifics. Good night," I added.

"Hey, before you leave," Carolyn interjected. "Karen told me about your client that might have some interest in one of my clients that was released today."

"Yeah, what about it?"

"I just want you to know that I am going down to the halfway house to pay her a visit. I will personally stress to her how important it is that she abide by the guidelines set for her probation, and that she must not see your client by any means or they will be violated on the spot."

Just like that, I developed a knot in the pit of my stomach. If I didn't know any better, I would've thought that they heard the nervousness inside of me rattling like a baby rattle. First of all, I didn't ask for none of this bullshit! I never wanted Karen or this bitch to get involved with my affairs with Seth. I knew the cat was about to be let out of the fucking bag. As soon as Carolyn sat down with Samantha and had that talk, I knew Samantha was going to run her motherfucking mouth about everything, including the conversation we had on the telephone a couple of weeks ago. When that happened, all hell was going to break loose, for real. Now, how was I going to handle that? I knew one thing, though. Seth and I were gonna have to work out an early retirement plan for me today, because I would not give the bitch in front of me the satisfaction of watching Karen fire me. No fucking way! After I thanked Carolyn for the heads up and asked her to keep me informed about how her meeting went with Samantha, I tapped

Marcus on the shoulder and told him I would talk to him in the AM. Then I flew out of there like a bat out of hell.

As soon as I got into my car, I got Seth right back on the phone. I could tell by all the commotion in the background that he was in his car listening to music. "Baby, you and I got some serious talking to do when I see you," I said, sounding out of breath.

"What's wrong?"

"My co-worker is going to have a sit down with your co-defendant next week, and believe me, our names are going to come up. If she starts running her mouth to her P.O. about us, then you and I are going to be history."

"Whatchu mean by that?"

"I mean, I will lose my job and we'll both be behind bars."

"Maxine, what could she possibly tell that lady?"

"For starters, she could tell her that you and I are in a relationship, and then about the argument she and I had over you a few weeks back."

"Nah, I don't think Sam would do that."

"And what makes you so sure? What, you been talking to her?"

"No, I haven't."

"You mean to tell me that she hasn't tried to call you at all today?"

"Nope, but I'm sure she will."

"Well, when she calls you, I want you to make sure that she doesn't open up her mouth. You need to understand me, because this shit is critical."

"Yeah, I understand. Now, why don't you calm down? Everything is going to be all right."

"Trust me, everything isn't going to be all right

until I resign from that place, which is the other thing I want to talk to you about."

"What's up?"

"When do you think you'll have all the money for me so I can start getting everything lined up to open up our business?"

"How much are you going to need?"

"I'm not sure. The way the economy is now, I'd probably need about twenty thousand at the least. Do you think you can swing it?"

"Yeah, I'm sure I can."

"When do you think you'd have it?"

"Give me to the end of the month," he said.

I let out a sigh of relief. "Good! Because I am ready to tell everybody at the federal building to kiss my ass!"

"Well, it won't be long now," he assured me.

We talked for a few more minutes about my aspirations to open up a pastry shop or any kind of restaurant that served gourmet food. Then we talked about what location might be good for business. While I was going on and on, Seth cut me off by saying, "Maxine, I gotta go, that's my moms beeping in on the other end."

"Tell her to call you back," I protested.

"I'm not gonna do that because it might be important."

"Well, just click over and see what she wants," I demanded.

"A'ight. Hold on." He clicked over.

After he answered his other line I just sat there with the phone pressed to my ear and wondered if it was his mother calling him for real. Because on some real shit, it might've been that bitch Samantha. But he wasn't gonna tell me that. I sat there and waited patiently for him to click back over. After waiting for seven consecutive minutes, this bastard never did click back, and I was steaming. I was literally about to go out of my fucking mind. I held my composure and dialed his ass right back. He'd better have a good explanation, or else I was going to let him have it. Since I had just hung up with him, all I had to do was press the SEND button again. His phone rang immediately.

"Hey baby, I am so sorry!" Seth apologized. "I tried to get my moms off the phone, but she kept talking and going on about how her joints was still hurting, even after she left the doctor's office today. Then she told me that she forgot to pick up her medication from the pharmacy, so she needed me to go by there and pick it up for her."

"When you plan on doing that?"

"Don't worry. I already told her I'm gon' have to do it later."

"Well, where are you now?"

"I'm about to pull up at your crib, why?"

"OK, good, because I'm about five minutes away myself."

"A'ight. Well, I'll see you in a few."

"All right."

Seth

Taking Losses

The next morning, Maxine went to work and I went back to my mom's crib to gather my thoughts. Maxine was driving me crazy as hell about this shit with Samantha being home. Not to mention, I wasn't gonna be able to keep my stamina up if I kept jumping from Samantha's pussy to Maxine's. I thought I was going to die when Maxine got on top of me last night. Man, I didn't know what the hell to do. I was already tired from busting three nuts in Samantha. When Maxine whipped my dick out and started sucking on it, I couldn't tell her to stop because I had already had enough pussy for one day, so I just laid back and rolled with it. I knew I wasn't gonna be able to do that too many more times. My dick wasn't gonna allow me to. And that's my word!

When I got to my mom's crib, she was in her recliner in the living room. She told me how upset Samantha was last night because I wasn't there to take her call.

"Why didn't she call me on my cell phone?"

"She said they only had pay phones in the facility, so that's why she called here."

"She called collect?"

"Yes."

"How many times?"

"She called four times."

"Well, why didn't you call me on three-way?"

"Seth, you know I don't know how to use that three-way mess. That's why I told her to keep calling back."

"What did she say, Ma?"

"She just said that you better not be with your probation officer because if she found out that you were, she was going to break it off with you."

"Did she try to call me this morning?"

"No. The phone only rang one time and it was one of them ol' telemarketers, trying to get me to do a survey."

"A'ight, Ma. Thanks," I said and kissed her on the forehead. As I was about to walk away, she grabbed my hand and told me to look at her.

"You know you're playing with fire, right?" she said.

"Ma, trust me, I know what I am doing."

"That's not the point, Seth. Maxine is going to try to put you back behind bars as soon as she finds out that Samantha is back in your life. Now mark my words, because I know what I am talking about."

"Maxine already knows Samantha is home, and she's not too happy about it, either."

"What are you going to do, son?"

"I don't know."

"Well, you better think of something because Maxine isn't gonna let you walk away from her without paying a price for it."

"I know." I shook my head in dismay because my mother was right. Maxine wasn't going to go down without a fight. I was going to have to come up with a clever plan to eliminate her without damaging myself.

After my mom and I had our heart-to-heart, I went upstairs to my room and lay down on my bed. Thoughts of me killing Mike's sheisty ass, among other things, were embedded in my mind. While I was in deep thought, my BlackBerry rang. I didn't recognize the number, but something told me to answer it.

"Hello."

"Where the fuck you been all night?" Samantha screamed through the receiver.

"I was out the way," I lied.

"Why the fuck you lying? You just told me yesterday at the hotel that you wasn't gonna fuck around out there anymore."

"Sam, I'm not lying. I did go out there."

"But for what, when you said you didn't have a need to?"

"I can't talk to you about it right now."

"Why not?"

"Listen, mommie, I had some business to take care of, so please stop beefing with me."

"Seth, don't try to turn this shit around. I know you were out with that bitch last night."

"No, I wasn't, Sam."

"Well, call her on three-way so I can ask her for myself."

"Come on now, you sound real stupid," I told her. "You know damn well I ain't about to do no dumb shit like that! What, you trying to get us both locked back up?"

"That bitch can't do shit to me!" she snapped.

"She can get your silly ass locked back up for harassing her."

"Trust me, she ain't gon' tell them people at her office shit because she knows I can rain on her damn parade."

"Look, Sam, come off that dumb-ass shit! You and I are back together now, so don't make something out of nothing," I yelled.

She finally managed to calm herself down. After I reassured her that it was only about me and her, she got the picture and didn't utter Maxine's name anymore during our conversation.

"Whose phone you're calling me from?" I asked.

"My roommate let me use her cell phone, but I can't be on it long because she ain't supposed to have it. If one of the house monitors walks up on me while I got it in my hand, they will take it from me. And you know I ain't trying to be responsible for somebody else's stuff."

"Check it out, I'ma pick you one up today so you can have your own."

"Wait. Don't get it until tomorrow, because that's when I will be able to leave this place."

"How long they letting you out?"

"Just for four hours so I can go to the Social

Security Office to apply for a Social Security card, and to the DMV to get a new I.D."

"They only giving you four hours to do all that?"

"Yep."

"A'ight. Well, don't worry about it. I'll come scoop you up."

"What time?"

"I don't know. You tell me."

"I'm not sure. I'm gonna have to wait until my counselor signs off on my pass."

"I'll tell you what; call me as soon as you find out what time they're gonna let you out."

"OK, let me go."

"A'ight, but are you going to be able to call me later?"

"Yeah, but it's gonna have to be from the pay phone."

"What time?"

"I am going to be in orientation until about five or six o'clock, so I'll call you back about six-thirty."

"A'ight."

"I love you."

"I love you too, mommie."

Seth

Like Old Times

Later on that day, I got a call from Mike. I told him I had been out of town but now I was back. He went straight for the jugular and asked me if I was ready to go back to work. I told him I needed a few more days because I had some shit lined up down south that I wanted him to get in on.

"What's good?" he asked with excitement.

"Yo, son, all I can say right now is that my cousin introduced me to some peoples that's trying to spread a lot of love."

"Where they at?"

"Down in Florida."

"Word?"

"Yep. And believe me when I tell you that those niggas are caked up, too."

"Where they from?"

"My cousin told me they from South America."

"Yo, if they're from South America, I know they got some real good shit."

"Yeah, I know."

"So, when you gon' hook me up?"

"Well, I'm gon' take a trip back down there in about another week, so if you ain't busy, you can go with me."

"Damn right! I'm down."

"A'ight. Well give me a couple of days to get back with my cousin so he can set a meeting up for us and as soon as I hear the word, I'ma hit you up."

"A'ight, dawg, don't forget."

"Come on now, Mike. You looked out for me and put me on, so that's the least I could do." Little did he know I had a death warrant for his ass, and as soon as I got the chance, I was gon' put one right in his head.

Once I made him believe that I had a plan in motion for us to make more money together, I flipped the script on him and asked him for the dough he owed me. Just like that, the nigga acted like he had amnesia.

"What money you talking about?"

"I'm talking about that dough you told me I would collect from that job out in Norfolk," I reminded him.

"Oh yeah, I got that for you."

"Good, because I'm gon' need that. I got a lot of shit going on and I'm gon' need every dime I can get."

"What's going on?"

"Man, this new chick I'm fucking with wants me to go in with her to start a business and she needs for me to hit her off with my half. I'm trying to scrape up all the dough I can."

"How much you gotta come up with?"

"Just $30,000."

"You ain't got that?"

"I did. But I fucked around trying to play Big Willy and lost most of it at the Hard Rock Cafe Casino in Hollywood, Florida a few days ago."

"Damn son, that wasn't a smart move."

"I know. And right now I'm paying for it, too."

"A'ight. Well, come by my crib later and I'll set you straight."

"What time?"

"Come by about three o'clock."

"A'ight."

After I hung up, I sat on the edge of my bed and wondered if Mike bought all that shit I was feeding him. All the excitement in his voice had me believing that he was looking forward to making new moves, so I could only assume that he took the bait. Time would tell, though.

Other than that, I could only wonder how much dough he was supposed to be pushing in my direction for that hit I put on Jay. I knew that nigga better not come at me with a little bit of pocket change, because I would definitely tell that nigga where to stick that shit. Murdering niggas nowadays paid anywhere from ten to one hundred grand, depending on how important that cat was. Regular niggas could get slaughtered for less than five grand, but I wasn't wasting my time with those types, because they weren't worth it. By the time you suited up, scoped out the area you were going to murder the nigga at, and then executed the mission, you felt just like you just went to war. For that little bit of dough, it wasn't worth it because you had to take so many risks. I would stick with the big dawgs and leave the smaller jobs for the amateurs.

Before I knew it, three o'clock was there in a flash, and I was right at Mike's doorstep a minute after. Lacy answered the door with a bright smile, which made me wonder if she knew how crooked her husband was. She seemed like a sweet and laid back type of chick. Lacy was always laced up in Christian Louboutin or something by Chloë or Oscar de la Renta. She was one bad-ass chick walking around carrying a big-ass load in her belly. Then again, my eyes could've been playing tricks on my ass. For all I knew, the broad could be a crooked-ass snitch like her buster-ass husband. If she was, she was going to fuck around and catch a few slugs in her head right along with her man if she didn't watch out.

"How you doing?" she asked.

"I'm doing fine, and yourself?" I replied as I stepped into the foyer.

"I'm fine, sweetie." She closed the front door behind us. "Come on, Mike's in the TV room." She escorted me in that direction.

When I walked into the room where Mike was chilling, I found him lounging back on his recliner watching the Steelers playing the Patriots. This nigga was so into the game I didn't think he realized I had walked into the room until Lacy said something to him.

"Mike, don't you see Seth standing here?"

Mike turned around in slow motion. "Oh shit, son! What's good?" He stood up to greet me.

I smiled as we shook hands. "Nothing much." I

watched his wife as she left the room. "So, who's winning?" I asked as I took a seat down on the loveseat right across from him.

"The Patriots is killing them niggas!" he said with happiness.

"Oh, so the Patriots must be your team?"

"And you know it!" Mike's face lit up as he said it.

"What quarter is it?"

"The fourth, and we ain't got nothing but two minutes left in the game."

"What's the score?"

"My boys are leading by fifteen."

"Oh yeah, the Steelers are finished," I agreed and then looked down at my watch to give this nigga a hint that I was kind of pressed for time. Of course, he fed right in to it.

"What's up? You got somewhere you gotta be?" he blurted out.

"Yeah, I told my girl I was going to meet her at her crib with the dough in the next thirty minutes."

"Where she live at?"

"In Chesapeake."

Mike smiled. "Damn nigga, when did you meet her?"

"I met her when I first came home but we only hung out a few times," I tried to conjure up a story. "And then about a few weeks ago, she stepped to me and told me she was ready to make it official."

"How she look?"

"Yo Mike, shorty is bad as hell! She's got that baby face like Rhianna, but she's got the body like one of them big butt video chicks."

Mike looked at me in amazement. "So, whatchu gon' do about your other girl, Samantha?"

"Shit, I'ma have her too," I responded nonchalantly.

"Yo dawg, you got it going on!" He reached into his pocket and pulled out a wad of money. "Here, take your paper!"

"How much is it?" I asked him.

"It's fifteen grand. That nigga only had forty-five grand in his crib, and I promised you a third, so that's your cut."

"A'ight, that's cool!" I stuck the wad in my pocket.

The game went to a commercial, so Mike turned all the way around in his seat and shook his head in frustration. I knew he was about to put me through test mode. I put on my game face and waited for him to come at me with his first question. This would be his opportune moment, since this was his first time we stood face-to-face since the shootout. Whatever he was about to say, I knew I had to be ready for him.

"What's wrong, son?" I coached him.

"Man, I just can't get my mind off losing all that dough Trina went to pick up from Jay."

"Yeah, I don't think I would be able to get that shit off my mind, either."

Mike sat there in silence and watched my facial expressions. I was kind of wondering what was going through his mind. Instead of dwelling on it, I changed the subject. "So, what's going on with the spot? Those niggas you got over there taking care of your business?"

"Yeah, they're doing their thing. But remember, it's still your spot, so anytime you ready to go back, just let me know."

"That's what's up," I said. Then I switched the conversation again and asked him how he had been since Trina was gone.

"Yo man, it's been hard as hell because I'd been fucking with her for a couple of years. I mean, she was like my right hand. She did shit for me my wife wouldn't even do."

"I'm feeling you. So, have you talked to any of her peoples since that shit went down?"

"Yeah, I talked to her moms a couple of times since then. I even went by there to drop off some money, since the family didn't have enough dough to pay for her funeral."

"Did she have any kids?"

"Nope, she sure didn't."

"So, whatchu gon' do now? I mean, are you still trying to find out who those niggas were that came through there, busting their pistols off at us and murdering her?" I watched his facial expression this time, but this nigga didn't flinch. He held his composure to a tee and played the part. I knew one thing: If Trina had not warned me about this clown-ass nigga, I would've been 'round there ready to kill somebody else for him. Not anymore, though, because this nigga was next on my list.

"I got a few cats on the lookout for me. And they know a lot of people, so somebody is bound to throw some names around. Soon as they do, I'm gon' be on them."

"Well, just let me know when you find out who they were because I want to get them myself. Those niggas tried to kill me along with Trina, so my beef is personal." I stood to leave.

Mike stood up too. "Yo, son, thanks for everything, man," he said and hugged me.

When the nigga patted me on my back I almost got sick to my stomach, but I stuck to the script. "You know I'ma always have your back," I replied with assurance and stepped back. "Well, let me get out of here." I turned to leave.

"A'ight. Well, hit me up as soon as you hear something from your cousin."

"I will," I told him and then I dipped out of there.

Seth

It Is What It Is

It seemed like the farther I got away from Mike's crib, the better my stomach felt. What really fucked me up inside was how sincere that nigga acted when I questioned him about still searching for the niggas who murdered Trina. And when that nigga told me that he was, that sealed the deal for me. That nigga was as good as gone in my eyes. The quicker I could cut off his oxygen supply, the better off I'd be.

The fifteen grand Mike gave me went straight into my stash. Right before I closed the metal box back up, I took one last look at my dough and smiled. "I'm gon' get me and Sam a lot of expensive shit with you!" I commented before I closed the top.

Sam called me exactly at six-thirty like she said she would, and she had a lot of shit to talk about, too.

"I just found out that they're gonna let me out

at eight o'clock in the morning, so I want you to be outside, front and center."

"A'ight. So, how was your day?"

"It was very boring. I had to see my counselor and the case manager, and we had to sit in this group meeting for three hours, so you know I wasn't too happy about that."

"Well, it's over now, so don't even sweat it."

"I know. You're right," she agreed. "So, whatchu been doing?"

"I had a meeting with Mike today, and then I ran a few errands for my moms, but that's it."

"What was Mike talking about?"

"Nothing much. I just went over to his crib and got some dough he owed me."

"So when am I going to spend it?"

"Soon, baby, soon."

"Well, can you take me out to lunch tomorrow after I take care of my business?"

"Come on now, Sam. You know I'll take you any-where you want to go."

"Well, can we go out of the country?" she asked me and then giggled.

"Out of the country?" Thoughts started racing through my head.

"Yes, I would love to get the hell away from here."

"And go where?" I coached her along to see where she was going with this.

"I don't know. But I'll tell you that anywhere beats here, especially since your P.O. is going to be breathing down both of our necks to keep us from being together."

"Don't worry about her. I got that under control."

"Yeah, I hope so, because I'm telling you right now if that bitch ever try to run up on me, or try to get my P.O. to violate me behind some dumb shit, I am gon' fly off the motherfucking handle and beat her ass."

"Calm down, 'cause you ain't gon' have to do none of that shit. Believe me, I'm working something out as we speak, so we are going to be a'ight."

"Look, I understand all of that, but I ain't gon' stop looking over my shoulder until we are far away from that bitch. Quiet as it's kept, if I had enough heart, I would walk out of this halfway house right now and I would never look back."

"Where would you go?" I asked her again.

"Probably somewhere where I couldn't get extradited back into the states, like Mexico or Cuba."

"You'd go there?"

"You damn right I would. To get away from all this shit around here, I would do it in a heartbeat," Samantha replied earnestly.

I sat back and thought about the possibility of that happening. I also thought about the chances of us getting caught, which were slim to none. I figured if we traveled to Mexico, all we had to do was cross the border, and that couldn't be hard.

Right when the pay phone was about to disconnect our fifteen-minute call, she asked me if she could call right back. I told her yeah, so we hung up, and within seconds we were right back where we had left off. For the next five phone calls, she wanted to talk about all the things we were going to do on her first weekend pass. She sounded so excited. If she knew like I knew, she hadn't experienced the type of excitement I was about to introduce her to.

After my last call with Samantha ended, I called Maxine because she blew my phone up the entire time we were talking. She sent me a couple of text messages, basically saying that she was not stupid and that she knew I was either laid up fucking another ho or I was on the phone with that bitch Samantha, and if she found out either was true, I was going to wish that I had never met her. Another message said that I'd better have a damn good reason why I was not at her house right now and that if I didn't call her with an explanation in the next ten minutes, she was going to have the U.S. Marshals at my door before I could blink my eyes. After I read her insane-ass messages, I got her silly ass on the phone.

"What's your damn problem?" I snapped.

"Where are you?" she asked, instead of answering my question.

"I'm at home."

"Well, why didn't you answer your house phone when I just tried to call?"

"That was because my moms was on it," I lied.

"I called your phone too and you didn't answer that one either," she screamed.

"Maxine, will you please calm down and stop yelling?"

"And why should I do that? It seems like when I yell and go off on your ass, you start acting like you got some damn sense!"

"Listen, Maxine, there is no need for all this. Just so you know, I was not out in the street fucking a ho, and I wasn't on the phone with Samantha."

"What were you doing then?"

"I was 'sleep part of the time, and then when I

got up, I jumped straight in the shower. I didn't notice you called me until after I came back into my room to get dressed."

"That sounds like a bold-faced lie!"

"Baby, I swear I am not lying to you. Wanna ask my moms? She'll tell you the same thing."

"No, I don't want to ask her anything because you'd probably get her to lie for your ass!"

I laughed to myself because she was right. My moms would lie for me in a minute and especially to Maxine, because she couldn't stand her.

"Listen, just tell me what I can do to make it up to you." I hoped this would calm her silly ass down.

"Don't play stupid with me, Seth! You know I wouldn't be bitching at you if you were where you were supposed to be."

"So, whatchu telling me is that I'm supposed to be at your house?"

"Exactly."

"A'ight, I'll be over there in a few minutes. Just let me get my moms situated."

"Seth, what time are you leaving?"

"Give me an hour."

"OK, but you better not be here a minute after that."

"A'ight."

Two seconds after I hung up with Maxine, I hopped my ass in the shower because I knew she was going to inspect me as soon as I walked through her front door. I made sure I had the Irish Spring smell on me and that it was strong, too. Of course, I fucked her real good and sent her silly ass to bed, but what she didn't know was our little rendezvous were about to come to an end.

Seth

Girl Fight

When I woke up the next morning, I saw Maxine going through the call log on my phone, so I snapped on her ass and asked her what the fuck she was doing. She got on the defensive, and instead of answering my question, she started throwing questions at me about what numbers belonged to who. Why was I on the phone with this person for this amount of time? The questions kept coming one after the other. When I got tired of listening to her ass, I immediately shut her down.

"Wait a minute," I shouted. "How the fuck you gon' question me about my shit? That's my moth-erfucking phone. You don't pay that bill, I do! I told you before to keep your hands off of it, but I see you ain't gon' be satisfied until I go upside your fucking head!"

"Do it, Seth! Do it!" she snapped back. Before I

knew it, she was standing over me while I was sitting up in the bed.

"You really want me to go back to jail, don't you?" I asked her with the most agitated expression I could muster. I mean, I was angry as a motherfucker. I honestly wanted to bash her damn head in, but I knew that if I put my hands on her, I was surely going back to jail. Instead of feeding into her shit, I got out of the bed, got dressed, grabbed all my things, and left. I didn't say anything the whole time, and she was pissed. Maxine threw so much shit around the house, I knew it was gonna take her at least a couple of days to pick up all the broken plates, vases, and the glass from the picture frames. She'd be all right, though. Ol' dumb bitch!

I hopped in my car and drove to the downtown part of Norfolk, since I had to pick Samantha up. It was 7:45 AM, so I stopped at IHOP and ordered her some takeout. I knew she loved herself a good cheesy omelet, so I ordered the steak and cheese omelet and told them to stick a cup of sour cream on the side. I also told them to give me a cup of freshly squeezed orange juice. Sam loved it cold, so I made sure they added a few cubes of ice as well. After everything was prepared, they packed it up in boxes and sent me on my way.

When Samantha came outside of the halfway house, she looked like a breath of fresh air. You could tell that she was fresh out the joint with her light, clear skin and long, flowing hair. Even though she picked up a few pounds from eating Ramen noodles, it went straight to her thighs and ass. I said it on the day she came home and we met at the hotel. Boy, did we have fun. When she got in my car she gave me a slow, wet kiss on the lips. My dick got hard instantly.

"Damn, mommie, you're getting my dick hard as a rock." I smiled.

I guess she didn't believe me because she reached down to my crotch and started rubbing her hand back and forth across my dick. "You sure weren't lying," she said.

"I told you," I replied, and then I put the car in gear and drove off.

"What's this?" Sam asked and picked up the IHOP bag from the floor in front of her.

"I picked you up a steak and cheese omelet with a side of sour cream and toast."

She smiled even harder. "Ahhh, you remembered how much I loved omelets."

"Come on now, Ma. You know I remember everything about you."

Still cheesing, she kissed me again and opened the Styrofoam container. While Samantha enjoyed her food, I found myself watching her every move. She acted like she was so happy and at peace. However, that feeling she had came to an abrupt end when I pulled up in the parking lot of the Social Security building and parked my car. Out of nowhere, Maxine snatched the driver's side door of my car open and started swinging on me.

"You lied to me!" she screamed, throwing blow after blow. "You said you wasn't gonna fuck with her! But you did it anyway. Then you disrespect me by having that bitch in a car I co-signed for your ass! I am sick of your shit!"

I didn't see Samantha hop out of the passenger seat because I had my head buried in the steering wheel, trying to stop Maxine from hitting me in my face. I recovered the instant Samantha pulled Maxine from off me.

"Bitch, what's wrong with you? You don't be putting your motherfucking hands on my man!" Samantha yelled at the top of her lungs, simultaneously slamming Maxine against the back door of my car.

Hearing the tone of Samantha's voice made me open my eyes to see what was going on. As soon as I regained my sight, I saw both Maxine and Samantha going for what they knew. Samantha had Maxine pinned down with one hand and punched her in the face with the other. Maxine was getting a few good punches in herself, but it didn't do enough damage to get Samantha off her. When I saw a small crowd gather around with a security guard in the midst, I rushed over and proceeded to break them up.

"Let her go, Samantha. She ain't worth it. You know she can get you locked back up for this shit!" I tried to reason with Sam, hoping she would release Maxine from her grip.

"Fuck this bitch! She ain't got no right running up on us like this," Sam panted.

"Oh, don't try to talk to your convict bitch now! It's too late, 'cause both of y'all's asses are going back to jail as soon as the police get here," Maxine yelled.

"Shut up, bitch! I am so tired of hearing your fucking mouth!" Samantha tried to muffle Maxine's mouth with her fist but when Maxine bit down on

Samantha's hand, Sam went bananas. "Owww, this fucking bitch is biting me!"

"Maxine, let her go," I demanded.

"If y'all don't break this up, I'm gon' call the police," the young black security guard warned us.

"This bitch is trying to bite a plug out of my fucking hand," Samantha screamed in anguish as she continued to pound the hell out of Maxine's face with her other hand.

"Help me, man! Help me break them up," I pleaded with the guy.

"Grab her," he said, pointing to Sam. "And I'll get her," he said, pointing to Maxine.

It took us a while, but we finally got them separated. Samantha's hand was pretty bruised up by Maxine's teeth, but Maxine's face looked a lot worse and she had scratches, along with black and blue marks, all around her mouth. Both of her eyes were black, and her hair was all over the place. Samantha had fucked her up.

"Say goodbye to your freedom, because both of y'all convicts are going back to jail today," she threatened while she was fixing her clothes.

"Shut the fuck up, bitch!" Sam yelled over my shoulders. "You're just mad because Seth doesn't want you and I just whipped your ass!"

"He ain't gon' want you either, after I get through with your ass!"

"Don't talk about it, bitch! Be about it!" Sam snapped, getting hyped all over again.

"Y'all gotta break this up or else I'ma call the police," the security guard said again.

Maxine said, "I want you to call them. While

you're at it, tell them I am a U.S. Federal Probation Officer, this man right here is one of my parolees, and when I was trying to make an arrest, his convict girlfriend here attacked me."

"Bitch, you're lying! You attacked him first," Sam said with rage.

"Yeah, Maxine, why you lying?" I interjected.

"You're a P.O., for real?" the security guard asked her.

"Yes, I am. Here's my badge." She handed him an ID with her face and credentials plastered all over it. Once he scanned over all the information printed on her I.D., he handed it back to her and said, "Do you need me to help you make an arrest?"

Before she answered, I looked at this nigga like he was fucking crazy. I mean, did he actually think that I was going to make her job easier by letting him take me into custody? Was this fake-ass, non-gun-toting nigga stupid or something? Before he could make a move, I settled the whole thing by saying, "Maxine, before you answer this cat's question, I just want you to think about the repercussions he is going to face if he puts his hands on me. Now, you know I ain't nothing to be fucked with, and I would seriously hurt him if you don't send him on his merry way."

Maxine stood still and acted like she was contemplating taking this guy up on his offer, so I reminded her again that if the nigga touched me, I was going to lay him out on the ground. I told Samantha to get back in the car and I followed her.

The security guard stepped aside when I started the ignition, but Maxine refused to move. "Trust me, you can run but you can't hide," she said. "Remember, I got eyes all over the place." She kicked a huge dent in the driver's side door with her boots. When I pulled off, she got on her phone and started dialing numbers.

"Don't go to your mother's house because the U.S. Marshals will be waiting for you," she warned me.

Seth

The Real Wifey

Samantha complained about her hand the whole time I was driving, and I swear I wanted to tell her to shut the fuck up, even though I knew that wouldn't have been the right thing to say under the circumstances. What she needed was a first aid kit or something. I pulled over to the nearest drugstore and got everything I figured she would need to medicate and bandage her wound. Afterward we rode down to Lafayette Park, found a parking spot by the tennis courts, and sat there trying to figure out what we were going to do.

"What's going through your mind?" I asked her right after I shut off the ignition.

"I'm just trying to figure out what I am going to do. I mean, I know the U.S. Marshals are going to be waiting on me when I get back to the halfway house, which makes me not want to go back there."

"If you don't want to go back, I won't take you."

"But where else am I going to go? Those people are going to put out an APB if I don't show up. And not only that, if I go back there today without a copy of my application from the SSI office and a receipt from the DMV showing them I'd been there, they are going to railroad my ass for real."

"So whatchu wanna do?"

Frustrated and confused, Samantha started crying. "Seth, I don't know what I want to do. Shit would've been a lot easier for me if you hadn't fucked with that bitch from the beginning. But, nah, you had to play big dawg and act like you were a fucking lover or something. And now I'm sitting here on pins and needles, trying to figure out if your stalker bitch is going to rat us out."

"Trust me, she ain't gon' rat us out."

"Trust you? Come on now, Seth. That sounds like a joke." She wiped her tears.

"Listen, I know I fucked up and I do a lot of shit without thinking about the consequences. But believe me, I'm about to turn all of this shit around." I pulled my BlackBerry out of its holster and dialed Maxine's number.

Samantha sat there in awe, not knowing what to say. I really didn't know what to say either, but as soon as Maxine answered her phone, the words came out of nowhere. I started by telling her how I would like to sit down and have a talk with her before she did something she was going to regret. Then I mentioned to her how sorry I was about how everything went down and that if there was any way I could make it up to her, I needed her to give me the chance to do it. Unfortunately, she wasn't as receptive as I anticipated. She started screaming through the phone like she was out of her mind and told me that if we didn't turn ourselves in to her office within the hour, she was going to have our faces plastered all over the six o'clock news.

"Come on now, Maxine. I know we can work this out without bringing the marshals into it."

"That bitch of yours attacked me and fucked my face up. Do you really think I am going to let her get away with it?"

"Look, I know you're upset, but I'm telling you right now, bringing in the marshals ain't gon' do nothing but add fuel to the fire," I warned her.

"Seth, do you think I give a fuck about you telling my supervisor about my relationship with you? I already know my career is over. So you are talking to somebody who has nothing else to lose. See, you betrayed me. You broke my heart. Then, on top of that, you lied in my face, knowing goddamned well you had every intention of getting back with her. That's why I am going to do everything in my power to make sure you regret you ever screwed around on me."

"So, you're telling me that there's no way I can make this right?"

"Seth, the damage is done."

"I understand all of that, but you're telling me that I can't make this right?"

"What could you possibly do to make it right?"

"I got a few things in mind."

"Like what? Let me hear one of them."

"Can we talk about this in person?"

"What's wrong? What, you can't talk around her?"

"She's not even around me."

"Where is she?"

"I dropped her off at one of her friends' houses until I can get shit straight with you."

"Oh, so since she's not around, you want to call. You got some nerve."

"Listen, Maxine, you and I could go on and on about how I betrayed you, but the fact of the matter is, you still love me. I know you want us to be together, so let's stop all this nonsense so we can sit down and try to work this thing out."

"It's too late for all that, Seth."

"No, it's not, so stop saying it."

"Seth, what do you want me to say?"

"I want you to say you'll give me another chance." She fell silent. I said, "Did you hear me?"

"Yes, I hear you."

"So, whatchu gon' do, because we need to make things right."

"Where are you?" she asked calmly.

"I'm in Hampton," I lied.

"Well, meet me at my apartment in the next thirty minutes."

"A'ight, I can do that. But let me ask you something."

"What's that?"

"Did you call the marshals on us?"

"Why?"

"Because I need to know."

She sighed heavily and said, "No, not yet."

"So, who were you calling when I pulled off in the car?"

"I was calling the marshals' office, but when I

couldn't get in touch with the person I was calling, I hung up."

"Let me ask you this."

"What?"

"Why did you lie to that security guard and tell him that Samantha attacked you because you were trying to arrest me?"

"Did you think I was going to tell him that we were lovers? That I was upset, started attacking you, and she got mad and jumped in it?"

"Why not? That is what happened."

"So what? He didn't need to know that."

"Yeah, a'ight."

"Are you coming or what?"

"Yeah, I'll be there."

"All right."

Immediately after I got off the phone, Samantha looked at me with the most vicious expression she could muster. I asked, "What's wrong with you?"

"So, you're really going to go see her?"

I started the ignition. "Yeah, I got to."

"No, you don't."

"Yes, I do," I said. I put the car in DRIVE and drove off.

"What are you going to do with me?"

"I'm gonna drop you off at the DMV so you can handle your business."

"And how am I going to get back to the halfway house?"

"I'ma give you some dough so you can catch a cab."

"So, you gon' leave me, just like that?" she snapped.

"What else do you want me to do, Sam? You know I got to go and see her so I can iron all this shit out."

"But what about us?"

Confused by the way she worded the question, I asked, "What about us? Whatchu mean?"

"You gon' go back to her?"

"Hell, nah! Are you crazy? I'm not ever fucking with her again. I told you it's about us, and that's how it's going to be."

"What are y'all gon' talk about when you see her?"

"If you wanna know the truth, I am gonna go sit down with her and sell her another dream. I am going to tell her that I'm not gonna ever see you again and that she and I are going to be exclusive from this point on."

"Oh, my God! You're making me sick to my stomach." Sam buried her face in her hands.

"Look, Sam, I know you don't want to hear all of this, but making her think that I am going to be with her again is the only way to get her off our backs until I can come up with a way to escape from this place. I don't know how she managed to follow us without me seeing her, but she did. So, I know she'll do it again, and I can't chance it."

"What does that mean?"

"It means that we're gonna have to lay low for a few days without seeing each other."

"No way that that's gonna happen!"

"Sam, baby, trust me; it's only for the best."

"What am I going to do in the meantime?"

"Don't worry. We're gonna talk to each other. We're just not gonna be able to see one another."

"But for how long?"

"Listen, I'm working on some shit right now, and if everything goes according to plan, we are going to be some rich-ass motherfuckers. And when that happens, I'm gon' snatch you out of that halfway house and we're going across the border."

"You're talking about Mexico?"

"Yep. But don't tell nobody. Not even one of those bitches at the halfway house."

"Shit, I promise I ain't gon' tell nobody," she said and finally smiled.

My meeting with Maxine was going fairly well until she got pissed when she said something about Samantha and I jumped to her defense. "I see this little arrangement of ours isn't going to work."

"What do you mean?" I asked her.

"I noticed that every time I say something about her, you always correct me or jump to her defense. I mean, look at my face. She did this to me. But you didn't jump to my defense about this."

"I did say something to her about it," I lied.

Maxine chuckled in a cynical way. "Did you fuck her?"

"How did I have time to fuck her when I'd just picked her up?"

"I'm talking about before then."

"Maxine, today was my first time seeing her," I said with a straight face.

"Well, I'ma give you one more chance, Seth. And I swear, this is your last time. You better tell that bitch it's over."

"I already did."

"When?"

"Before I dropped her off at her friend's house."

"I don't believe that."

"Well, I did."

After I dropped more lies on her, telling her how much I loved her and that I was stupid for messing up what we had, I could tell that she really wanted to believe me. But since I had damaged our trust so much, I was gonna have to do a lot of showing and proving. After our little chat, I talked her into letting me bathe her in the shower, you know, to take the edge off. When she encouraged me to hop in there with her, I knew I had her right back where I wanted her. I pulled out a pocket camera I bought on the way and pressed the record button. I was getting some real good footage and I had her talking her ass off about our relationship. She just didn't know she had incriminated the hell out of herself. And boy, did it bring me much pleasure.

Seth

Plan A

Maxine took off work for two weeks so the injuries on her face could heal, which meant she was all up my ass. I couldn't breathe for nothing in the world. She was everywhere I went, and it was getting on my nerves. I couldn't even go over my mom's house without her tagging along. I told her that I needed to take care of some business with Mike. Now she wasn't too happy about it, but I told her that this was something that I really needed to take care of and that she couldn't go.

"What time are you coming back?" she asked.

"Give me a couple of hours, a'ight?"

She sighed and said, "All right."

When she gave me the green light, I kissed her on the lips and hauled ass. As soon as I got into my car, it felt like I had just gotten released from jail. I mean, this bitch was smothering the hell out of me, and I had to find a way to get the fuck away from her, and I was gon' have to find it quickly before Samantha gave up on me. Today made five whole days since I had seen or talked to her. My mom had been keeping me informed of what was going on with her. Just yesterday, she told me that Sam found a job at Ziespot clothing store in MacArthur Mall. I drove downtown so I could see it for myself. Mind you, the whole time I was driving, I was looking through my rearview mirror. I was not going to let Maxine's stupid ass mess up this surprise visit, because I had some making up to do.

When I first walked into the store I didn't see Samantha, so I walked up to the lady behind the counter and asked if Sam was working. She told me yes, but she had stepped out for a minute to go to the bathroom.

I asked, "Which way are the bathrooms?"

"When you go out of the store, turn right. After the third store, you'll see the signs on your right."

"A'ight, thanks." I left the store, but guess what? I didn't have to travel far at all, because as soon as I walked out of the store I saw Sam walking right toward me. I rushed up to her before she could get back into the store. "Miss me?" I asked and grabbed her into my arms.

"No," she said, trying to play hard.

I started kissing her all over her face. "Yes, you do, so stop fronting!"

"Get off of me, because I know you've been with her." She tried to push me away.

"Sam, stop trying to push me away. I've been missing the hell out of you, so don't do this to me.

Baby, you have no idea what I've been through these last few days."

"No, I don't, but I'm sure you're going to tell me."

"Listen, we don't have time for that right now. Tell me what time you get off."

"Tonight I get off at eight. But tomorrow and Saturday, I'm gon' have to work until we close at ten o'clock."

"What time do you come in?"

"Tomorrow and Saturday, I gotta be here at two o'clock."

"A'ight. Well, check this out. I want you to be prepared to leave the halfway house for good on Saturday."

"Where are we going?"

"We're going across the Mexican border."

"Stop playing with me, Seth."

"Sam, I am dead serious. When you leave the halfway house on Saturday to come to work, make sure you take all your important documents and paperwork with you. Don't leave none of that shit behind."

"What about all my letters?"

"Yeah, bring that too. Don't leave any kind of paperwork behind."

"What about the clothes you bought me?"

"Fuck that shit! With all the money I'm about to take from that nigga who tried to get me killed, I could buy you a Saks Fifth Avenue."

"Wait a minute, what are you talking about? Who tried to kill you?"

"Not now, Sam; this ain't the place to talk about it."

She wasn't going for that excuse. She wanted to

know what was going on and why somebody wanted to kill me. She pulled me to the wall alongside the next store, but before she made me talk, she looked around to make sure no one was within five feet of us. "Seth, you are not leaving out of here until you tell me what happened," she demanded.

I hesitated because I really didn't want to scare her and have her start to act paranoid every time she was in my company. I wanted her to always feel safe around me, so I was very leery about telling her. But then she mentioned to me that I should never keep anything from her because of what we had been through, and then I reconsidered. "A'ight, this is what happened," I began. "Remember I told you about the cat named Mike I was doing business for?"

"Yeah, I remember. What about him?"

"Well, after all the money I made for this nigga, he hired a couple of cats to kill me so they could take all the money I made for myself."

"But why would he do that?"

"Because I found out that he tricked up millions of dollars he owed to some big-time motherfuckers. They gave him another shipment and basically told him that if he wanted to keep his life, he had to work the dope off for free. Since he couldn't move all of it by himself, he got myself, Jay, and several other dudes to help him move the dope. When he figured he was finished with a nigga, he'd either get you killed or knocked off by the police. Either way he looked at it, you were gone, so that gave him access to run up in your spot and take your stash."

"What exactly did he do to you?"

"Well, one night he asked me to do a job for him,

and I didn't know it until later, but he was setting me up to get killed. But his little mistress got the bullet instead."

Stunned, Samantha asked, "Did you kill her?"

"No, baby, I didn't. She got caught up in the cross-fire while those niggas was shooting at me. Before she died in my arms, she told me everything I'm telling you."

Samantha stood against the wall in disbelief. "Oh, my God! And I thought you got yourself into something when I found out how crazy Maxine was, but this one takes the cake."

I put my arms around her and said, "Listen, I know this is probably too much for you right now, but just remember that this is gonna all be over real soon and then we'll be able to leave this place and never look back."

"Have you figured out how you're gonna get him back?"

"Yeah, I've run a few things through my mind, but nothing's concrete."

"Have you figured out where you're gonna do it?"

"Well, he owns this strip club in Portsmouth called Magic City, so I was thinking about getting him right when he was about to leave the club. Then I figured too many police be around there, so that wouldn't be a smart move."

"So, whatchu gon' do about your mother? Is she going with us?"

"Nah, baby, she can't go 'cause she'll slow us down. But I'ma leave so much dough behind, she's gonna be a'ight."

"Baby, I love you!" She threw both of her arms around me.

"I love you too, mommie."

Once the plan was set in motion with Samantha, I figured that there was only one thing left for me to do. After I left the mall, I called Mike. He was the last piece to my puzzle, and as soon as I could repay him for what he did to me, I'd be able to move on.

"What's good, son?" he asked.

"Yo, Mike, I just called to tell you that I just got off the phone with my cousin, and his peoples said that if we could fly down there this weekend, they'd make it worth our while."

"A'ight, so when you want to leave?"

"Well, I'ma call the airlines right now and see if I can book a flight leaving Saturday evening."

"A'ight. Well, let me know if you can get one and how much it costs."

"A'ight."

Seth

Biting Off More Than I Can Chew

After I got off the phone with Mike, I called several airlines and found the perfect flight plan to use for bait. The lady at Southwest gave me the schedule of flight 3401, leaving out of Norfolk at 8:17 and flying nonstop to Miami. She also told me that this last-minute, round-trip reservation would be five hundred dollars. I thanked her for her time and got Mike right back on the phone.

"Ay yo, son, I just booked my flight."

"For real?"

"Yeah." I gave him the flight details.

"How much was it?" Mike asked.

"Five hundred."

"Word?"

"Yep."

"What time does the flight leave?"

"It's a nonstop flight and it leaves at eight-seventeen."

"A'ight. Well, I'ma get Lacy to call them and purchase my ticket right now."

"A'ight, I'ma holler at you later."

"OK."

I decided to go by my mom's crib to see how she was doing, since I was by myself. All the other times I came through, I had Maxine next to me, so we couldn't talk like we really wanted to. When I got into the house, she was in the kitchen, pouring herself a cup of coffee. As usual, I gave her the "I love you, Ma," spiel and a kiss, but this time she wouldn't let me near her. She pushed me right out of the way when I tried to kiss her.

"Dag, Ma, why you pushing me away?"

"We need to talk," she said and took a seat at the kitchen table.

"About what?"

"Have a seat," she said. After I sat, she said, "What in the world happened to Maxine's face, Seth? Now, you know I raised you better than that. I am not gonna tolerate no man putting their hands on a woman. I don't care how crazy or possessive she is, because if that's the case then you can leave her."

"Ma, calm down!" I grabbed her hand. "You know I don't be putting my hands on women."

"Then what happened to her?"

"She and Samantha got into a fight. Somehow Samantha got the best of her and beat her up."

Shocked, she said, "You have got to be kidding me. Samantha jumped on Maxine and beat her up?"

"Yes ma'am." I laughed.

"And when did this happen?"

"A couple of days ago."

"And you mean to tell me that Maxine didn't get her locked up for it?"

"She was getting ready to, but I talked her out of it."

My moms shook her head in disbelief. "I'll tell you the truth; I thought I'd never sit here and hear you tell me that you had two women fighting like cats and dogs over you."

"Ma, it ain't even like that."

"Oh it's like that. And if you know like I know, you'd better be trying to figure out a way to prevent it from happening again. The next time, somebody will probably get killed."

"Trust me, there isn't going to be a next time."

"And how you supposed to keep that from happening?"

"I'm working that out right now as we speak," I assured her and then we went into another conversation. I sat around with her for about an hour and then told her I'd be back to check on her later. On my way out the door, she gave me a kiss and that made me happy.

Seth

Gotta Take One Step At A Time

From the time I got up Saturday morning, I had been feeling kind of weird. I knew it was because I was about to leave this place behind for good, so all I could do was take everything in stride. While I was getting dressed, I suggested to Maxine that she go out and pamper herself at an all-day spa while I went out and handled some business with Mike. She was reluctant to get an all-day treatment, but she did say that she'd go to a spa that provided a three-hour special. I handed her five hundred-dollar bills and told her to have fun.

"Call me when you're done, and that way I'll be able to let you know when I can break away from Mike."

"OK, I can do that," she assured me. Within twenty minutes of our conversation, she was in her car and on her way down the road.

I left right after she did, but I went in the opposite direction and headed to my mother's house. Thank God she wasn't home, because there was no way I would have been able to explain to her that I was on my way to murder a nigga and then I was leaving town for good. When I got into the house, I went straight up to my bedroom and grabbed all my money from out of the vent. Then I grabbed a couple of shirts, three pairs of my favorite jeans, some boxers, T-shirts, and a pair of sneakers, and threw all of it into a large duffel bag. I also grabbed a couple pictures of my mom and a few other family members and stuffed them into the duffel bag, too. After I did all the necessary packing, I went into my mother's room. I grabbed one of her personal deposit slips from her bank and slipped it into my pocket. I wanted be able to deposit some dough into her account later on today, before I left town for good. When I was leaving, I stood in the foyer and turned around to look at all the pictures my moms had on the wall and soaked it all in. I did this because I wanted to remember everything just like it was. When I had this mental picture in my mind, I said goodbye and walked out the door.

Once I had everything packed up in my car, I drove straight to a used car lot right up the street. It was called E-Z Autos, and the cat who owned it was crooked as a motherfucker. I think he was an Arab. I knew that all I had to do was bring him at least forty-five hundred in cash and he'd put me right in something suitable to my taste. I didn't have to show him a pay stub or let him run a credit check. He didn't give a damn about none of that, and all he wanted was to see the green. After we made the trade, I signed a few promissory notes for the balance of the car, along with some legal documents for the DMV and a form stating that I would purchase car insurance as long as the car had a lien on it. After I did all of that, homeboy put me in a 2002 Land Rover. It was black in color and it was spacious as hell. I figured it would be perfect for my travels, so that was why I picked it. After homeboy stuck a set of thirty-day plates on my truck, I was set to go. "Hey man, can I leave my car here until later?" I asked.

"Yeah, sure. Just park it over here behind the building," he said, pointing to the exact location he wanted me to go. After I parked, I was out of there.

The next stop was my mother's bank, which was Bank of America. She'd been banking there for a long time, and I remembered when she first got the account, back in the day, when it was called NationsBank. When I walked into the lobby, one of the tellers recognized me and asked me to come to her window.

"How are you doing today?" the young black chick asked.

I smiled. "I'm doing good, and yourself?"

"I'm fine. Now, how can I help you?"

"I would like to deposit this amount in my mother's account," I said and handed the chick fifty grand.

"Boy, this sure is a lot of money," she commented.

I smiled again. "I know."

"You sure you didn't rob another bank?" she teased.

"If I did, I wouldn't have brought it here, because I would be on my way out of town."

She chuckled. "Now, that makes sense. Wait right here; I'm gonna have to send this through one of our currency machines."

"A'ight." I watched her walk over a few feet to a small gray machine. A couple of seconds later, she fed the machine every bill I gave her until it stopped running and the sum totaled fifty grand. I saw the numbers big as day.

"OK, so you want to deposit fifty thousand dollars into your mother's account?"

"Yes, ma'am."

"All right." She started typing away at her computer keys. Next, she separated the twenties, the fifties, and hundreds and then placed them in labels. She stuck them all in canisters and dropped them into a drawer right below her top drawer. Afterward, she printed out a deposit receipt and handed it to me. "Here you go," she said.

"Thank you so much," I said and left.

Throughout today's journey, Maxine made it her business to call me every thirty minutes, it seemed. She called me while I was at my mom's crib and she called me while I was at the used car lot and I answered my phone both times. When I was inside the bank I couldn't answer my phone, so she started calling me back to back until I answered.

"Where you at? And why haven't you been answering my calls?"

"Maxine, I was inside a bank and you know they don't allow you to be on your cell phone when you're inside their lobby."

"Whatchu doing at a bank?"

"Maxine, I was with my mother," I lied.

"Well, where is she at? I don't hear her in the background."

"That's because I'm outside and she's still in the bank."

"Seth, don't be lying to me."

"For these last few days, have I given you any reason not to believe me? I mean, I have been with you every single day, and the only time I stepped away was for a couple of hours, to take care of some business. I told you I needed to get my money straight so we could open up our business. That's it. So get all that dumb shit out of your head. I am not out here doing nothing wrong and I am not with Samantha, so give me a break, please."

Hearing the frustration in my voice, she softened her tone. "So, how long are you going to be out?"

"Well, I just got off the phone with Mike and he wants me to take a quick run with him to Roanoke so he can pick up some money from a couple of cats out there."

"But what does that have to do with you?"

"The thing is, he doesn't want to go out there by himself, just in case those niggas are thinking about doing something stupid."

"How long is that going to take?"

"Probably about a couple of hours, at the most. If we leave about five or six o'clock, then I should be back no later than ten."

"Baby, I don't know about that. That doesn't sound like a good idea."

"Come on now, Maxine. After I make this trip with him, you won't ever hear me mention his name again. I promise I won't do another job for him, OK? Is that a deal?"

Maxine hesitated a moment and then she said, "All right. You have a deal."

We talked for a few more minutes and then she told me she had to go because one of the ladies at the spa was waiting to give her a facial. Before we hung up, I gave her the OK to call me as often as she liked, just to prove to her that I wasn't out with Samantha or any other chick. She agreed and then we hung up.

Seth

It's My Time To Shyne

Right after I hung up with Maxine, I called Mike and asked him if he was ready to head out. He acted like he was excited as hell, and I couldn't get that nigga to shut up if I had to. I told him that I'd swing by his spot to pick him up around six-thirty, since our flight didn't leave out until eight o'clock that night. When he agreed, I told him I'd holler at him later.

In the meantime, I decided to get Maxine squared away. I went back to her crib while she was still out and gathered up all the evidence I needed to get her silly ass fired from her job. First, I grabbed a few pictures she had of us posed together at my birthday party, and another one while we were on vacation in Las Vegas and then I attached a letter explaining who I was. I stuck them inside a manila envelope and then I placed the video disc of us making love in the shower in there too, and sealed it. On the front of the envelope I printed *To: Carolyn Granger*. I figured she would be the perfect person to receive the package since she hated Maxine's guts, not to mention, she was on the verge of becoming her supervisor. Then after I put the address on it, I put a couple of postage stamps up there, stuck the envelope under my arm, and exited her crib. The first mailbox I came upon, I dropped it off and then I drove off. By this time on Monday, Maxine would definitely be packing her bags.

Since I had some time to waste, I headed back out to P-Town to see what the spot was looking like. When I pulled up on the other side of the horseshoe and saw the police had it blocked off, I made a U-turn and parked on the opposite side of the street. Then I got out and walked to the other side of Dales Homes on foot. People were standing around all over the place, so I stood among the crowd to see what they were watching. When I saw several big white boys wearing FBI vests walking in and out of Melody's crib, I knew shit was serious. I put my head down and turned around to leave because I didn't want anybody to see me. The last thing I wanted to do was bring attention to myself. Shit, those motherfuckers were probably looking for me. Right after I turned around to leave, Faith was standing right beside me. I ain't gon' lie, she scared the shit out of me.

"Why you always walking up on me like that?"

"I scared you again, huh?"

"You damn right!" I said and started walking.

She started walking alongside me. "I know you're glad you wasn't in there, huh?"

"Come on now, what kind of question is that?"

"You know they been in there for about two hours now?"

"Word?"

"Yep, and they took out a lot of shit, too."

"Who did they arrest?"

"They got those two new guys that just started working over there and they got Melody too."

"But I thought she was their snitch?"

"She wasn't snitching for them. She was a snitch for Portsmouth Police."

"Ahh damn! Well, she fucked up now."

"Yep, she sure is."

"So what's up with Hakeem and Bishop?"

"Ain't nobody seen them since they ran off with them boys' dope."

I laughed. "How much did they run off with?"

"I don't know, but Melody been running her mouth, saying that one of them new boys gave Bishop and Hakeem both two hundred pills. He told them to go on the other side of the horseshoe and catch the sales that were filtering over into Lincoln Park. But when they left, they never came back."

"Ah man, I know Mike was mad about that shit!"

"Yeah, I believe he was, because the very next day, he came out here and all I heard was a whole bunch of commotion inside the house."

"Well, you know what? That's their problem and I'm out of here."

"You think I can hold something before you go, because I know I ain't gon' ever see you again."

"Yeah, you sure can." I pulled out three hundred dollars and handed it to her.

"Damn, I wasn't expecting this much." Faith smiled with excitement.

I smiled back at her and said, "Go take care of your business."

"Shit, ain't no good dope out here. The feds got all the Black Label packed away in a brown paper bag in the back of their car."

"Then you better head on over to Norfolk."

"You know what, Seth? I am so tired of getting high. I really would like to have my life back so I can see my baby girl."

"Where is she?"

"I don't know. I haven't seen her in a couple of years now."

"How old is she?"

"She's going on eight now."

"So whatchu gon' do about it?"

"I want to get clean."

"You sure?"

Faith's eyes got watery. "Yeah, I'm sure."

"A'ight. Well, if you want me to, I can drop you off at a rehab center over in Norfolk."

"You'd do that for me?" Faith smiled again and tears started falling from her eyes.

"Yeah, so wipe your tears and come on." We got out of there.

Seth

Taking Back What Belonged To Me

Seeing the feds shut Melody's spot down made me feel so good that I was out of the game for good. However, I was having an eerie feeling about those same feds running up on Mike before I could get to him. I called Sam and got her to act like she was sick so she could get off work early. When she walked outside the mall to meet me, I ran everything down to her and told her that we needed to get out of there as soon as possible.

"Whose car is this?" she asked, while I was driving.

"I just bought it from E-Z Autos earlier this morning. But I left my car up there, so I'm gon' take you back up there so you can drive it off the lot."

"Where are we going to take it?"

"Let's park it at the airport's parking garage and leave it there."

"All right. Well, let's do this," Sam agreed.

As soon as we got to E-Z Autos, we were there and gone in seconds. The way Sam and I drove, we got to the Norfolk airport in no time. After I parked my car, I hopped out and met Sam at the exit gate. "Get over on the passenger side," I instructed her when I approached the truck.

"What are we going to do now?" she asked, as she slid over to the other seat.

"I don't know, but let me call Mike right now," I said as I drove off.

"Whatchu calling him for?" Sam asked, sounding agitated.

"I just want to feel him out and see if anybody called and told him that the feds ran up in his spot." I dialed his number and from the moment he picked up his line, I scrutinized every word that came out of his mouth.

"What's up, son? You ready?" I asked.

"I don't know if I'm gon' be able to go now, man."

"Why not? What's wrong?" My heart was beating because I knew he was about to tell me about what happened to Melody, and that he was gon' have to bail out of town on his own.

"My wife said she ain't feeling too good, man, and I think she might be getting ready to go into labor."

"You bullshitting!" I was mad as hell. I mean, this shit couldn't be happening at a worse time. What the fuck was I going to do now? I knew the feds were moving in his direction, so I needed to get that paper before they got it.

"No, I'm not."

"When is the baby due?"

"Next week. But, you know babies are gon' come out when they're ready."

"A'ight. Well, I'ma tell you what; I'ma come by there and get my cousin on the phone so you can talk to him, and then you can decide whatchu gon' do from there."

"I'm telling you right now that I'm not gon' leave my wife if she keeps having these pains."

"Oh I understand that, but I'ma still come by there so you can talk to my cousin yourself."

"A'ight, that's cool," Mike replied and then we hung up.

Frustrated, I slammed the phone down.

"What's wrong now?" Sam asked.

"That nigga just told me that he thinks his wife is in labor."

"So, whatchu gon' do now?"

"I'm just gon' have to run up in his crib and get him before the feds do."

"Are you sure you're ready to do that?"

"I ain't got no choice."

While I was in transit, Maxine called me. Samantha sat in the passenger seat, pissed off, but thank God, she didn't say a word.

"Where are you?" she asked me.

"I'm taking care of business." I was short with my reply.

"Is that guy Mike with you?"

"Yeah, why?"

"No reason. I just asked."

"Where are you?"

"I just got in the house, so I'ma take a quick nap

and when I get up, I'ma cook our dinner. Is there something in particular you want to eat?"

"Nah, not really."

"So, you wouldn't care if I made cooked liver and onions?"

"That's cool."

"All right. Well, I am going to let you go."

"A'ight."

"I love you."

"I love you too," I told her and I hung up.

Before I could even put my phone back down, Samantha backhanded me right across my face. "Damn! What was that for?" I yelled.

"I am so sick of you and your bitches!" she snapped.

"Come on now, you know I had to play the role."

"Yeah, whatever!" She turned to face the window.

I didn't bother to say anything else to her for the rest of the drive to Mike's house. As soon as we pulled up in the driveway, I told her to follow me into the house just in case I needed her to handle Lacy. We climbed out of the car and walked up to the front door. Mike greeted us at the door and escorted us back into the den area of the house. When we entered the room, Lacy was lying back on the recliner with a blanket placed on top of her. I said hello and introduced Samantha to them. After all of the formalities were out of the way, I looked back at Lacy and asked her how she was feeling.

"I'm not too well," she told me and then she moaned as if she was having excruciating pains. "I think I am going to have this little girl before the night is over."

"For real!" I said, acting like I was excited for her.

"Y'all have a seat," Mike said. Me and Sam sat down beside each other and then Mike said, "You wanna go ahead and call your cousin?"

Shocked by what he asked me to do, I hesitated for a second, but not long enough for him to notice that something was wrong. "A'ight," I finally said and pulled my phone out.

Samantha sat there, speechless as I pretended to dial a number that supposedly to belong to my fictitious cousin that lived in Miami. While all this was happening, Mike sat across from us and acted like he was waiting patiently to get on the phone. "He answered yet?" he asked me.

My heart started beating uncontrollably. "Nah, his voice mail came on," I told him.

"Why didn't you leave him a voice mail?"

"Because he doesn't listen to his messages," I replied.

Mike stood up from his chair and at the same time his wife Lacy pulled back the blanket covering her. When I looked up and saw a sawed-off shotgun, my eyes almost popped out of my head. I stood to my feet and asked them what the fuck was going on.

"Sit your motherfucking ass down, nigga!" Mike demanded. He pulled a 9 mm Ruger from the back of his pants and aimed it at me.

I looked back at Samantha to see her reaction and when I noticed how scared she looked, I felt helpless as hell. But what was I going to do?

"Didn't he tell you to sit your bitch ass down?" Lacy got to her feet and when I saw how sticky this situation had gotten, I sat back down on their couch.

Meanwhile, Mike had a lot of shit to say. "You

thought you were going to come in here and take my money, huh?"

"Whatchu talking about, Mike?"

He looked at Samantha and said, "Take his gun from him."

When Sam grabbed my pistol, I almost lost it. "What the fuck is going on?"

Sam stood and aimed the pistol at me. "Nigga, did you really think I was gonna leave the country with you? Especially after all the shit I've been through with you? Nigga, you ain't did nothing but cause me a lot of fucking pain. First, it started off with a couple bitches in the street, then you got real greasy and started fucking my sister. But it didn't stop there because while I was locked up, I had to hear about you fucking your P.O., and then I had to fight the bitch. And while all of this is going on, I found out later that you were fucking the bitch Melody too!"

"What the fuck you talking about? That's a lie!"

"Shut the fuck up, Seth!" she interjected. "Mike and Melody was setting your dumb ass up the whole time. But it's all good because after today, I ain't gonna have to worry about your trifling ass no more. Mike told me everything."

I sat there in awe and Mike burst into laughter. "Damn, Seth, I thought you said you were loyal!"

I began to panic so I looked back at Samantha and said, "Look, Sam, you know me and you can work this thing out. We have been through too much to let it go down like this."

"Work it out! Nigga, I ain't working a motherfucking thing out with you! I'm done with your ass for good this time."

"So, you set me up?"

"Yep, I got fed up with your bullshit! After all the shit happened between me, you, and Maxine, I felt like it was time to cut your ass off. I called Mike at the club and told him everything. Then after I spilled the beans on you, Mike turned around and told me everything about the little relationship you and Melody had. I know all about how you were spending all day at her crib, selling dope out her house and fucking her at your leisure."

"It wasn't even like that and he knows it," I said to her but gritted my teeth while looking at Mike.

"You know what, Seth? I could care less how it was. You were fucking her just like you were fucking Maxine, end of story. And now I'm gon' make you pay for it." Sam pulled back on the chamber to load the first bullet.

Watching everything unfold before me, all I could do was think about my mother and how she would feel when she found out that I was dead. And what would be even sadder was when she found out that I had been dealing drugs all over again. "You know he's going to kill you right after he kills me," I warned her.

"Yeah, I know," she said and turned the pistol and fired it at Mike. He fired back twice but he missed Sam by a couple of inches. When he fell to the floor, she kicked the gun away from him.

Lacy's eyes grew two inches when Samantha unloaded my burner on her husband, so she aimed her shotgun at Samantha. Right before Lacy pulled the trigger, I jumped to my feet and knocked it out of her hands. When she tried to grab it off the floor, I got to it first and hit her in the face with the butt of it. It knocked her out cold. But before I could stand up straight, Samantha hit me in the back with one slug after the next. *Boom! Boom! Boom!* I collapsed helplessly on top of Lacy and pain shot through my body like an armored truck. I screamed at the top of my voice. "Uggghhhh, you fucking shot me!"

"Shut the fuck up!" Samantha told me and kicked the shotgun over by the wall. "You thought I was playing with you, huh? Well, I wasn't, so die!" She pulled the trigger once more. When I saw the explosion from the barrel of the gun, I knew that in less than a second I was gone. I closed my eyes and waited for the inevitable. And just like that, I took my last breath.

Samantha

Payback

I stood there and watched Seth take his last breath. Believe it or not, it didn't affect me at all. I actually pushed him off Lacy as if he were an old rag doll. When he fell onto the floor, I helped Lacy up. When she regained consciousness, I had the barrel of my gun pointed right at her head. "Now, we can do this two ways," I said. "You can open up the safe and give me all the money and I can walk out of here, or you can die. Which one is it going to be?"

She started crying. "Please don't kill me and my baby."

"I won't if you open up the safe."

"OK." I walked her over to the first door and waited for her to type in the password and when it clicked and unlocked, my face lit up like a Christmas tree.

"Now, you got one more door," I said. After we entered the first room we walked up to the second door and just like the first time, she keyed in the password. We heard a clicking sound and then it unlocked. I walked into the room, saw all the money piled on top of a wooden pallet, and my heart skipped a beat. All I could think about was how in the hell I was going to get all this dough out the house. I also thought about what I was going to do with Lacy in the process. Seeing her pregnant gave me second thoughts about killing her. But then again, if I decided to let her go, she could point me out in a lineup. Then I'd be facing a life sentence in prison for murder, and that wasn't how I wanted to spend the rest of my life. Without further hesitation, I aimed the barrel of the gun straight at her chest.

She started crying. "Wait, I thought you weren't going to kill me?"

"I lied," I said and pulled the trigger. *Boom! Boom!* She collapsed onto the floor and I stepped right over her.

Before I grabbed the money out of the safe, I picked up the blanket Lacy was using earlier, wrapped the money inside, and carried it out to the truck. One after the other, I loaded each stack into the back of Seth's truck. The shit was heavy as hell, but I got the job done in a flash. Afterward, I wiped down the sofa I was sitting on before everything went down. I also wiped my fingerprints off Seth's gun and placed it in Mike's hands, since Seth had two gunshots in his back. I wanted to make it look like Mike was the one who shot him. I grabbed Mike's gun off the floor and placed it in Seth's hands, since Mike had been shot a couple of times too. Then, after all that switching and moving shit, I closed both doors to the safe because I couldn't afford to give the police the slightest inclination that there had been a robbery. Once I felt my mission was completed, I was gone.

On my way out of there, I drove right by four undercover cop cars. They were following each other, so I knew that they had to be heading to Mike's house, and that scared the hell out of me. I remained calm, though, and continued to look forward until the last car rode by. When the cars were no longer in sight, I took a deep breath and pressed down on the accelerator and got the hell out of Dodge. I could only assume that one of the neighbors called them after they heard the gunshots. I just hoped they didn't see me when I pulled out of there because if they had, it wasn't gonna be long before I got picked up. I guessed I would find out soon enough.

Two days had passed and I hadn't heard anything from anyone except Seth's mother. The poor lady was bawling her eyes out over the phone when she called the halfway house to talk to me. I kept a straight face and pretended to cry too. She told me that the FBI went into a house to arrest Mike but found him dead, along with his wife and Seth. She also told me that the FBI found kilos of drugs in the house so she wanted to know what kind of people he was involved with. I told her I didn't know shit and that she needed to contact Maxine. As soon as I mentioned her name, Mrs. Richardson told me that Maxine called her crying yesterday. She said that she had just gotten fired from her job because

Seth sent her supervisor pictures and a video of them making love. I wanted to laugh my ass off, but I held my composure. After a few more words were exchanged with Seth's mother, I ended the call. Right before I hung up, I told her I put in for a pass to come to his funeral but they denied it. She told me not to worry about it because Seth probably wouldn't want me to remember him that way anyway. I didn't put up a fuss about it. I said OK and told her to take care and we finally hung up.

A week later, I was walking inside MacArthur Mall to go to work and I ran into Maxine coming out. She gritted on me really hard, so I gritted right back on her. She stopped in her tracks and said, "You got something to say to me?"

"If I did, don't you think I would've already said it?" I replied sarcastically.

She walked closer to me. "I know you heard about Seth getting killed."

"What about it?" I asked sarcastically as I gave her a nasty stare.

She smiled and said, "I guess neither one of us ended up with him, huh?"

I smiled right back at her and said, "I guess not." Then I walked off.

Little did she know that I was the one who took his cheating ass out. Too bad she'd never know about his murder and the money I took from him, in addition to the $5.7 million I snatched up from Mike's crib. I was sitting on a gold mine, and I could have cared less about any of that bullshit she was talking about. All I had on my mind was how I was going to spend all that money I had stashed in the basement of my mom's crib.

First and foremost though, I made sure my old roommate Ms. Blair was straight when she went back to Trinidad. That was the least I could do considering she gave me the blueprint on how to take what belonged to me and how to kill a nigga in the process without getting caught. Payback sure feels good! But, being a rich bitch feels even better!

If you enjoyed *A Sticky Situation*,
don't miss Kiki Swinson's

Playing Dirty

and

Notorious

Available now wherever books are sold

Playing Dirty

From the Beginning

"Okay, Yoshi, it's your time," I whispered to myself. I ran my hands over my Chanel pencil skirt to smooth out the wrinkles. Then I turned toward the large bathroom mirror and checked my ass—along with my silver tongue and beautiful face, it was one of my best assets. I stood in the old-fashioned marble courthouse bathroom, making sure I looked as stunning as always before I made my way to the courtroom. My assistant had just texted my BlackBerry to tell me the jury was back with a verdict. The jury had only deliberated for one day. For a defense attorney, that could spell disaster. But that rule stood for regular defense attorneys—and I'd like to think that I was in a class by myself.

The trial had had its moments, but through it all I shined like a star. On the second to last day, I had all but captured the jury in the palm of my hand. I used my half-Korean background and my native Korean tongue to appeal to the two second-generation Asian jurors. My mother would've been so proud. As a proud Korean, she always wanted me to forget that I was half Black. She spoke Korean all the time. It had everything to do with the volatile relationship she had with my father before he packed up and left New York to go back to his hometown in Virginia when I was only eight years old. Him leaving the family devastated my mother, but I was okay with it. I got tired of listening to them fuss and fight all the time. And it seemed like it always got worse on the weekends when he came home drunk.

That wasn't the life my mother's parents had in mind for her after they emigrated all the way from Korea to Brooklyn, New York. I'm sure they felt that if she was going to struggle, then she needed to struggle with her own kind. Not with some African-American scumbag, alcoholic, warehouse worker from Norfolk, Virginia, who only moved to New York City to pursue his dreams of making it big in the music industry. My mother, unfortunately, picked him to father me. When I got old enough to understand, my mother told me that as soon as my grandparents got wind of their relationship, they disowned her. But as soon as my dad packed his shit and left, they immediately came to her rescue and wrote her back into their will. They were so happy that nigga left, they got on their knees and started sending praises to Buddha.

I couldn't care one way or the other. I mean, it wasn't like we were close anyway. From as far back as I could remember, I pretty much did my own thing.

After school I would always go to the library and find a book to read, which was why I excelled in grade school. After graduating from high school, I thought about nothing else but furthering my education in law. I had always aspired to be a TV court judge, so I figured the only way I could ever have my own show was to become an attorney first. So here I was defending my client, the alleged leader of the Fuc-Chang Korean mafia, who was on trial for murder, bribery, and racketeering. Now I knew he was guilty as hell, but I pulled every trick out of the bag to make the jury believe that he wasn't.

"Ms. Lomax, the jury returned its verdict after just one day of deliberation. Are you worried?" a reporter called out as I made my way down the hallway toward Judge Allen's courtroom. A swarm of reporters surrounded me, shoving microphones in my face. I never turned down an opportunity to show up on television.

"A fast verdict is just what I expected. My client is innocent." I smiled, flashing my perfect white teeth and shaking my long, jet black hair. And right after I entered the courtroom, I switched my ass as hard as I could down the middle aisle toward the defense table. All eyes turned toward me. I could feel the stares burning my entire body. My red Chanel suit was an eye-catcher. It showed off my curves and it made me look like a million bucks. When potential clients approach me for representation, they are not surprised to learn that I charge a minimum of $2,500 an hour. They don't even blink when the figure rolls off my tongue. The way they see it, you never put a price on freedom, and with my victory rate, how can they lose?

Right before I took my seat at the defense table, I looked at my client, Mr. Choo, who was shackled like an animal and guarded by courtroom officers. He appeared cool, calm, and collected, unlike the men in black across from him. The prosecutors sat at their table and fiddled with pens, bit nails, and adjusted ties. They looked nervous and frazzled, to say the least. I was just the opposite. In fact, I was laughing my ass off on the inside because I knew I had this case in the bag.

The senior court officer moved to the front of the jam-packed courtroom, ordered everyone to stand, and announced Judge Allen. I looked up at Judge Mark Allen, with his salt-and-pepper balding head and little beady eyes. Mark is what I call him when he's not in his black robe. As a matter of fact, it gets really personal when he and I get together for one of our so-called romantic interludes. Last week was the last time he and I got together, and it was in his chambers. It was so funny because I let him fuck me in his robe with his puny five-inch wrinkled dick. He thought he was the man, too. And when it was all said and done, I made sure I wiped my cum all over the crotch of his slacks. Shit, Monica Lewinsky ain't got nothing on me. I wanted him to know that I had no respect for his authority or his courtroom. After I let him get at me, and I bribed a few of the jurors, all of the calls in the courtroom went my way. The prosecutors never had a chance. . . . It was amusing to watch.

The judge cleared his throat and began to speak. The courtroom was "pin drop" quiet.

"Jury, what say you in the case of the *State of Florida* versus *Haan Choo*?" Judge Allen boomed.

The jury foreperson, a fair-skinned Black woman in her mid-fifties, stood up swiftly, her hands trembling. "'We, the jury, in the matter of the *State of Florida* versus *Haan Choo*, finds as follows: to the charge of first-degree murder . . . not guilty.'"

A gasp resounded through the courtroom. Then the scream of some victim's family members.

"Order!" Judge Allen screamed.

The foreperson continued without looking up from her paper. "'To the charge of racketeering . . . not guilty. To the charge of bribery . . . not guilty. And to the charge of conspiracy . . . not guilty.'"

Mr. Choo jumped up and grabbed me in a bear hug. "Yoshi, you greatest," he whispered in broken English.

"Order!" the judge screamed again. "Bailiff, take Mr. Choo back to booking so he can be released." He had to go through his motions to set Mr. Choo free. I looked over at the prosecutors' table and threw them a smile. I knew they all wished they could just jump across the table and kill me. Too bad they hadn't taken what I had offered them after the preliminary hearing. Both assistant district attorneys were new to the game and overeager to take on their first high-profile case. Out of the gate they wanted to prove to their boss that they both could take me on, but somebody should've warned them that I was no one to fuck with. With a smile still on my face, I strutted by them and said, "Idiots!" just loud enough for only them to hear. Then I threw my hair back and continued to strut my shit out the courtroom.

After I slid the city clerk's head administrator ten crisp one-hundred-dollar bills, it only took about an hour to process Mr. Choo's release papers. Money talks and bullshit runs the marathon! And before anyone knew it, Mr. Choo and I were walking outside to greet the press. He and I both were all smiles, because he was a free man and I knew that in an hour or so, I was going to be $2 million richer; that alone made me want to celebrate. But first, we needed to address the media. Cameras flashed and microphones passed in front of us as we stepped into the sunlight. Mr. Choo rushed to the huddle of microphones that all but blocked his slim face from view. "Justice was served today. I am innocent and my lawyer proved that. I no crime boss, I am family man. I run my business and I love America," he rambled, his horrible English getting on my nerves. I waited patiently while he made his grandstand and then I took over the media show.

"All along I told everyone my client was innocent. Mr. Choo came to the United States from Korea to make an honest—" *Bang, bang, bang, bang, bang, bang!* The sound of shouts and then screams rang in my ears. Then I heard someone in the crowd yell in Korean, "You fucking snitch!" The shots stopped me dead in my tracks; my words tumbled back down my throat like hard marbles, choking me. I grabbed my arm as heat radiated up to my neck,

"Oh shit, I'm hit!" I screamed. I dropped to the ground, scrambling to hide . . . and saw Mr. Choo, his head dangling and his body slumped against the courthouse steps. His mouth hung open and blood dripped from his lips and chin. Before I could figure out what to do next, someone snatched me up from the ground. I didn't know where we were headed— my thoughts were on my throbbing arm and my racing heart. Then suddenly my vision became blurry and the world went black.

My career changed after Mr. Choo's trial. Shit, after having almost lost my damn life, I would not accept anything less than the best.

After the shooting, the law firm of Shapiro and Witherspoon was thrown into the media spotlight like never before. I became known as the "ride-or-die bitch attorney" that would take a bullet to get a client off. I became the most sought-after criminal defense attorney in Florida. Sometimes I didn't know if that was good or bad. But one thing was sure, my life changed and my appetite for money and power grew more and more intense. I started living each day as if it were my last.

Years ago, I never thought I would have turned out to be the way I was today. When you look at it, I had become a heartless bitch! I could not care less about anyone, including my own damn mother. Even when having a nightcap with my flavor of the night, I never let my feelings get involved. Once I put the condom on him, I reminded myself that it was only business and that my client's freedom was on the line, so everything worked out fine. That's how I kept men in line. After the shooting, I vowed that my heart would remain in my pocket forever.

Notorious

Life in VA

I can't believe that just a week ago I was living in my man Lance's beach house in Barbados. I had plenty of money to burn on whatever I wanted—jewelry, clothes, anything. That may sound like the good life, but it wasn't. I was hiding out in Barbados, on the run from the Feds, the Miami-Dade police, and my client, Haitian mob boss Sheldon Chisholm. The Feds and police were trying to pin a whole bunch of shit on me, including the murder of my best friend, Maria, who was a DEA agent, and the murder of my house-keeper. And Sheldon wanted my head for promising him an acquittal and dropping the ball on his case. I'd been my firm's most successful attorney, and I'd had dozens of police, court clerks, ADAs, judges, you name 'em, on my payroll, but someone got to them all, and my career took a serious hit.

When Lance got murdered outside a night club

last week, I knew I couldn't stay at his house in Barbados. I didn't think his murder was random; I knew that whoever killed Maria and my housekeeper and got to the people on my payroll also killed Lance. That meant someone was on my trail.

Since the court had confiscated my passport, I used an illegal one to re-enter the US. My plan was to head to Virginia, where I had family, and lay low until I put together a plan to prove my innocence and get my old life back.

I'd crossed a lot of state lines to get to my father's hometown in Virginia. During my travels, I picked up a newspaper in Texas that had my picture plastered across the front page. At that moment, my world stopped and I thought back on my life. Just a few months ago, I'd been a successful attorney in Miami with millionaire clients and an expensive appetite for the lavish lifestyle. I was at the top of the food chain. I was an unstoppable force with judges and DAs on my payroll. But then that all went up in smoke when I allowed greed and a cocaine addiction to take control of my life. Damn! I wished I could turn back the clock. But since I knew that was unrealistic, I folded the newspaper in half, stuffed it underneath my arm, and got the hell out of there really quick.

Instead of hopping on another flight, I rented a Toyota Highlander from Enterprise, stuffed all my things into the back of it, and drove the rest of the way to Virginia. It took me approximately twenty-two hours to get to my destination. Along the way, I prayed that my father's people hadn't heard about my brush with the law and the reward that they were offering. It had been a long time since we had been together, so I was like a stranger to them, which I'm sure would have made it easy for any one of them to turn me in. I knew what I had to do, and that was to keep my eyes and ears open. And the first time I sensed that something wasn't right, I was going to haul ass without even looking back.

I was tired as hell when I finally arrived in Norfolk, so I stopped at the Marriott hotel downtown near Waterside Drive to get some rest. It was around three in the afternoon, so I was able to wear my sunshades in front of the hotel clerk without looking suspicious. After I paid the man with cash, I headed up to the fifth floor room to unwind. I started to call my cousin Carmen right after I unpacked, but then decided to wait until I got me a nap. So that's what I did. But my rest didn't last long. I got a call from the front desk asking me if I wanted concierge services, and after I told the woman on the other end that I wasn't interested, I immediately hung up the phone. But for the life of me I could not go back to sleep. I looked at my watch and realized that it was a little after seven, so I got up from the bed and decided to make the call to my father's family. The only number I had was the number to my father's mother's house. My grandmother has had that number for as long as I could remember, and it had never been disconnected. So, I figured that when I called her I could get Carmen's number and we could hook up.

The phone rang about four times before someone picked up. I hadn't been in contact with my relatives in ages, so I didn't know what anyone's voice sounded like. I said hello and asked to speak with Mrs. Hattie.

"Can I ask who's calling?" the woman asked.

"This is her granddaughter, Yoshi," I replied.

"Wait a minute now. I know this ain't my cousin Yoshi from New York."

"Yes, I am the one," I said, grinning.

"Oh, my God. I can't believe it's you."

"Is this Carmen?"

"You damn right it's Carmen. Who else would it be?"

I smiled. I'd almost forgotten how Carmen could be. "How have you been?"

"I've been doing okay. What about yourself?"

I couldn't tell her the truth—that I was on the run. So I said, "Nothing has changed. I'm still a lawyer, winning case after case, trying to make a name for myself."

"Wow! I remember when we were kids and we used to talk about when we grew up we were going to be lawyers. But you were the only one who stuck with it. You must be living the life."

"Trust me, Carmen, life as an attorney isn't a bowl of fucking cherries. Girl, it's a constant grind, doing a lot of research, staying on top of your paralegals to make sure they are doing their work, and then on top of that, you've got to make sure you keep away from the psycho-ass clients. They will try to kill you." I couldn't help thinking back on the shit I went through in Miami with Haitian mob boss Sheldon Chisholm.

"Ahh, it couldn't be that bad. Shit, I would love to have your life any day."

"You can't be doing *that* bad."

"Yoshi, I am thirty plus, working as a fucking waitress at the IHOP on Twenty-first Street. I live with

Grandma and I don't have a car. Now tell me I'm not in a fucked-up situation?"

Before I responded to her question, I thought about it and the answer was clear. She *was* in a fucked-up situation. Not as fucked-up as mine, but she was right behind me. I never would have pictured Carmen's life to be like this. Before my father died, he and I used to visit his people during the summer. Back then, everyone thought Carmen was the smarter one. She was prettier, too. All the boys wanted her to be their girlfriend, and they never considered looking at me. I was an attractive little girl growing up, but the boys couldn't get over the fact that my eyes were really chinky and I was bony as hell. Those little neighborhood bastards chose Carmen over me every single time because she had all the right curves and a really big butt. I wondered where those boys were now. Probably strung out on drugs, in jail on drug charges, or deployed over in Iraq, fighting a fucking war that Bush started. Whatever their status was right now, it sure wasn't helping Carmen out, because the way she just laid out everything, shit was really messed up for her. I just hoped she didn't try to come at me with her hand out because I was strapped. I only had enough money to last me until I could make my next power move.

Now, don't get me wrong. I'd help her as much as I could, but I would not purchase her a car, and I would not put her up in her own apartment, so she'd better not ask.

So instead of making any comments about her situation, I said, "You're going to be all right."

"Easy for you to say. You're the big-time lawyer,

living the life of a celebrity, and probably got a man with a lot of money, too."

"No, I don't. In my profession, you can't keep a relationship because men are always intimidated by success. So for the most part I've been single."

"So, what's going on? Last time I heard, you'd gotten hired on to some big-time law firm, making seven figures a year."

"Yes, that's true. But I think I've gotten kind of burnt out with all the mind-numbing cases. It's really hard trying to compete with other attorneys, especially when you're trying to make partner in your firm. People don't play fair. So anyway, I decided to get out of there for a while and take some time off."

"So, what are you going to do?"

"I wanted to come and see you guys."

"Come on and see us, because we ain't going nowhere."

"Well, give me thirty minutes and I'll be there."

"What do you mean, you'll be here in thirty minutes? Where are you?" Carmen got excited.

"I'm in Norfolk at the Marriott hotel downtown."

"Oh, my God! Are you serious?"

"Yes, I'm serious. So let's get together so we can continue to catch up. I would love to see how everybody else is doing."

"Are you driving?"

"Yes, I have a rental."

"Okay. Well, you can come by the house and pick me up. That way you can see Grandma and the rest of the family."

"Does Grandma still live in the same house from when we were kids?"

"Yep, she sure does. The house is blue now, but other than that, ain't nothing changed but our ages."

The thought of my grandmother still living in that old house made me cringe. I honestly couldn't imagine anyone living there for as long as she had. I remembered back when I used to visit her how the floor would squeak because the hardwood flooring was old and had never been maintained. I also remembered her having wooden paneling on her walls, space heaters in every room of the house during the winter months, and one big air conditioner in the living room during the summer months. Everybody used to pile up in that small-ass room when it was hot. I just hoped conditions at that house had gotten at least a little bit better. Because if it had gotten any worse, then the house sure needed to be condemned.

"Okay," I said. "I'll be there in thirty."

"Okay," Carmen said; then we hung up.

It took me only about thirty-five minutes to hop in the shower and get dressed. I could not let on that I was a fugitive, so I slid on a pair of dark blue Chip & Pepper jeans, a black wool Max Mara turtleneck, and a pair of black Fendi riding boots. It was kind of nippy outside, so I also threw on a wool blazer with patches on the elbows. After making sure my weave looked straight, I headed out.